THE
OPPOSITE
OF AMBER

THE
OPPOSITE
OF AMBER

GILLIAN PHILIP

BLOOMSBURY

LONDON · BERLIN · NEW YORK · SYDNEY

Bloomsbury Publishing, London, Berlin, New York and Sydney

First published in Great Britain in April 2011
by Bloomsbury Publishing Plc
36 Soho Square, London, W1D 3QY

A CIP catalogue record of this book is available from the British Library

ISBN 978 0 7475 9992 0

Typeset by Hewer Text UK Ltd, Edinburgh
Printed in Great Britain by Clays Ltd, St Ives Plc, Bungay, Suffolk

1 3 5 7 9 10 8 6 4 2

www.bloomsbury.com

For Sarah Molloy
(and for Jamie & Lucy,
because it always is)

They found the fifth girl right after the snow melted.

There hadn't been a body for a while, and there had never been two in the one place before. He'd left them all over the country, up till then. All over the country and all over the years.

The fifth girl was caught under the water, under the bank, where the flow was fast and it washed everything away, all the traces. That's why they could say for sure it was the same man: because it was the same neck of the woods as the fourth girl, and because she was in water too.

The fourth girl they'd found in the sea. Not far out. They found her bumping gently against the rocks, tumbled in the shallows, her hair all tangled with green weed like a mermaid. A child might have thought she was a mermaid, with her pale greenish skin rippled in watery sunlight, but it wasn't quite summer, so it wasn't a child who found her, and everyone said that was a blessing at least, and it could have been worse. The dog that stood and barked and raced up and down and raised his hackles and refused to fetch his stick – at least he belonged to a retired lady doctor who might be

1

assumed to have seen a bit of life, and a bit of death to boot. And that was a mercy.

It seemed less of a mercy when they found who she was, when they saw their mermaid was still a child herself, or very nearly. And later, a good bit later, they said she was a mistake. When they saw it all more clearly, they said he'd got it terribly wrong with the fourth girl: it was a double tragedy because she was a normal girl, she wasn't like the others, she was just in the wrong place at the wrong time. And it seemed like that had shocked him into sanity for a bit, because he didn't kill anyone else for a long time, or not that they ever discovered.

In the end, though, it seemed he couldn't stop himself. In fact they wondered if he'd had to go and do it again to make it right, do it properly this time and to the right person, and that was why there was a fifth girl in the same town.

Because he got it right the fifth time – I heard a woman say so when I sat behind her on the bus last week – he got it right and went back to his pattern, and the fifth girl was just a prostitute again. And to keep it right, to make it the same, he put her in the water too.

Not the same water, that's true; but it's a good idea, if you don't want to leave traces, to put a girl in water. It's the opposite of amber.

Not that the fifth girl wasn't quite well-preserved, because the place where he left her was winter water, crazed with ice-feathers and dusted with snow. The traces from her body were gone, the ones that said his name, but she had an extra skin of ice that protected her. The water's surface was an icy coffin lid, like the one that covered Snow White, and she looked perfect like Snow White, or nearly.

Not altogether, of course. You can't look so very perfect, and nobody's kiss was bringing her back, but she looked as good as she could. Her blonde hair was full of ice and it glittered when they pulled her out into the sun; and quite honestly, the man who found her looked so pale and drained and shocked to stillness, she looked almost better than he did.

Summer

One

'Nobody pushed him,' said Jinn. 'It's nobody's fault but his. Silly arse.'

This was simplistic beyond even my big sister's standards, but I didn't say so.

I wasn't inclined to say much about anything. The Alex Jerrold incident had only confirmed this policy. Open your mouth – and I know this isn't a nice image – you open a can of worms. Keep it shut, and you are less likely to make some tosspot throw himself off a roof.

You see, the thing about Alex Jerrold is that he might have jumped anyway.

The thing about me is that I'll never know.

This is because I'm never going to ask him. I could ask him, because even jumping off a roof he couldn't get right. He's lying there in his parents' house like a broken doll, waiting for me to ask him. But I wouldn't like his answer.

I didn't want to discuss Alex Jerrold and his incompetent suicide attempt, and I didn't know why Jinn had to bring it up, not on a day like this. We were watching the tide race upriver but there weren't any benches free in the

Dot Cumming Memorial Park, so we were on our backsides in the grass. We didn't mind because the grass was dry, and the black-glossed benches looked almost sticky in the heat; on one of them, just to the right of us, a woman's flowery bottom had spread as if it had begun to melt. There was a good chance she was fused to the wood and would never get up again. She was that big. It was that hot.

Jinn had got us ice creams and a bottle of cider that was already losing its refrigerator chill. My cone had a flake: I didn't want it but I couldn't exactly chuck it in the river, not while Jinn was looking, not when she'd spent extra on it just to make me happy. She had bitten off the pointy end of her cone, the way she always did, and used it to scoop out a miniature ice cream from the top. I watched her put the baby cone whole into her mouth and crunch it, shutting her eyes to chew. I loved watching her do that; it was my favourite part of ice cream. That was what made me happy, not chocolate flake. Jinn had forgotten I'd grown up. Also, she always kind of forgot I was too old for ice cream. Which was great.

A fighter jet from the airbase screamed overhead, followed a couple of seconds later by another, but the deafening roar faded fast and left me with no excuse for keeping my mouth shut. Jinn wasn't saying any more because she knew I'd have to say something in the end. I didn't want to disappoint her so at last I said, 'Not really.'

'Not what, Rubes?'

'Not his fault.' My tongue stuck to my mouth. It was the heat. I licked at my ice cream. God, it was hot. 'There was a few people –'

'Shouting at him to jump?' She shrugged. 'Oh yeah, I know. They didn't mean it.'

'How do you know?'

'And anyway,' she said again, 'nobody pushed him.'

My mouth was dry already from too much talking. 'He wasn't thinking straight.'

'How do you know?' Jinn cocked her head at me. 'You weren't inside his head.'

Shows how much you know, I wanted to say. 'Why would they tell him to jump if they didn't mean it?'

'Dunno. Got a bit up themselves? Got excited? Wanted to impress somebody?'

I gave Jinn a sharp look, but she didn't return it. Jinn had never asked me right out about Alex. I think she was respecting my privacy or something. Waiting for me to want to talk about it. Well, she'd die of boredom waiting for that.

She sucked the last of the melted ice cream through the hole in the bottom of her cone, threw it towards the river, and flopped back with a happy sigh. A seagull caught the scrap of cone before it hit the water. That reminded me of Alex Jerrold, but then everything did. Nothing dived through blue space to catch Alex, white wings slicing the deadly emptiness. Alex landed.

I sat up sharply, punched in the stomach by a visual memory. 'Can we do something else?'

'Like what?' Jinn opened one eye.

'Beach?'

'You can't sit still these days,' she complained.

No, indeed. But then if it was up to Jinn, we'd never move our arses from July till September; we'd just lie in the grass, her telling stories, me listening. Jinn loved summer. Nothing bad happened in summer, she said.

She had a point. Lara died in winter, because it was dark. And this last winter, of course, Alex Jerrold jumped off a roof and broke two vertebrae, a femur and both hips. Mind you, that wasn't something you could blame on the light conditions. Everybody could see fine.

I was itching to get to the beach now, but for a while Jinn fooled around, refusing to get up, going all heavy and limp when I tried to drag her. At last, when I could stop laughing, I prised her off the grass and we sauntered towards the river, Jinn swinging the cider bottle at her side. It was a bit of a hike. At Breakness the river was wide and shallow, flowing in a wide extended loop that cut off the beach from the town. The pretty high street had shops on one side only and the little Dot Cumming park on the other. After that, in the VisitScotland brochures, it looked like you could step right on to the beach, but in real life there was the broad curve and delta of the river mouth. Only beyond the river could you get to the peninsula of dunes and the flat white beach and the sea.

Oh, we had to work for our beach summer in Breakness, we did. So did the tourists, which was probably why they stopped coming. That and cheap flights to St Lucia, of course. At Breakness you found a parking place in the crammed High Street, unpacked your barbecue and your windbreak and your Swingball, and then you either staggered round to the rickety bridge, or you took off your shoes and waded across. Life, if you weren't born here, was basically too short.

At this point in the day, though, the water only came halfway up our calves, so wade is what Jinn and I did. Because the tide was surging inland, the flow towards the sea wasn't too strong, but the two currents were squabbling and the surface was churned into violent little waves. My feet sank in the sand. It was so soft it was almost like floating; no hard rock to ground on. And compared to the cold grip of the river on my ankles, the yielding sand was warm between my toes. I loved that sensation.

'Watch out for the quicksand,' said Jinn.

OK, I loved that sensation up to a point. I shoved her, annoyed that she'd broken the floating spell, and she stumbled and giggled.

'Oh, Rubes, there's no quicksand here. You know that fine.'

'I know,' I lied. All the same I hurried through the river and out, splashing my rolled-up jeans. What did she know? Quicksand lived in estuaries. It could just appear. I was fairly sure about that.

Neither of us was in the mood for walking far, so as

soon as we'd scrambled up through the sandhills, we sat down to look across the sea, wriggling our backsides into the shifting dune to make ourselves semi-permanent. Jinn took a long thirsty swig of cider before passing the bottle to me. I tilted it to my lips but it was warm and I never was crazy about the taste. Jinn took it back quite happily.

'I shouldn't encourage you anyway. You're underage.'

Ice cream and cider had made me sleepy. The sunlight was an unrelenting white blaze, the glitter and thump and rush of the waves hypnotic. There were swimmers and bodyboarders in the water, and kids on the shoreline, emaciated by the dazzle. I could hear the fizz and thump of someone's radio beyond a striped windbreak. God's sake, why did they need a windbreak in this weather? A kite sagged on the end of its line, refusing to rise further in the windless air, hovering, then nosediving to earth.

I wished Jinn didn't have to go back to work in the afternoon. I wished she was still at school so we had the whole holidays together like we used to. Shit happened, for sure, but I objected more than anything to shit's bad timing. If Lara hadn't died when she did, Jinn could maybe have gone to university and then she'd have had the holidays too, same as me, or nearly.

'Nah,' Jinn would say. 'I'd've had to work the holidays. That's what students do.'

True. And anyway, thinking of possible good outcomes from Lara's silly death made me feel kind of bad.

I had to keep reminding myself that I missed her. She was flaky and impossible and absolutely the most incompetent mother I could imagine, but she was *there*, and she was fun, and she made absolutely the best hot chocolate in the universe: the kind with marshmallows and squirty cream so thick and tottering, you could hardly get your mouth to the chocolate underneath. And the cream is so cold out of the fridge, it's almost a shock when the chocolate below it is hot. And that actually is the absolute best hot chocolate, though she would never have wanted to hear me say that, because Lara took the mickey out of people who overused words like 'absolutely' and 'actually'. I didn't overuse any words, but I'm not sure she was so crazy about that either.

Hey, she couldn't have it both ways.

Actually my mother's name was Lorraine. She didn't like that name (she didn't like 'Mum' either) so she insisted on being called Lara (in honour of Lara Croft, not the Russian babe in *Dr Zhivago*). If she'd fallen out with someone, and whoever it was wanted to wind her up, they'd go back to calling her Lorraine. This would drive her demented, so she'd cut the culprit dead in the street, and the spat would become a miniature feud till both sides got over their dudgeon and so-and-so started calling her Lara again.

I liked my mother's new name and I was a little jealous that she hadn't saved it for me, but instead I was named after one of her favourite country and western songs. This was not a bad outcome: if I'd been a boy I was going to be Elvis, and I'm not sure Elvis Carmichael works.

Jinn's real name was Jacintha, and she hated it. Jacintha was a character in one of Lara's favourite soaps: some martyr of a female doctor with an eternally unfulfilled crush on a male one. Jacintha the Doormat was still aching after this man when I started watching *Medics* at about the age of seven: that's how long the scriptwriters had spun it out. A couple of years ago Jacintha the Doormat finally fell under a bus and died in the arms of the devastated thick bloke, which was a relief all round. When she was eleven Jinn swore to me, in the light of an LED pen-torch under the bedclothes, that she would never follow the Path of Jacintha, and that she was changing her name forthwith. We sealed the pact with blood pricked from our thumbs. Lara didn't mind this act of rebellion, since even she had tired of Jacintha the Doormat by then. She didn't even mind the thumbprints of blood on the sheets, but then Lara never did mind household technicalities.

So Lorraine became Lara, and Jacintha became Jinn. I was the only one in my family who kept my name the same. Ruby Intacta.

I had my eyes closed against the sea-glare by now, but I wasn't asleep, so when a shadow blocked the sun, I knew it. As soon as the vivid rash-red inside my eyelids was gone, so was the day's warmth, and a shiver ran across my skin like a whisper. I didn't especially want to open my eyes, but I was too nosy not to. Rubbing the prickling goose-bumps from my arms, I blinked and propped myself up.

I was the one in his shadow, but he wasn't looking at me. It was my air he'd sucked the warmth out of, not Jinn's, but I might as well not have been there at all. Jinn, still in the sunlight, had her hand up to shield her eyes, and she was smiling at him.

As my eyes adjusted I could see why. There wasn't much I could see of his face but at fifteen I knew a nice outline when I saw one.

'It's muck, that stuff.'

'Aye. Horrible. Want some?' Jinn wiggled the bottle.

She and the boy were talking like I'd come in in the middle of a conversation, so maybe I had been asleep after all. As he slumped in the sand beside Jinn, I twisted round to get a better look at his face.

Not all-get-out handsome, and a bit skinny, but his golden eyes were sparky in that you-know-you-want-to way, and he gave good teeth. His smile was broad and catching. It was all for Jinn, though.

'Hi, Jinn.'

'Hi, Nathan. Long time no.'

Oh. Right. Not the middle of the conversation, then; or perhaps it was just that the conversation had been on hold for a few years. I crinkled my eyes to give the boy a second, closer look. Oh yes indeedy. Nathan Baird, the unmistakeable. I thought he was gone for good. But I suppose Nathan Baird never did anything for good.

'Is that your wee sister?' Like he'd only just seen me.

'Uh-huh.' Jinn put her arm round me.

'Ruby Red. I like your hair.'

I'd smiled back at him before I realised what I was doing, so I had to twist my face into a scowl double-quick, as if it had only been going into some sort of spasm in preparation for a deadly glare. I couldn't stop my hand going to my hair, though, and pushing it up in spikes. Ruby Red actually was the colour it said on the bottle; that's why I'd picked it, because it had my name on it. I wondered if Nathan knew that. I wouldn't put it past him.

My hair was a dark, vivid, unnatural red, too dramatic for my pale skin. I liked it that way. I'd enjoyed the whole process. My hair's choppy and tangled and short, so there was plenty of dye and I was careless and the colour had trickled down my face like blood. I looked like something out of Stephen King, and I went on looking that way for a few days, because the dark scarlet trails left stains, as if I had an invisible axe lodged in my skull. The blood trails had of course long faded, but I'd shortly be dyeing it again. I'd got a real kick out of all the funny looks.

I didn't want to discuss my hair with Nathan, so I ignored him, and he got the hint and ignored me back. Unfortunately, he didn't leave. I was hot and sandy, and I'd have liked to go and cool my feet in the water's edge, but I didn't like Nathan Baird, never had. He so clearly wanted to be alone with Jinn that I wanted to thwart him.

I lay back against the dune and closed my eyes again,

16

but annoyance had made me even hotter. And I was thirsty. It was stupid of Jinn to get warm cider I wasn't strictly old enough to drink. I reached for the bottle, half-buried in sand, and took a swig of it anyway; as I expected, it gave me an instant throbbing ache in the back of my head.

Sod it, I had to go and paddle.

Neither of them took any notice as I stood up and brushed sand off my backside. They were too busy giggling and mock-punching each other. Boys turned Jinn into a chittering idiot, they really did. Especially Nathan Baird: he'd always had that effect on her. I'd have thought his two-year abscnce would have given her the wisdom of perspective. Rolling my eyes I stalked off – not easy in dry sand – and headed for the water's edge.

The water wasn't cold in the shallows, just deliciously cool. I stood there and let the waves roll in over my feet and up over my ankles, sinking millimetre by millimetre in sand. Now I was woozy with pleasure. Even the cider-throb in my head had vanished. I glanced back at Jinn and Nathan, but they weren't watching me. Doing a double-take, I screwed up my eyes.

Their heads were close together but they weren't kissing. He'd given her something and they were both examining it. As he drew back she reached behind her neck, fumbling with the something, till Nathan pushed her hands aside and fumbled with it himself. Chancer.

I wanted to race back through the sand and demand to

know what it was. Ten years earlier I could have done that. Ten years earlier, of course, she wouldn't have left me to wander down to the water's edge by myself.

A shattering noise exploded in my right eardrum. Right beside me a dumpy toddler was screeching, because her idiot older brother and his retard pals were splashing her. Before I could drown her or them, the brother took pity, seized her small fingers and tugged her back to their mother.

I was cross and deaf but it didn't last, because I was ambushed by a tactile memory so vivid I had to stare at my own hand to reassure myself.

No, it was fine, I hadn't fallen through the space–time continuum after two mouthfuls of Woodpecker. What I had was the hand of a fifteen-year-old, tipped with turquoise nail varnish, but for an instant it had felt like a tiny hand folded in a larger one.

The memory of the incident was so physical it left me breathless. It was my first memory ever, maybe that was why. A sea just like this one, in all the details: the colour of the waves, licks of foam on glassy ripples, easy to jump. I remembered the green stripy ball bobbing out to sea, and howling for it. I remembered the cold of the waves, and the fear of the sea out there where waves didn't break, and my grief for the lost ball.

And I remembered Jinn's warm hand enclosing mine. I had no memory of her nine-year-old face, just my hand in hers as we jumped the waves together, Jinn laughing so that I started to stop crying. We'll get it back, she said. Just a bit further. Don't be scared.

A pack of boys nearby were using a bodyboard to skim the shallows, but I wasn't interested. It took all my concentration to jump the waves and it had become a very serious game, and I was biting the tip of my tongue. We were going to get the ball back, the green-and-white striped ball, but I had to hop clear of every wave, the way you'd never step on the pavement cracks. Jinn was helping me now because we'd gone deeper, and I was up to my fat little waist, and she was laughing as she lifted me high over each swell. I didn't even shriek or giggle, because it was all so deadly serious, and if I stepped on a wave, something terrible might happen.

And then it did. One of the bodyboard boys knocked into Jinn and she stumbled, and my hand slipped out of hers.

It was such a loss, abrupt and awful. My hand without hers felt like it was adrift in space. I fell over just as a bigger wave tumbled in, rolling me over and lifting me. I didn't know which way was up and I didn't know where the shore was, what distinguished rock and sand and sea. I only knew that Jinn's hand was no longer there, but it wasn't me I was afraid for, it was Jinn.

My mouth and nostrils filled with water, but we weren't so very far from shore; it was just that I was little and terrified. When I was seized by Jinn and the boy together, I was howling with fear for her. I screamed and screamed for Jinn till her laughter and tickling fingers turned my wails into giggles.

I never did forget the feeling of her hand leaving mine. I dreamed it on and off over the years. I'd never see it but I'd feel it, or rather I wouldn't feel it. The emptiness in my fingers, and the loss, and Jinn bobbing away from me like a green-and-white striped ball.

Two

If Jinn and I were changelings, as I sometimes suspected (neither of us seemed to have Lara's genetic code), we were changelings from different eggs. Either that, or the exact same egg, and I got all the bits that weren't Jinn.

It wasn't just the age gap. Jinn was quick and shining bright; Jinn was motor-mouthed and nurturing. It didn't really matter that Lara was scatty and a bit flaky (and a bit of a tart, to be honest), because from the earliest I can remember, Jinn catered for my every need. Actually she catered for my every whim, to the point where she anticipated it, asked for it, spoke for me. There was never any need for me to speak, and I knew I could never say anything as well as she did, so I didn't bother. I didn't resent her or anything. I was proud to be spoken for by Jinn, sparky and bold. I was spoilt voiceless.

Jinn had a distinctively pretty face: one that changed when she smiled, but not too drastically. She had the same pale northern skin as me, but her blonde hair was just the right degree of unruly. My hair was mouse-fair and not distinctive, so that's why, as soon as I got up the nerve, I dyed it. To start with I went orange-ginger ('Cinnamon', it said on the box). I thought I'd never get the shade just right, till one day like a message from the follicle gods I saw the box with my name on it. I loved that dark dramatic burgundy, and it made me a bit recognisable, because I have one of those faces that people forget. Very ordinary eyes, non-specific cheekbones, a forgettable nose. Nathan Baird wouldn't have known who I was without Jinn at my side.

Which would have been fine by me.

I didn't like how close Jinn and Nathan were sitting when I trudged back to the dune, but when Jinn saw me coming she stood up abruptly and dusted sand off her cropped jeans.

'I have to go to work.' Unnecessarily she checked her watch.

Good, I thought. I was hot and thirsty all over again, and I wanted a freebie from the mini-mart, and it was high time Jinn ended the conversation anyway.

'I'll walk you,' said Nathan.

Oh, bollocks, I thought.

Nathan couldn't walk if you paid him; all he could do was strut. No wonder, because I noticed Jinn was wearing a new necklace: a pebble of amber enclosing a surprised-looking mosquito. She kept lifting her hand to touch it. The amber was glassy-gold, pure and unflawed, bigger than the top joint of my thumb. The chain was thick links of silver.

'Where did you steal that?' I asked him.

Jinn slapped my arm quite hard. Nathan said, 'Oh, it *talks*,' and then ignored me.

I fell behind, sullen and jealous. This time Jinn didn't wade through the river: too undignified in front of Nathan Baird, and I had the nasty feeling she was playing for time. Instead she took the long way round, across the rickety bridge. *Trip-trap trip-trap across the rickety bridge.* As I stepped off the end of it I looked down, like always, for the troll.

No troll, but Wide Bertha was standing outside the mini-mart having a smoke. She stood in a little witch's circle of tab-ends, arms crossed over her solid overalled breasts but one hand dancing in the air, flicking the cigarette, pulling it in for another deep drag. Beside her the man from Molotov Mixers was unloading his lorry. One crate on top of another; a crash like shattering windows every time. The noise of it reverberated off the pavement and the sun-baked walls and echoed into the sky but Wide Bertha didn't flinch. She gestured her fag at Jinn.

'You're early, love.' But she didn't smile the way she usually did. She gave Nathan Baird a hard stare.

'That's because I love my job so much,' said Jinn. 'I couldn't wait to get here.'

Crash went another crate. Bertha rolled her eyes and tapped her fag and resisted smiling. 'Well, don't let Kim leave early. You cover for her too much. She's to finish her shift.'

'Aye, no chance.'

Bertha ignored Nathan entirely. *Crash.* 'Hello, Ruby. How's it going?'

'OK.'

Making a face like a bored bull mastiff, she rolled her eyes again. One day, I reckoned, Wide Bertha's eyes would work loose and start rattling around in her head like lottery balls. 'You want to curb that wicked tongue of yours, Ruby. Do you never shut up?'

I looked awkwardly at the traffic. *Crash.*

'She's going through a phase,' said Jinn, ruffling my burgundy hair like I was a kid. 'A fifteen-year phase.' I shook her off, and she laughed and blew a kiss at Nathan Baird and went into the shop.

Bertha sucked on her fag, giving Nathan the evil eye, but he grinned and sauntered off.

'What's Jinn doing with him?'

I shrugged.

'He's a bad lad.'

'I know.'

'So does your sister, the silly cow.' Bertha pinched out the end of her half-smoked fag and tucked it carefully back into its box, studying the big black letters: SMOKING KILLS. 'What's he doing back here? They should have kept him. Thrown away the key.'

I watched his swaggering back view. I wondered why he'd been in prison, and what he'd done. I wondered if it was something terrible, like murder, or something romantic, like robbing a bank. Or a bit of both. I could imagine either, and against my own wishes I decided he'd look good doing it.

Whatever he'd done, he'd done it down south, where he'd moved with his father. So I'd never asked, because I wasn't interested, and now it was too late to ask without looking fantastically ill-informed. I had a vague recollection of why they'd gone south in the first place: something to do with an ill-judged swindle and a gambling debt and old man Baird getting on the wrong side of some bloke up in Glassford. Nobody had thought they'd ever come back. I wondered if old man Baird was dead, knifed in some bar brawl in Sheffield or wherever they'd gone. Nathan's mother was alive (as far as he knew) during his Breakness days, but she'd gone off when he was ten years old so she could be dead by now, just like ours.

Two more fighter jets split the sky; it was such a beautiful day they were non-stop enjoying themselves. As the racket faded the Molotov man wiped his forehead on one bare arm, transferring sweat to sweat, then tucked his damp polo shirt and his protruding stomach back into his waistband. He was pink-faced with effort, but he was always a bit pink-faced: smooth-cheeked, dark-haired and slobbishly handsome, with those long beautiful lashes and sad eyes that some men are blessed with. Wide Bertha said he looked like George Clooney, which was stretching truth till it snapped, but if you inflated George Clooney with a bicycle pump there might have been a passing similarity. At any rate, Bertha fancied the pants off him.

Bertha was married, of course, to a pallid housebound man with disability benefits and a Sky subscription, but Molotov man was only in the neighbourhood once a fortnight, and I don't think their flirtation ever actually came to anything. There was no harm, said Bertha, in looking.

And no accounting for taste, says I. But only in my head.

She pulled out her fag packet and offered him one, blocking the half-smoked one with her thumb. He tucked his newspaper under his arm and lit her cigarette first, then his own. She'd selected a new one for the occasion.

'Awful about that girl,' said Bertha.

'What?'

'Her.' Bertha jabbed at his newspaper, dislodging it from his armpit. I angled my head as he shook it out, catching sight of half a blurred face, half a bright smile, one eye glowing red in the flash of a camera.

'Awful,' he said. 'Makes you think.'

'Makes you think what?' asked Bertha.

He shrugged. 'You ought to be careful, Bertha. Walking home at night and that.'

'Like he'd want to rape and murder me!' She roared with laughter, then seemed to decide that was in bad taste. Pressing her lips together, she humphed. 'You needn't worry. Nothing that exciting ever happens in Breakness.'

He gave her a serious look, touched her hand. 'All the same.'

'Kirkcaldy, that's another planet. Aw, look at her, she had a kid.' Bertha smoothed out the paper and flipped a page. 'Two years old. The wee soul.'

'You locking up the shop and taking the money at night and that. You watch out.'

'I'd like to see anybody try.' Wide Bertha flexed her biceps. Somewhere under the blanket of fat, muscles shuddered. 'Anyhow, he's not after money. She was a working girl. Like the one that got killed last year in Cambuslang. You don't kill prostitutes for money.'

'No,' he said, frowning at the paper. 'Young. Look at her.'

'And I'm an old bat. It's the likes of Ruby need to be careful.'

I shrugged and returned her smile.

'That's right,' said Inflatable George the Molotov man. 'She's right, Ruby.'

I didn't want to stand here shaking my head and muttering about some dead prostitute in a ditch two hundred miles away. It depressed me, mostly because my moral meters were badly calibrated right now, and I didn't know what to say. It was another good reason not to say much at all. What could I talk about? I felt sorry for the girl in the ditch and her sad dirty end, but I couldn't do anything for her and it wasn't my place to be indignant. What did she expect, anyway? That's the kind of thing that happens when you do that kind of thing.

Jinn came out of the shop and into the brightness, tilting her face to the sun, half-closing her eyes, I didn't like the way a light had gone on inside her skin since Nathan Baird had cast his shadow across the day.

'Five minutes.' She blinked at Bertha and smiled.

'Ten. Let Kim do extra. She buggered off early yesterday and she thinks I don't know it. Do you girls want a Molotov?'

I hesitated. I wanted a drink, but I'd rather it was a colour found in nature.

'I'll get them,' said Jinn.

'There's cold ones in the fridge. Make a note, will you, love?'

It didn't mean we were paying for them, just that Bertha liked to keep things orderly. Wide Bertha was a great believer in writing everything down, but it wasn't as if she was mean with the occasional drink, or a bag of crisps here and there.

Anyway, since I was getting the Molotov for free, I could hardly complain. Maybe they tasted better with vodka, the way Jinn drank them in the evenings. I wished I liked the taste of alcohol more: maybe it took the edge off the chemical sweetness. Molotovs came in colours rather than flavours, all of them practically radioactive: Last Mango, Blue Lagoon, Pink Flamingo and Mellow Yellow. Jinn had brought me a pink one because they were the least offensive, but a flamingo in that shade of fuchsia would need shooting. I tipped it down my throat and tried not to notice the taste. At least it was wet and cold. Other people liked them. If they didn't, Inflatable George wouldn't get to come up and see Bertha so often.

Jinn kept looking up the street, the way Nathan Baird had gone, but at last she drained her Molotov and disappeared back into the shop. I didn't hang about after that; it wasn't as if I wanted to chat. I left Bertha and George leaning together, bums against the warm stone wall, heads close together over the tabloid, flirting glumly over sudden death.

Three

Jinn and I lived in a grey stolid house at the end of a row. It used to belong to all three of us – though of course it really belonged to the council – and after Lara died, they let us stay on because Jinn was nineteen years old and just terrifyingly competent. The social workers and the housing department people kept coming by for about three months, and then they shrugged and smiled and left us alone.

Inside it wasn't much to look at. Beds, chairs a bit too big for the room, a TV, occasional tables. A few photos, candles on a shelf, a china horse with a chipped ear. What else can I say about it? Embossed wallpaper in outdated pastels. A dead wasp on the windowsill. It was a house in a million and it wouldn't have stood out from any of them. But there were two bedrooms and there was all the space we needed, because if we needed more we went outside. A little garden clung to the front and side of the house, where Jinn grew easy things like nasturtiums and snapdragons and Livingstone daisies: the kind of plant you buy in trays, three for a fiver at B&Q.

We had the most colourful garden in the street. Jinn would stick shiny windmills in the soil that glinted in the smallest sunlight, and she'd buy odd-looking plastic frogs and rabbits and an occasional fairy. She hung up wind chimes and forgot to take them down when gales raced in off the sea, so the chimes got all tangled and wouldn't ring till she'd unravelled them. There was one little stone gargoyle who looked as if he had something stuck in his throat and was about to throw it up. He'd made Jinn laugh out loud in the garden centre, laugh so hard that people stared. She said he couldn't stay in the garden centre after that, it wouldn't have been fair; people would have laughed at him all the time and as he clearly had no sense of humour, he'd be hurt. (She actually meant all this. Go figure.) So even though he was expensive, and made of what felt like real stone but was probably concrete, the ugly little git had to come home with us.

Jinn got the gardening bug from Lara. Lara used to spend ages in the garden, pulling out straggly weeds and then frantically trying to push them back into the soil when she found a faded label and realised they were flowers. She never did anything very constructive. After Lara died and Jinn took over, the garden exploded into colour. Not a hundred per cent natural colour, it was true, with the poison-green plastic frogs and the rainbow windmills whizzing in the breeze, but it glittered and sparkled like a funfair at the end of the grey row. Little kids liked to peer over the low hedge till their mothers tugged them away. I was proud of it, and very proud of Jinn.

Jinn planned to grow vegetables too: you could pile up tyres, she said, and you could fill them with compost and they were easy to keep. She hadn't got around to this yet but she'd collected a few old tyres that were dumped in a corner of the backyard and got immediate complaints from the grumpy old bugger next door, who said we were turning the place into a scrapyard. Jinn told him to eff off, and as the council didn't give a toss about some old tyres (they probably didn't give a toss about the G.O.B. either), we kept them. All the same, Jinn found an old blanket to throw over the tyres, pinning it down with bricks, and that seemed to mollify the G.O.B.

'Who says you can't be self-sufficient in a town?' said Jinn that day, when she came home from work. Out in the hallway, the front door finally shut with an explosive noise. It always did that. It swung painfully slowly on its hinges, and then it slammed with a colossal bang. If we waited to close it quietly we'd die of boredom, but it still gave me a shock, every time.

In the kitchen, Jinn upturned a plastic bag and shook it out. Wizened potatoes tumbled and rolled on to the Formica tabletop.

I leaned on the worktop. 'What are those?'

She gaped at me and let her jaw go loose, like somebody really thick.

I rolled my eyes. 'I mean, what are they for?'

'I'm going to plant them. In the tyres.' Jinn opened the corner cupboard and started loading potatoes into the blackest depths. Pulling a newspaper apart, she tucked the pages around the potatoes, layer after layer. 'They were only going to get thrown out.'

'They'll rot,' I said. I rescued an old bit of paper that I hadn't read. Dear Deidre was on one side, a missing girl on the other. I folded it up and started to read Deidre.

'No they won't. They'll sprout and we can plant them.'

I hoped she wasn't contemplating goats again. Jinn contemplated goats regularly, and far too seriously. I reckoned the G.O.B. would have something to say about that.

'Anyway, we'll see. They're not worth eating. Whatcha want? Macaroni cheese?'

Jinn liked cooking and she didn't use packets if she could avoid it, so she danced around the kitchen while she stirred and melted and got flour over everything. I set the table, blowing off its fine coating of flour-dust. We shimmied and boogied and snaked round each other as we worked, and Jinn kept turning up the volume. Tonight it was *Twenty-Four Hours from Tulsa*, her favourite song. Jinn liked a lot of old music. She was crazy about Gene Pitney and Dusty Springfield and Johnny Darrell, about Motown and Phil Spector and cheesy country songs. If she wanted to wind me up she'd play *Ruby Don't Take Your Love to Town*, singing along in a melodramatic voice. It didn't wind me up, because I didn't mind; I could see the people in the song, like watching a little movie, and those are the best songs.

I wasn't sure about my namesake though. Ruby didn't seem altogether adorable and if her boyfriend was tempted to shoot her, frankly I didn't blame him. She'd painted up her lips and rolled and curled her tinted hair, and I didn't know how that would look. Because at first I thought she had *tented* hair I imagined you couldn't see her eyes, like she had just a slit of an opening in the hair hanging down across her face. You'd never know what Ruby was thinking. You notice she never answers him, she just slams the door. Maybe she knows the thing about opening your mouth and letting the words out.

When Alex Jerrold threw himself at my feet, all the way from the community centre roof, I'm not sure if I was surprised or not. Well, no, I *was* surprised, but I shouldn't have been. I'd asked him to do it, so it shouldn't have been as big a shock as it was.

Take a running jump, I had said.

Alex Jerrold couldn't take a joke, that was his trouble. It wasn't much of a joke, it's true, and I wasn't laughing at the time, I was kind of embarrassed and I just wanted him to go away. I'd laughed moments later though, because I'd seen Cameron Foley grinning and rolling his eyes and I wanted to draw his attention.

After Alex jumped, after he landed, nobody looked at

anybody but Alex. There was a small collective intake of breath – silent, but I felt it physically, as if the atmosphere had been displaced for a moment.

It was all a bit of an anticlimax. I might have thought (if I thought at all) that he'd spend longer in the air. I might have thought that he'd drift down like a snowflake, or a skydiver. But he didn't do anything so elegant, and he never got near the sky. Alex Jerrold fell through the space between buildings, the space between roof and tarmac. He jumped and landed, and there was no time between the two.

He didn't land quite at my feet, of course – he was maybe ten metres away. We had to stand back and stare up, you see, and there were people yelling at him to jump – silly beggar, all mouth, doing it for effect, never have the balls for it. There were other people there with their hands over their mouths, holding painful breaths, but I didn't take any of them seriously because I was looking at Cameron Foley and he was kind of smiling at me, kind of curious. He wasn't really interested in Alex. He'd just thought he was funny for a moment.

And then Alex stopped being funny. He tipped forward and his hands flailed out to break his fall and the air caught him and then the truck did. He couldn't even aim and hit the tarmac; he missed the great wide continent of it and hit a truck roof. But he still landed like a bag of meat. He didn't bounce.

Cameron Foley stopped laughing, and he stopped look-ing at me.

That's when the sirens started.

That's when I ran.

So much for impressing Foley. Hell for leather, lickety split, and I was still running six months later. I wasn't even an elegant runner: I ran, naturally enough, like a girl.

It's amazing how even in quite a small town you can avoid people. Outside of school I hadn't seen Foley since that day, and I hadn't spoken to him anywhere. I wasn't sure I wanted to. He'd been there too, after all. He'd stood in the community centre car park, shielding his eyes at the white sky and the roof and the boy caught in between, ogling it all like some reality TV show. Foley watched Alex Jerrold jump and land and he didn't catch him any more than I did.

I'd been crazy about Foley for months if not years. I'd hung around the car park that day not for Alex's sake, not to save him from himself, but because I wanted Cameron Foley to notice me. I wanted to be able to think of some-thing smart and short to say, I wanted the moment to kick-start a beautiful relationship, and Alex was no more than scene-setting, a backdrop. (*Backdrop*. Bad choice of word.) I'd told Alex to Take a Running Jump because I wanted a clear run at Foley, and Alex was in the way.

So when you consider all that, when you consider how my adoration of Foley contributed to the rejection and the leap and the whole damn thing, it's ironic that I was now trying to avoid him.

It wasn't that I didn't still like him; it was more that he reminded me. And I didn't know what he thought. And I was ashamed.

The petting zoo at the Provost Reid Park up in Glassford was not the most romantic place to bump into him again. And I didn't think he could still take my breath away, but that's what he did. I was holding it, because I'm not keen on the smell of goat shit, but when his voice behind me said, 'Hello, Ruby,' it knocked the held breath out of my body.

I was forced to take another goat-scented lungful of air. 'Hi.'

The goat enclosure was rank. I wrinkled my nose and looked doubtfully at Foley's little sister. Mallory was six years old, mouse-haired and so skinny her supermarket jeans were falling off her. Foley had knotted a pink belt round the waist to try and hold them up.

'What are you doing?' he asked.

I nodded at Jinn. 'She likes the goats.'

'No accounting for taste.'

I laughed.

Jinn and I got into the petting zoo for nothing at the weekend, because the boy on the gate fancied Jinn and because she brought all the tired out-of-date fruit and veg from the mini-mart (except for the potatoes, obviously: she brought those home to keep the gargoyle company).

Her original excuse for the petting zoo was me (I suspected that like with the ice cream, I *was* an excuse). Like some bored dignitary she'd pay duty visits to the dilapidated aquarium and the chickens and the guinea fowl and the pot-bellied pig. But she'd always end up with the goats, playing staring games with the evil-looking male.

'Look, Ruby. It's like he's human!'

No, it wasn't. The billy goat had a smirking grin and slitted pupils sunk in sulphur-yellow eyes, which certainly made him expressive, but if I ever met a human with that goat's expression, it would be lickety-split all over again. The nanny was if anything worse, with her wicked aggressive face. Jinn loved those goats.

'I'm going to keep goats,' she kept saying. 'I'm going to keep *these* goats.'

I didn't know what her idea was. I hoped the lifespan of a goat was short.

'They don't need a lot of space,' she said.

They needed more space than we had.

She was reaching over the fence now to scratch the billy goat between its eyes. I caught a glint of clear gold: her new amber pendant, bouncing against the hollow of her throat. I'd forgotten about it, and the shock of seeing it again made my heart trip. I swallowed reflexively. I didn't like that necklace and I didn't like Nathan Baird. Anyway, I felt sorry for the mosquito. I could imagine it having a hot happy mosquito day, landing for an instant on liquid amber resin, and thinking its last thought: *Oh shi—*

Mallory ran to the goat pen and Jinn picked her up, looking, I thought, as if she was about to feed the child to the goat. Instead she lifted her high enough to scratch the animal's head. I could picture Jinn as a mother; it was perfectly feasible, but the mental image made me kind of jealous. So I leaned on a fence and watched the guinea pigs instead, and the peacock that strutted inside the fence like Nathan Baird, then flapped ostentatiously on to the fence to perch and preen. I remembered how Jinn had once persuaded me to scratch the goat's head. It was so hard, like rubbing a rock beneath a thin covering of hair. I remember not thinking it was real.

'You can eat every part of a goat,' said Foley.

I said, 'That's pigs.'

'Oh.'

I liked the way he was finding words difficult, but you can always tell if that bothers a person or not. He couldn't think of much to say, but he wasn't saying stupid things to fill in the spaces. He couldn't think what to say, so he said nothing. When I realised he wasn't planning to talk, and he wasn't going to try and make me talk either, a funny shiver ran across my scalp and my whole body seemed to breathe out and relax, like Jinn taking the lid off Lara's old pressure cooker.

We watched the guinea pigs for maybe five minutes, which could have felt incredibly awkward, but didn't. Under all that fur the things were probably the size of voles. Shrunken little men in velvet and ermine.

At last Foley said, 'Not a lot of eating on those.'

'No,' I said.

And for the first time in ages, I felt I wanted to add something. I wanted to make one of those slender word-chains that kept a person at your side. I wanted to make a rope out of words and loop it round his wrist, invisibly, so he wouldn't get bored and walk away. Words look fragile, insect trails of ink, but they're strong. Words bind people together or bludgeon them apart. Words are a grappling hook, flung skywards to yank a boy off a roof. What I wanted was the daisy-chain words, but unfortunately I couldn't open my mouth except to lick my lips.

It was very frustrating. I could think of several semi-smart things to say but I wasn't quite sure of them, so I couldn't get them past my throat. I kept expecting Foley to sigh or whistle under his breath or stand up and edge away, but he didn't.

Out of the corner of my eye I could see the peacock wobbling towards him, but I was too busy fretting over my next slice of wit to warn him. It was practically at his arm before it let out a tooth-buzzing, ear-ripping screech.

Foley would have leapt into my arms if I'd been ready to catch him. As it was, he crashed sideways into me and I had to grab the fence and him to stop us both falling in a heap. He staggered upright, swearing impressively, but he didn't loosen his white-knuckle grip on my arm for at least two seconds. It was worth the circulation loss. When he realised, he let me go, but he didn't move away because the peacock was still perched there, a metre away, looking pleased with itself. Foley eyed it. I could feel the warmth of his body pressed against mine and I could see his pulse beating hard in his throat. If he pressed any closer our skins would fuse.

'Jaysus,' he said, making a wild swing at the bird till it flapped down.

I noticed he still didn't move away. He stayed in body contact, biting his thumbnail as he watched the peacock swagger off. He shivered. He cleared his throat and shook his head and said 'Jaysus' again.

I sniggered – couldn't help it – then turned it into a cough.

Foley made a face. Then he wrinkled his nose.

'I'm hungry,' he said. 'Come on.'

Jinn was perfectly happy to be left with Mallory and Mallory felt the same way. We left my sister giving Foley's sister a lecture on goat husbandry, and sauntered out of the petting zoo and into the main park. Pooling our resources at the burger van, we bought two hot dogs, a Mars bar and a large Coke, then sat on the dilapidated roundabout and ate. Foley still didn't seem inclined towards idle chat. He pushed on the ground with one foot so that we creaked round a hundred and eighty degrees. Now instead of trees and colour-coordinated shrubs we were looking out across the rugby pitches, where thirty kids from the Academy were trying to kill each other,

41

egged on by a Bruce Willis lookalike in a blue tracksuit. The sun was hot on the back of our necks. I felt positively blissful.

Foley popped the ring pull on the Coke and passed it to me. 'Did you think he'd jump?'

I just about spat in the Coke can. 'Who?'

'Alex Jerrold,' he said, taking the Coke back off me. 'Did you think he was going to jump?'

'No,' I said.

'Seriously?'

I took a deep breath. 'Seriously no.'

I thought he'd say something else then, but all he did was turn the can in his fingers and kick us round in a half-circle again so we were watching the kids on the swings and the sun was back in our eyes.

'I didn't think he'd jump,' I said again. 'I never thought he'd jump. Not while we were all there.'

Silence again. It pressed against my ears like something physical.

'What about you?' I asked.

Foley turned the can upside down: empty. He shook it, and a few drops scattered. Methodically he squeezed the sides of the can, turned and squeezed, turned and squeezed. He did it over and over till the Coke can had a waist. Then he squashed it hard, top to bottom, flat hand to flat hand.

'I dunno,' he said. 'Maybe I did. I was the other way round though. I thought he might jump *because* we were

42

all there. I thought I should go away, cos there were too many of us there. I thought if I went away he might not jump, but if we all stayed he might.'

'Well,' I said, 'one of us had to be right.'

'I didn't mean to laugh,' he said.

'No.'

'I hope that didn't make him jump,' he said.

I looped a short lock of hair round my finger, tightened it, tugged it. 'No. No, I'm sure it didn't.'

He dug his heel harder into the ground, jolted us round again. Back to Bruce Willis and the rugby match. The roundabout creaked and groaned.

'Did you ever see him?' asked Foley. 'Since then, I mean?'

I shook my head.

'It wasn't your fault,' he said.

I shrugged.

'No more than anybody else, anyway,' added Mister Frigging Tact. 'Nobody made him jump.'

I tightened the loop of hair again, till it hurt. I twisted it, and again. I felt the roots give. I felt strands of hair start to come out of my scalp.

'I laughed too,' I said. 'Didn't mean to, but I did.'

'Well,' he said, 'it was funny. God knows why, but it was funny. Right up until.'

He stopped pushing the roundabout and hitched himself up on to it, so I did the same, hugging my knees. We sat peaceably, watching boys scramble and collide as Bruce

Willis bellowed in frustration. I did like this Foley. I liked this boy who didn't feel he had to talk.

'He might have jumped anyway,' said Foley at last.

'Don't suppose he'll ever tell us,' I said.

'Got to live with it,' said Foley. 'Got to live with it.'

That night I saw Alex Jerrold jump again and again. I couldn't get to sleep without him jumping off the high shelf of my mind and plummeting on to the truck roof of my dreams and waking me up with the shock of it. After a while I lay with my eyes shut, watching him jump over and over, waiting for immunity to kick in. I don't think immunity did, but after a while sleep did. I knew I was asleep, I could sense it, so I wasn't properly out of it. It was that semi-conscious state when you think you can control it, you think you can manipulate your dreams, and that makes it worse when they're stronger than you are. You've been fooled all along, you've been lulled into passive complacent dreaming and you don't mind watching.

So when I saw the figure leap into thin air, when I saw it miss the truck and hit the tarmac and collapse in on itself, and I saw the dead face wasn't Alex, it was Jinn, I woke up screaming till my throat hurt, and still no sound came out.

You remember news stories for funny reasons. I do, anyway. I usually remember some pointless conversation I was having when it came up, or some party I was at, or some song that was playing on the radio, or the hairstyle of the checkout girl when I read the paper in the queue at Tesco. I wouldn't have remembered the first girl – because heaven knows you can't remember every name and every killing – except that I'd gone out during the school lunch break to get myself a sandwich and a bag of Worcester Sauce crisps, but when I walked into the newsagent, there was Foley standing at the counter with Annette Norton.

Second year at Breakness High and already I fancied him, hopelessly, pointlessly. To be fair, he couldn't be expected to know I existed, since if I saw him coming I'd duck my head and put on speed and hope to God he wouldn't see the colour of my face. Still, on a couple of occasions, quite meaninglessly, he'd opened a conversation with me. Just a sentence, you know? A hello, a how's-it-going, a did-you-do-that-homework? Occasionally it was a little more profound and required some thought like: bloody hell, Mrs

Carver has an arse-elbow identification problem, what do you think, Ruby?

He would never get to find out what I thought, of course. He must have been mad to try and get a word out of me but I thought it was lovely and flattering that he kept trying. So my maniacal crush on him was not based solely on his jawline or the slightly-too-big nose that reminded me of some actor. I'm shallow but I'm not just a damp patch on the point of evaporation. I did actually like him because he was actually *nice*.

So when I saw him giggling with Annette Norton I couldn't help but treat it as a personal betrayal. Despite having shared all of two syllables with him so far I regarded him as mine, so it was a lance to my heart to watch his treasonous hand sneak into hers. Also, he whispered something to her and his tongue just about made contact with her eardrum. Also, he bought her a bag of Worcester Sauce crisps.

Red with shame, horror and homicidal loathing, I couldn't let him see me. I shoved my Worcester Sauce crisps back into the big cardboard box with the rest (how could I ever touch them again?) and turned my back on the pair of them. I don't think they saw me as they left the shop: too wrapped up in each other, the tossers. And meanwhile I just stared and stared at the red tops in the newspaper rack, and after a while I got over myself a bit and wondered who the brown-haired girl in the photo was, the one with the stripy T-shirt and the vast smile, and because I had time to kill along with Annette Norton, I picked up a copy and read the story.

And I know this is a very roundabout and self-centred way of remembering something, but give me some credit, at least I do remember it. I remember feeling almost as sorry for her as I did for myself.

So this was the first of the girls. They had her on Page One because she'd been missing, they'd appealed for her return, her father had gone on TV and asked her to get in touch. So it was a bit of a story already, though it had gone right over my head.

As it turned out, though, she'd been on the game. Which explained a lot. It explained why she'd been out so late, and why she would get into a stranger's car; somebody had come forward and said they saw her do it but it was the outskirts of town, there wasn't any CCTV and there wasn't a record. Her father cried and said he hadn't known, he hadn't known, but she didn't deserve it, she didn't deserve this.

She'd lain in a drainage ditch for a while, with the leaves of autumn drifting down on to her in layers of red and gold and brown, but it had rained a lot that September and the ditch flowed deep, so they only found her when the farmer went to clear it. They didn't know who'd done it, they said, but he was clever, because the water had worked away the traces. He was clever and clued-up. Or maybe he was just, you know, very, very lucky.

Four

Small towns, eh? Funny how you can suddenly *want* to bump into somebody and you still can't do it. From trying to avoid Foley I'd switched to hankering after him, but after that time at the petting zoo, I didn't see him for days. This I blamed on Mallory. It was better than imagining the alternative, which crept up on my brain day after day: that I'd misread him, that he'd actually been bored with me that day and desperate to get out of my company. Still, I went over and over every moment in my head and I couldn't forget the way his body stayed pressed against mine, even when the big scary peacock had gone.

I clung on to that memory, screwed my nerves into a tight ball and walked over to his house. There was no way I could make this look casual or accidental because the Foleys' house was at the end of a rutted track that didn't go anywhere else. It was a seventies-style bungalow faced with fake stone, neat and tidy except that when you got closer you could see the doors were deeply scored with claw marks, as if the occupants had barricaded themselves in against werewolves. I hesitated with one hand on the gate, very nervous now and not quite willing to walk the minefield of dog turds.

Out of the corner of my eye I saw Mallory, one hand on the neck of a gigantic German shepherd, the other clutching a brush. She examined me with a critical eye. There was a delicious smell in the air: roasting beef and onions.

I screwed up my courage to address a six-year-old. 'Is that your tea nearly ready?'

'Nah. It's Apache and Mojave's.' She pronounced it like it looked: *Moh-jave*.

I didn't ask which one she was brushing. They looked the same to me. 'Is Foley in?'

The critical eye turned sly. After a thoughtful pause she said, 'Cameron?'

'Yeah.' I caught myself blushing. I forgot his family would call him by his first name. He'd always been Foley to me and everybody else at school, except the teachers.

Mallory was still sizing me up. 'How much is it worth? *Ow!*'

Foley, who had just turned up, clipped her ear. 'Hello, Ruby.'

'When I grow up I'll sue you,' said Mallory.

'*If* you grow up it'll be cos I'm a feckin' saint,' said Foley.

Mallory jerked her head in my direction. 'Is she coming in or not?'

'No, I'm going out with her.'

'So I'm coming too.'

'No, you're not.'

'I am. You can't leave me here. Apache and Mojave haven't had their tea.'

'What, like they're going to eat you?'

Mallory gave her brother a trembling, sweet smile. 'Won't they?'

'You'd choke them.' He rolled his eyes, shot me an exasperated look, but he was weakening. 'You haven't had your tea either, Mal.'

'It's only frozen pizza and it hasn't even got pepperoni. You can get me a better one at the chip shop.'

I sniffed the beef-scented air again, puzzled.

'Apache and Mojave have got a show next week,' Mallory told me, in a talking-to-a-retard voice. Just as she said it, the door of the bungalow opened and the enticing smell drifted strongly into the garden.

'MALLory! Have you got MOH-jave?'

The German shepherd rose and stretched, then padded unhungrily towards Mrs Foley.

'I'm putting on the pizza, kids,' she shouted. 'Be ten minutes.'

Foley looked at Mallory, who whimpered pitifully. He rolled his eyes.

'S'OK, Ma,' he called. 'We're going out.'

I don't know why, in summertime, we wanted to hang out on the ice. I don't know why anybody did, but the rink was always packed. I suppose it's something you can do without holding a long conversation. It's where you can get a pizza without having to stand in the chip shop queue while the smell of fat sinks into your clothes. And what's more, you can entertain a small girl for hours on an ice rink, without actually having to, well, entertain her. Mallory didn't give her brother and me a backwards glance, just shot out on to the ice, small, slick and immortal.

Annoyingly enough, her brother was almost as cocky as she was. He was showing off, I thought, as he raced three times round the rink to warm himself up, swerving easily, flipping into reverse and dodging elegantly backwards around the tottering beginners. When he passed me the third time, he skidded to a graceful halt, throwing up a fan of ice.

'Miss Torvill,' I said.

He smiled.

He had his own skates, unlike those of us who had to wear the clunking plastic rink-hire ones, which were only tangentially the shape of a human foot. I couldn't skate for more than half an hour in them. Foley could skate for ever. He could skate for ever backwards. Sometimes I could hate the boy.

All the same, I smiled back.

His hair had grown a couple of centimetres since I'd sat behind him at the exams in June. I liked that, even though bits of it were a mess and half-obscured his dark eyes. He offered me a hand.

'I'm not going to fall over,' I said.

'I never said you were.'

God, I could win awards. I could be Miss Gauche in the All-Time Gaucheness Contest in Gauche County, Awkwardsville. The boy wants to hold your sodding hand, Ruby. Get on with it.

I don't want to give the impression I'd never had my hand held by a boy before. I'd never had my hand held in Cameron Foley's, that was all. And as I may have mentioned, I couldn't think of anything to say around boys, so I got so fixated on the contact of a hand, my own would start to sweat, which of course made me even more self-conscious and tongue-tied. This was such a vicious circle, my hand would slip out of his simply through the laws of friction and traction and whatever the physics term is for sweaty palms.

The phenomenon didn't seem to be a problem with Foley. My hand felt perfectly comfortable in his, as comfortable as the silence between us. My fingers were linked through his fingers and so long as he didn't go too much faster, I might get through several circuits without falling on my backside. I hoped so, because I wasn't sure I could untangle my hand to break my fall. It seemed too firmly locked in his.

I was already too attached.

Again he did that confident skid-to-a-halt-in-a-fan-of-ice thing, and as he switched direction he caught me, folding his arms across my body. Natural enough, then, to fold my arms over his. We leaned against the battered barrier and watched the other skaters. There was a girl in the centre of the ice, spinning and dancing and whirling. I watched her, bewitched by envy, as she gripped one foot behind her own head and pirouetted impossibly.

'Hey,' said Foley, and nodded.

I tore my eyes away from the ice dancer and looked where he was looking.

Well, there was a surprise: Jinn tottering on to the ice with Nathan Baird. Usually Jinn would only go to the ice rink in winter, and then under duress. She used to take me because I insisted, but she herself was rubbish at it. I didn't take lessons, I just practised not falling over, and eventually I got better. Jinn didn't even bother with that. She was happy to sit up on the metal chairs overlooking the rink, which were almost as comfortable as the skates, and watch me circle the ice, style-free but more or less sure-footed.

Jinn didn't like getting cold and however energetic and wrapped-up you were, cold rose from the ice like an invisible mist. So she'd sit there and shiver, watching and smiling at me. I told her she'd be warmer skating, but of course she said if she fell – and she would – her bum would freeze to the ice.

But there she was now, doing her damnedest to stay upright in front of Nathan Baird, struggling along in the clumsy skates that gave you verrucas. She could hardly walk in them, let alone skate, so she was almost breathless with laughter.

I never knew Nathan Baird could giggle as well. Jinn was arse over tit as soon as she let go of the barrier, and Nathan tried to help her up, only to join her in an inelegant heap. They tried to get up, holding on to each other's arms, but then they collapsed again, weak with hilarity.

'Will I go and help?' came Foley's voice in my ear.

I shook my head, bringing my ear into brief, tantalising contact with his lips. I liked him right where he was.

And it was funny, but I didn't want him to help them. He'd only get in the way. I wanted Jinn and Nathan Baird to go on fooling around for ever.

I couldn't even watch the ice dancer any more; I couldn't see anything but Jinn. She wasn't wearing a flirty skating dress or a glittery hair tie but she had a rhinestone sparkle that came out of the inside of her, and her shrieking laughter was like frost crystals scattering. Her pale hair glittered with ice where she'd lain flat on her back, corpsing, undignified but beautiful.

Beside her, Nathan, laughing too, looked bloody awful. *Awful.* That wasn't like him. But however bad and hungover he looked, he was laughing and he was happy. You could tell that too: sparkling happy. Inner rhinestones. He must have caught them off Jinn. Like verrucas.

Five

'Hey, Ruby Red,' said Nathan Baird.

God's sake. I was thinking seriously about changing my hair colour again. He was standing in the narrow aisle of the mini-mart, idly picking up cans and packets, reading the contents lists, blocking the way. He wore a black T-shirt with a faded Batman logo. I hadn't bothered with a basket, so my arms were full of a loaf and a two-litre bottle of semi-skimmed and a six-pack of Coke. I hovered, glowering at him. He knew I was still there but he didn't move.

I couldn't be bothered trying to shove past; I knew he'd make it difficult for me. Backing off, I went down the other aisle. But by the time I got to the checkout, Nathan had got there first. He was leaning on it, picking up gum and turning it in his fingers, waiting for the last customer in the queue to take her credit card receipt so he could flirt with Jinn. When she didn't move fast enough, he practically elbowed the woman out of the way. Jinn gave him that scowl that wasn't angry enough to be real. He leaned on the counter, smiling his shit-eating smile.

The smile was still good, but I thought he wasn't looking so well these days. His skin had a sweaty look and the whites of his eyes weren't so white. I was hoping Jinn would go off him now that he'd lost the vivacious sexiness, but Nathan Baird was one of those guys who looks good sleazy.

Out of doors, in the sunlight, he was diminished, but somewhere as restricted as the mini-mart he had the sort of presence that makes your heart go faster and your stomach lurch. Reluctant magnetic attraction and fear all mixed up together. Charisma, Jinn called it. I didn't trust it or him. He was nervous about something, too; his fingers trembled.

Also, I didn't like him always being at our house.

I don't know quite how that happened. I only know I came out of my room one day because I heard the music from the iPod dock in the kitchen, and I thought Jinn must be starting to cook and I'd go and help, like always. *Good Vibrations* usually meant tacos or pasta with chilli: something summery and hot.

But when I went through to the kitchen, Jinn didn't see me. She wasn't cooking; she hadn't got past picking up the wooden spoon, which she wielded like a lady with a fan. Nathan Baird was dancing with her, doing the shimmying boogieing thing in my place, and her arms snaked round his neck, and she beat the spoon lightly against his taut butt in time to the music.

She laughed.

Cold dread trickled from my breastbone down into my guts. I thought about what Wide Bertha said, about Nathan Baird being no good. I thought about what he'd been doing all the time he was away, what got him put in prison that I didn't want to ask about. I hoped he was going to leave soon so that Jinn and I could go back to being Jinn and me.

Draping his arms loosely over Jinn's shoulders, he danced her in a semicircle so that he was looking right at me. It took him a few seconds to smile, and I didn't like it when he did. He gave me a slow wink.

'I'm hungry,' I said.

He didn't take his eyes off me, but I saw them open wider when Jinn smacked his backside with the spoon.

'The children are hungry, Mr Baird.'

Distracted from me, he became more human. His eyes lost their hostile focus, his smile softened. Jinn lifted his arms and dropped them gracefully off her shoulders.

'Aw,' he murmured at her ear. As they walked past each other, her to the cooker and him towards the door, he raised a hand so that it caught strands of her hair that flickered through his fingers. He was looking at me again.

'I'll help,' I told Jinn.

'No, I'm fine. Go and sit down till it's ready.'

Reluctantly I went through to the lounge, feeling Nathan behind me like a big bundle of electricity. I sat down right in the middle of the sofa and splayed my hands out at my sides. I didn't think he'd try and sit with me, but I wasn't taking any chances.

He gave me an amused grin, as if he could read my motives, and slumped into the swivel chair beside the TV, one leg hooked over the chair arm. He tossed the remote control up and down in his right hand, then clicked the screen on, but it didn't make any sound. He did nothing about that, just went on looking at me.

'I like your sister,' he said.

I shrugged, staring at *The Weakest Link*, at mouths opening and shutting in silence, the sneer on Anne Robinson's face, the curl of her lip. Nathan's twin.

'I like your sister,' he said again.

Stung, I snapped, 'Me too.'

'Are you jealous?' he grinned. 'Ruby Red.'

I made a face that I hoped was contemptuous.

'You haven't changed since I was at school.' Yawning, he stretched his arms above his head. I wanted to snatch the remote control off him but I didn't dare. 'Do you still not speak? Do the teachers know you're there? They used to talk about you – I heard them. They felt sorry for you. Not sorry enough to do anything about it, of course, but they thought you were dead weird. Just as well you had your sister, eh? Don't know what you'd do without Jinn.'

I stood up. 'I'll go and help her.'

'Tom Jerrold's back as well.'

That made me sit down again, because my knees wouldn't keep my legs straight. My jaw had gone slack as my knee joints, which wasn't a nice thing to be aware of in the face of Nathan's jeering, but I couldn't think for a minute how to rearrange my face. At last I swallowed. 'Why?'

'Work. He's got a junior partnership in Roscoe Geddes. Wants to be near his family, now his brother's out of hospital.' Nathan was watching me out of the corner of his eye as he played with the remote. Suddenly he pointed it at me. 'Click! Put your jaw back.'

I did. Then I didn't know what to say anyway, so I shrugged again.

'That was crap, what that wee tosser Alex did. Think so? Imagine jumping off that roof.'

'Wasn't his fault,' I said.

'Bloody was! Who jumped? Miserable wee git. Couldn't even do the job properly. Was there not a high enough roof in Glassford? Mad as a frog. Was he on drugs?'

I shook my head.

'Really? You think not? Even madder wee git, then. Must be a sight more miserable now, you think? Stuck in a chair the rest of his life.' He laughed. 'So what did he look like, then? Drunk?'

'He was just sad,' I said, before I realised what I was getting into.

'In the old-fashioned sense,' said Nathan. 'Or, nah, both kinds. Did he shut his eyes?'

I shook my head, feeling my spine curl in, hoping I'd soon be an impenetrable ball, like a woodlouse. I could have used a shell.

'Really? Did he not? Did you look that closely?'

'No,' I mumbled.

Nathan winked at me. 'Nobody's perfect, eh, Ruby Red? Don't feel bad. Even if you were horrible to him, poor wee soul. I wonder if Tom feels bad? You know, being away and everything. Going away and getting a job and that. Mind you, maybe Alex depressed the arse off him as well.'

What with all Nathan's baiting, I'd forgotten how the subject of Alex came up in the first place. The reminder about Tom felt like a kick in the stomach. I half-rose, glanced in a panic towards the kitchen. I could hear the crashing of pans and the slap of Jinn's bare feet and she was singing along to Marvin Gaye.

'He was in Edinburgh,' I said. 'Tom.'

'Yeah. Imagine leaving Edinburgh and coming back here! If you didn't have to.'

'Why did you? Come back?'

He widened his eyes. 'Imagine you asking!' He laughed, then laughed again, as if my nerve really tickled him.

He didn't answer, though. He kicked the chair back round to face the TV, and turned up the sound and changed the channel to the six o'clock news. A weepy woman was talking at a press conference; her husband had his arm round her shoulders and the policeman beside her was wearing a professional Grim Face. I recognised them: the parents of the third girl. That was months ago. Must be a development? An arrest?

Oh, no, it was a reconstruction. Somebody who looked like Girl 3 from the back was walking down a leafy street, pretending the ranks of press cameras weren't there, swinging her white lookalike Prada bag at her side. She turned down a lane, and a young couple turned out of it and glanced back at her, and walked on in the opposite direction, and Girl 3 walked on to meet a reconstructed Death, and that was it.

(I'm calling her Girl 3, but that's the smart-arsiness of hindsight. Girls die all the time. I didn't connect them; why should I? I'm not sure anyone else did either. Except for the obvious person.)

I put one hand over one ear, only half-trying not to listen as the reporter recapped the tale of her miserable death – as if we hadn't heard it a hundred times, as if we didn't know everything but the most vital plot point. I wondered, if they never found her killer, whether the story of her end would change and mutate, like a myth, like Chinese whispers.

Nathan shook his head, like he was disgusted at the sheer unpleasantness of the world, like he hadn't just watched the whole thing with fascination. The story changed to something political, so he flicked through the channels till he found *The Simpsons*. He didn't ask me what I'd like to watch. Like it was his TV or something! That should have forewarned me.

He sighed as they interrupted Marge and Lisa for adverts, and muttered it again, almost to himself.

'I really like your sister.'

* * *

So he never left. At least, he left only to get his things. It wasn't that he actively moved in, just that more and more of his stuff migrated into the sitting room and the shower room, and suddenly he wasn't staying every third night, or every second night: he was there the whole damn time. That's how you can get a family member without even knowing it's happening.

He didn't give Jinn anything for his rent, his argument to me being that he wasn't taking up any extra room. I disagreed. He took up my space. He took up my space beside Jinn on the sofa. He gave an edge to the air. It wasn't a big house and it had just fitted the two of us, dilapidated but snug. Nathan Baird sucked the pleasure and the oxygen out of the place, and he took up more than a Nathan Baird-sized piece of space. I hated finding him in the kitchen in the morning, shirt open to show his ribcage or just stripped to the waist. He wasn't interested in me and he knew I wasn't interested in him: he flaunted himself to taunt me. I'm sleeping with your sister, he was saying. Get over it.

It's not that I couldn't see why she fancied him. I did get that whole scrawny, sleazy, bad-boy charm. I just wished Jinn didn't. She'd always been crazy about him, even at school. At school he hadn't been inclined to attach himself to just one girl, but he'd been more conventionally attractive then. Now he seemed happy to be with Jinn, and no wonder. Where else could he get a rent-free roof over his head and home-microwaved meals? Because once he moved in, she didn't have time to make macaroni cheese any more. She was too busy having sex with Nathan Baird.

'What's your problem with me, Ruby?' he said more than once.

My problem was that Jinn was happy. My problem with Nathan Baird was that he was right, I was jealous. We were not a three-person family. Not these particular three people.

And he couldn't even leave Jinn alone while she was working. He hung around the mini-mart too much, and Wide Bertha didn't like it. And so here we stood now, fighting silently over Jinn's workspace as intently as we fought over possession of her at home.

I dumped my groceries on the counter and lasered him with my glare, but he took no notice. He leaned across it and kissed Jinn's nose, which made her laugh.

'I'll get those for you, Ruby.' Jinn didn't even look at me. She just wiggled her fingers in my vague direction, all her focus bound up in his lean hard smiling face.

I watched them, unwilling to move, partly out of a stubborn need to be noticed, but mostly because the look that passed between them fascinated me.

I liked Foley – I'd liked him for ages – but I hadn't looked at him like that yet. I wondered if I ever would. I wondered if it was fakeable, and as I wondered that, I let myself study Nathan's face instead. If it was fakeable, was he faking it?

There was only one way to find out, and that was to try

it out on Foley some time. Nibbling my lip, I concentrated on memorising it. The intensity and the exclusivity. The smile that wasn't entirely a smile, that was starting to segue into seriousness. I wondered if this was the first time they'd looked at each other and truly, honestly loved each other, because that was the impression I was getting.

It was only because I was watching so closely, only because I was part of the atmosphere and I never opened my mouth. It was only because Jinn was so used to me I might as well have been an extra arm or something. They'd forgotten I was there and that was how I saw her slide four packs of Embassy Regal into his waiting hands.

I wanted to tell Wide Bertha, but how could I? Bertha was crazy about Jinn, thought the sun shone out of her arse, and was incredibly cocky about having kept her despite the lure of Tesco up in Glassford and their employee bene-fits package. The thing was that Jinn was crazy about Bertha too, so the concept of her stealing from the woman was almost beyond my comprehension. The thing that niggled at me most, the thing I fought against considering, was that Nathan Baird didn't even smoke.

It was a fabulous summer that year. Summer was Jinn's lucky season, so the best summer for years should have been her best luck in years. I suppose it was, if you count falling in love with Nathan Baird, but I didn't and neither did Wide Bertha.

It turned out Wide Bertha wasn't stupid either.

'I've banned Nathan Baird,' she said, out of nowhere. 'He's not getting back in my shop.'

She was sitting with me and Foley on the grass; she had taken an early lunch break so she could enjoy the sun. Mallory was rampaging with a small boy, shoving him into flower beds and getting shoved back, shrieking with offence and hilarity. It was blazing hot and Bertha had taken off her shoes and was dipping her swollen ankles in the little landscaped stream that ran through the Dot Cumming Park on its way to the river and the sea. I could hear the crash of crates from the shop; Molotov Mixers were selling fast in this weather, so Inflatable George was back again. He was nearly finished, so I knew he'd be joining us shortly, which was another reason Bertha had taken the early break.

Foley lay back on the grass. 'Should've banned him before,' he muttered.

'Thanks for your timely advice,' said Bertha tartly. 'I'm well aware of that.'

'What's he been doing, nicking stuff?'

'And distracting my girls.' She shot me a sharp look. 'Eh, Ruby?'

Meaning, distracting Jinn. I wondered if she knew that distraction wasn't the only problem. I just concentrated on the sea, at the play of the breeze out there, stroking the surface of the water and making it shudder, like rubbing a cat's fur the wrong way. I thought it must be a lot cooler out at sea. I thought about my green-and-white ball and wondered if it had ever got to America. Obviously I was thinking about anything except answering Bertha.

'That wicked tongue of yours.' Bertha shrugged and lit another cigarette. I wondered what she did with the half-smoked ones, because as carefully as she tucked them away, she never seemed to use them again.

'It's not like your sister to be stupid,' remarked Bertha.

Foley opened one eye and caught mine. I gave him a tiny shake of the head, willing him not to say anything. Bertha didn't know about Jinn stealing for Nathan, I figured. She just meant Jinn made stupid boyfriend choices. And who were we to argue?

Fortunately Foley was telepathic with me now. He didn't ask.

'Finished, George?'

Up till that moment, when he settled down at Bertha's side, I hadn't known Inflatable George's name actually was George. He was losing his shyness around her, and now he sat very close, leaning protectively into her in a way that announced that her space was his space. I'd have expected her to draw back like a big defensive crab in overalls, but instead she leaned into him. Now their shoulders were touching, it was obvious, but they didn't look embarrassed. Certainly not half as embarrassed as me.

'Hello, Ruby,' said George. He ignored Foley. His pink cheeks were pinker than ever in the sun.

'I bet there are lots of good words in your head, Ruby,' he said.

'Yes,' I said.

Bertha sighed. 'She likes to keep them to herself, does our Ruby. I sometimes think it's a bit rude.'

When she stood up and stalked off she had a green patch on her ample backside. Normally I'd have called her back and we'd have had a giggle, but for once this didn't seem like the moment.

'She'll be OK,' said Inflatable George, who hated a scene. 'She's a bit upset with your sister. Jinn'll get over that waster Baird, won't she? She's too nice not to.'

He was nice too. I smiled at him. I hoped he was right, and I felt bad about making Bertha stomp off in a huff just as he'd arrived, so I made it a really genuine smile.

'She should be in a Molotov ad,' he said, nodding. 'Your Jinn. I always think that.'

I felt quite swollen with pride that he thought so, as pleased as if he was the company chief executive in charge of marketing instead of just a delivery driver. The Molotov ads were all sunlight and laughter, girls and boys who glittered with light and health, who chased each other across the sand and fooled in the shallows, and threw friendly arms around one another, and tipped bottles of Molotov to their perfect laughing lips. They never got drunk and threw up behind a sand dune. There had been complaints about those ads: some fat bloke had stood up in the Holyrood parliament and huffed and puffed about glamorising alcohol.

But the ads hadn't been banned, and the fat bloke lost his vote, so he went off and drowned his sorrows in the parliament bar. And the Molotov girls and boys went on playing in their eternal sunlight with the breeze whipping their golden hair and the light glowing out of their skin. They were like angels, naughty angels, and the soundtrack was pretty cool too. Jinn would be a perfect Molotov beach girl.

'She should do something like that. She should go to drama school. Or be a model or something.' Inflatable George stood up and squished his fag end into the grass with his toe. He smiled shyly at me.

I could see he was desperate to go and chat up Bertha some more, so there was no need to talk. I just smiled back. When he was gone Foley, still lying prone on his back, blew out a relieved breath.

'Peace at last,' he said.

'Don't be mean.'

'He's a sad bastard. He follows her about like a puppy.'

'I think it's sweet,' I said. I'd been going to try out the Nathan Look, but I was cross with Foley now.

'Yeah, all right.'

'They're not doing any harm.'

He opened one eye again and grinned at me. 'You don't think they're shagging?'

I blushed. The very thought! 'Don't be ridiculous.'

'Why not? Bertha's stuck with that waste of space at home. I don't even think Mr Bertha's that ill.'

I suspected much the same, but I was in no mood to agree with him.

Foley rolled his head round to look at me. 'Oh, sorry I'm sure. C'm'ere.' He flapped an arm out against the ground.

Being annoyed with him warred with feeling sorry for myself and in need of a hug. They warred for, oh, four and a half seconds, and then I wriggled closer and lay back into his arm. He didn't look at me, just curled his arm round my neck and stared up at the sky, so I still couldn't try out the Nathan Look. I was changing my mind about that, anyway. I was starting to think it wasn't fakeable.

'You want to relax or something?' There was an edge of irritation to Foley's voice.

Oh, right. All my muscles were squeezed up tight, and I was grinding my teeth. On one of the benches beside the water, her Tupperware begging bowl right in the path of strolling pedestrians, there was a woman in a dirty floral dress, squeezing random notes out of a reluctant accordion. My spine was that accordion, all the vertebrae crushed tightly together. As she released it and it gave a painful howl, I made my spine go limp too.

'What's Jinn playing at anyway?' he said.

'Dunno.'

'You know he was done for stabbing somebody. Down south. Nathan Baird.'

A cold shudder went down my backbone; Foley must have felt it. 'That what it was? What, *dead*?'

'Nah. But not for want of trying. He's a bastard. Takes after his dad.'

'How did he get out then?'

'Dunno. Served his time, I guess. Jinn must be OK with that.'

'Suppose so.' I swallowed, and found it difficult. 'I suppose she knows. She's happy anyway.'

'Oh well,' said Foley, thick with irony. 'Long as she's happy.'

'There's happy and happy,' I said.

After all, Lara was usually pretty cheery, but not in a good way. Bad-happy is when you don't care a toss for life and the world and your problems, because you've forgotten they're there. Bad-happy was Lara's state of mind when she walked in front of that Vauxhall Astra. Bad-happy was presumably also the state of the driver, who was three times over the limit, but owing to the state of my mother, my scope for indignation was limited.

Well, Jinn was proper-happy. She wasn't like Lara and Foley had no business implying she was.

'Sorry I said that,' he muttered, telepathic again.

'No worries.' And instant forgiveness.

'I wish you were staying at school,' he added.

I turned my head and gazed at him. I gazed at him so intently, I could sort of feel the Nathan Look creeping in, without me even meaning to do it.

But his eyes were shut.

Six

So here's the thing about words. Words can mean everything and nothing. Words meant everything to Alex
Jerrold, who hung on every one from every source, sifting
it for meaning and sincerity and an excuse to be hurt.
Words meant nothing to my mother. Lara loved words for
the sound of them, the ring of them. That was all. She
used an awful lot and she liked to teach me new ones but
in the end all they were was words. She liked words to
play with one another, and she didn't care if they made
sense or told a story worth hearing. And even ordinary
words, she only liked for their own sake. Like *I'll take
care of you* or *I'll be there for you.*

This was why I was careful with words. People shouldn't
treat them so lightly. Sticks and stones have nothing on
words. There are far too many of them about, and not
enough like *regurgitate* or *muslin* or *hollyhock* or *descant.*
Those are what I call words. Not *I love you.*

The real *I love you* was the way Nathan smiled at Jinn
and she grinned right bang into his eyes. I was starting to
hate him from the deepest level of my innards. He wasn't

just taking up space now. He had brought a whole atmosphere with him.

Nathan had been shacking up with us all summer. Foley
was going back to school tomorrow, so I couldn't even
hang out at his place as much as I had done the whole
holidays, with his parents away all the time at dog shows.
I was bored and lonely and I couldn't wait to start work in
Glassford. If I'd had the nerve I'd have stayed over at
Foley's when his parents weren't there, but I was still
nervous of upsetting Jinn and anyway, Foley seemed to
think it would corrupt Mallory.

And when it came right down to it, I didn't want to
sleep with him, not yet. Nathan and Jinn were putting me
so far off sex I was going to end up in a convent. Squeak
squeak, grunt, muffled cry, silence. Only not that quick.
Yerch.

I had a month or so to go till I started work and my
SVQ course at a proper salon, and I was almost wishing
I'd done a fifth school year just to get away from Nathan
for a few extra weeks. I'd decided to go straight to work
because I'd found a salon that did training on the job and
I couldn't bear the thought of further formal education,
but I'd have done just about anything at that point to get
away from Nathan. I'd have gone back to playgroup.

I stood in the kitchen and stared at his naked back as he
yawned and scratched his shoulder. He was thinner than
he'd been when he arrived, and his skin was sheened with
sweat. I could smell him from across the room. It wasn't

73

a bad smell; some girls might even have liked it. But it was too male and too unwanted.

'Well, hello.' Nathan didn't turn round; he just knew it was me because of the hostile silence. So much for the Air of Mystery I'd hoped I was cultivating.

I took a breath, changed my mind, then sucked in a second breath. 'We've got a shower. It's right next to the toilet.'

'How very daring!' He gave me a mocking look over his shoulder.

'You stink.' I'd started so I might as well finish.

'I ooze pheromones, darling. It's not the same thing.' He clicked on the kettle, then turned and came towards me. I was too surprised to react and besides, I was damned if I was going to back off.

He propped a hand against the door frame and leaned over me. I could have drawn a finger down his freckled, sweaty chest, had I been so inclined. Instead I put my hands behind my back and glared up at him.

'I just don't fancy you, Rubes.'

'What?' I was going to have to do something about my loose jaw-hinge.

'I mean, I like you fine. Just don't fancy you. So you can stop feeling all threatened.'

I wanted to put my hand against his ribcage and shove him hard across the room, but that would have involved touching his skin, feeling the warmth of blood and what there was of his muscles. His sweat-smell was all over the inside of my nostrils and I hated him for it, and for what he'd said.

'Piss off,' I snapped.

'Your wish,' he said. 'My desire.' Ever so slowly he eased himself away from the wall and pushed past me, leaving traces of himself on my clothes. It made me shiver, and that made me even angrier. The shower-room door slammed behind him and I heard the hiss of water. In turn I went into my own room and slammed the door, rather pointlessly. Good luck to him, if he wanted hot water at this hour.

Why didn't he get a job, anyway? Then he wouldn't be taking showers at half past eleven and he wouldn't have to be asking Jinn to steal sixpacks of WKD. I glowered at the small stack of bottles in the corner, glowing as blue as opaque jewels in the halogen spotlight. I wanted to take one of those bottles, smash it against the wall and glass him. And me a non-violent person.

I doubted Jinn would approve of me glassing her boyfriend, so I texted Foley instead.

Got M, he texted back.

So what? He always seemed to have Mallory. She seemed to be some kind of chaperone. I wasn't unhappy about it because I wasn't sure I was ready to get in any deeper with Foley at the moment, and besides, she was a mascot. With a small child around I felt like the kind of human being who could be responsible for another one.

But before I could text him back and tell him I didn't mind about the brat, my phone bleeped again.

Fd th dux?

It didn't sound like a bad idea and it didn't cost anything. I went back to the kitchen and hunted around for some scraps, raking deep into cupboards, and suddenly felt my fingers sink into something cold and yielding.

I yelped in disgust. When I pulled the thing out, it used to be a potato. It was still a potato. Its body was withered and squishy, and it was pushing out green and yellow tendrils like pustules, like the most satisfying zits you ever squeezed. They ought to be planted, but Jinn had forgotten potatoes, she'd forgotten goats.

Nathan's kettle had boiled. I lifted it and poured the water down the sink. Petty but satisfying.

What to do with the dead potato, though? I picked scraps of newspaper off it, mentally apologising for its meaningless existence. Briefly I wondered if I could feed it to the ducks, but I might poison them.

Briefly I wondered if I could feed it to Nathan Baird.

I didn't want to deal with the potato so I shoved it back in the cupboard with its friends. One day, I thought. One day she'd remember the sodding potatoes and the tyre garden and then we'd be happy again. One day, when we were back to being us.

The ducks at the Provost Reid Park in Glassford were fat and overfed and uninterested. Ducks were spoiled these days. Not like when I were a girl. Oh, I remembered feeding ducks that were actually grateful for your mouldy crusts and the hard fairy cakes out of the shop, and the ingratitude of this lot aggravated me. They didn't even care that the screaming gulls were having a gang fight because gulls didn't know the meaning of 'overfed'. They just sculled fatly around the pond, while the gulls teemed overhead like something out of a Hitchcock movie.

Mallory must have been having the same thoughts as me, because she'd given up on the ducks and had started forming little pellets of bread, squeezing and rolling them till they were like ball bearings, then hurling them at the gulls. She was not a bad shot. She actually hit one, hard, on its beak, making it wobble off balance and shake its white head and shriek with rage.

'You keep it up and the council might give you a job,' I said.

'Oh, it *talks*,' said Mallory, echoing Nathan Baird.

'The mouth on you.' Foley flicked a bit of crust at her. It missed, and Mallory fired back a pellet of bread intended for the gulls. It smacked him right on the eye.

'Ow! Ah, ya wee –'

She took evasive action, dodging her bum neatly away from his swinging palm and making a run for the play-park. We followed, Foley swearing blue murder at her and rubbing his eye.

'Thank Christ she's got school tomorrow.'

'You and all.'

'Yeah. What are you going to do with your time now that you won't have my scintillating company?'

'Me? I was thinking of getting a life.'

This was true in only one sense. Frankly, I was panicking at the prospect of getting a life. I knew a few others who were leaving school and going to college in Glassford but nobody else was starting at the salon. Nobody else was starting actual *work*. And now that the moment was upon me I was a lot less sure about leaving school for the big bad world. I'd have choked on my pride and gone back to school after all, but it was too late now. Imagine tonguetied Ruby trying to talk herself out of what passed for a decision. Not a chance.

I'd have liked to explain all this to Foley but I was still awkward around him, for different reasons now. I couldn't stay away, but sometimes I couldn't think what to say to him, or if I did think of something to say, I didn't want to say it. And yet we were a sort-of couple, and had been right through the summer. Well, a threesome if you counted Mallory, which we had to.

Foley was now paying me all the attention I'd ever wanted, but my contrary brain (or some part of my anatomy) had gone *whoa*. That didn't mean I wasn't still hauled by some mysterious magnetism into his company. There was definitely an attraction in the fact that he didn't feel the need to talk, and didn't feel the need to make me talk either. It saved my tongue from getting knotted and stuck to the roof of my mouth like Velcro.

So after a bit of nervous coughing and throat-clearing,

and turning to each other at the wrong moment, and bumping shoulders too hard and muttering apologies, Foley and I finally got our movements coordinated enough for a decent snog.

It was maybe three weeks after Mallory stunned the gull. I think it helped that Foley had been back at school for a bit and here I was, never having to go back again. That couldn't help but give me a slight superiority. It definitely helped that we were Mallory-free: she had some kind of after-school activity (Art Club, I think, which if I knew Mallory would involve drawing coded rude bits on pictures that the teachers wouldn't recognise but her evil little boyfriends would). So we were going to go and meet her out of school, but in this downpour the brat could wait.

Yes, the weather gods had aligned themselves in my favour too. Usually the weather got finer after the schools went back, but this year it was the other way round.

I was kicking my heels till my job started. Wide Bertha could give me a few hours' work at the mini-mart but she couldn't afford to give me a regular gig at the moment, not with summer over. September had turned nasty, in a dull wet way, and Foley and I were sheltering under the concrete arches of a little shopping arcade in our estate (*arcade* and *estate* are excellent, beautiful words but they are not honest. If you say 'I have an arcade on my estate', it conjures up an arch of clipped privet, framing sunlit parkland that hazes into blue distance. This is not what I'm talking about).

The damp roughcast walls were even damper than usual, because the wind had swung round and was driving the rain at us. I could hear it pattering on the metal shutters down over the Chinese takeaway, which didn't open till early evening. The Fu Ling restaurant sign had been vandalised again. Predictably enough, this happened a lot. The owner would haul out his stepladder at least twice a month and climb up patiently to scrub out the spray paint. I don't know why he bothered. I thought he should change the name to Golden Dragon or something, but when I suggested it he just smiled and nodded and didn't do anything about it. I could talk to this guy because he was even more taciturn than I was. There was a chance he didn't even speak English but you'd never know either way. It was his tiny wife who did all the talking when we got a takeaway. She never shut up. I liked Mr Fu Ling; we were comrades in the world of the monosyllabic.

Anyway, there were Foley and I leaning against the Fu Ling shutters, waiting for the rain to ease off a bit so we could go and meet Mallory (though I reckoned she'd be safe walking home on her own; God help anybody who tried abducting her). In contented, dripping silence we people-watched: pasty old guys with yellow fingers going into the bookmakers with the boarded-up window; old ladies shuffling into the Co-op, ground down to half their original size but still up for a long gossip with the woman at the till, while the teenagers behind them huffed and fidgeted and stuck stolen gum and sweets into their pockets out of sheer boredom.

There was no sign of the weather giving us a break, and I think Foley must have come over melancholic at the sight of all that rained-on human mortality, because he sighed a huge unexpected sigh and turned and kissed my left ear. This time he didn't get awkward and jerk his head away when I turned. This time he didn't shut his eyes. This time, when I turned, his face stayed where it was, gazing right into mine.

We were a good height together and he had incredibly watchable eyes. I smiled. He smiled. I was not about to risk puckering up if he was going to blush and pull away at the last moment, because I have a very low embarrassment threshold and I had a feeling the relationship, such as it was, would not survive another missed kiss. I remembered a different incident with Alex Jerrold, after all. I remembered that like it was yesterday.

So I put my hand up to Foley's head. His hair was quite short – certainly compared to Nathan Baird's unkempt straggle – and it had a nice silky feel. He was vain enough to use conditioner, then. I had a closer look at it, now that I had him still, deciding I liked the softness of it through my fingers. And since he really did have excellent movie-star eyes, and that nose, and his lips weren't bad either, I gave him a hesitant kiss.

He gave a little start, like I'd electrocuted him or something, but swiftly grounded himself, and kissed me back. Interesting. The current came whizzing back through me. Foley was a good kisser. I congratulated myself on my taste, and was about to hunt for his tongue when his found mine.

Words. Who needs 'em?

All the same, after that interlude, we found them easier. I'm not saying Foley and I had had a silent relationship for the previous four months, but it wasn't endless chat. We both liked it that way: casual, intermittent conversation and laughs more frequent than the talk justified. A good snog loosened both our tongues. He got into a habit of startling me with his conversational openers, a habit which might have been deliberate. He didn't even refer to the kiss, but he started with the left-fielders then and there.

'Imagine Alex trying to top himself. I always thought he'd be the one that killed people.'

I had to do a swift reorientation: of my nerve-endings, my leaping innards, my brain. 'What?'

'Alex Jerrold. I thought he'd stock up high-powered rifles and handguns and then he'd come into school and shoot seventeen people and a teacher.'

'That's eighteen people.'

'Right, yeah. You know what I mean.'

Well, I did. You could imagine the stunned townsfolk

blinking into the camera and going, 'He was a loner, you know. Quiet. Odd, now you mention it.'

He'd have done it for effect. Or we'd have assumed so. 'Alex Jerrold does it for effect,' everybody at school said. The whole silent, strange, oddball thing. I saw aspects of Alex that were a lot like me, which was partly why I enjoyed the baiting he got and did nothing to discourage people.

As far as I was concerned he was a drama queen, which was exactly what Jinn used to call me. A drama queen with no dialogue. 'Ruby, you're such a drama queen!' That was when I was sulking, which was when my quietness grew palpably more malevolent. 'Get over yourself!'

Which was precisely what I was trying to do. Get over myself. When I was small, I was not endearing. If I capered adorably, adults would give me a quizzical look, either pitying or slightly alarmed. This was how I got to know that I was short on the charisma stakes.

Jinn had all the charisma a family could need, but I wasn't jealous of her. I was glad there was someone in the family who gave good vibes. My vibes were like bacon that's been left in the fridge that tiny bit too long and has a strange, frightening aftertaste. My vibes were like music that's so slightly off-key you don't know why it's wrong. I was proud of Jinn for being the exact right chord, and I was grateful that she drowned me out.

I knew that if I tried to be loud and outgoing I'd get it wrong, so I stayed quiet, hoping it would give me the alternative gift, an Air of Mystery. All it gave me was an Air of Extreme Gaucheness, but it was better than making an arse of myself. I kept words in my head, good ones, but all for me. Alex Jerrold, the silly bugger, let his loose. He wasn't shy, or gauche, or awkward. He was Aloof. He was a not-very-talkative tosspot who thought he was different. Well, he was that all right.

Secretly – very secretly – I quite liked Alex Jerrold. Not in a romantic way, I hasten to add, but we could have been mates. I was aware that after Alex, I was possibly the second-weirdest and second-least popular person in school.

So I could either befriend the boy, or join the majority and have my safe second place secured by the more extreme dorkiness of Alex. Loathsomely enough, I went for the latter. I knew all along that if I was mates with Alex that would make me the same as him, which was out of the question. Even though I liked him, he was everything I hated about myself. And the fact was, he was an irredeemable twat, whereas I had an Air of Mystery. We weren't in the same category.

And of course, in the end, I told him to jump off a roof.

Not that I said anything, as he hesitated up there, blinking at space. I didn't want to make things worse by saying another word, and I was perfectly sure I'd get it wrong anyway. So I let the others taunt him and I let him fall. I let him jump.

It comes to the same thing in the end.

* * *

I knew I ought to go and see Alex. I should go and ring his doorbell and face the cold wounded eyes of his mother, the reproachful stare I'd last felt when I passed her in Glassford High Street six months ago. I had this inkling that if I got through and talked to him, he might start to forgive me, and I'd start to feel better enough to forgive myself.

I wasn't ready to forgive myself. And to be forgiven, by Alex Jerrold, was a more mortifying prospect than I could bear. I imagined it would be like one of those Victorian paintings, with me kneeling at his sickbed in a pool of yellow light, pressing his limp, forgiving hand to my tear-stained face.

I got as far as the end of the road that led to the smaller road that led to his house, then chickened out. I never did get further than the big copper beech on the corner; once past it, I'd be a lot more visible, and pale Alex, reclining on his Victorian sickbed, might by some magic of mirrors and weird angles catch sight of me. So I turned on my heel, like I always did, and went to the library instead.

Spinal injury websites and I were old friends. I liked reading about new research and new possibilities, but even when it was all Renal Complications and Survival Rates and Outcomes After Ten Years, I couldn't look away. The scratch of guilt's jagged claw across my guts made me feel better, paradoxically. I should be feeling guilty, I should be feeling bad. And you never knew, I might find something the doctors, his parents, the consultants and the physiotherapists had somehow failed to spot. I went back to those websites as a dog returneth to its vomit, which is an expression that has always appealed to me.

The librarian, who was part of my penance even on a good day, gave me the evil eye as I pushed open the doors. Oh, yeah. I pulled my phone from my pocket and switched it off. Last time I was here she'd thrown me out because it had gone off and she had her period or a bad hair day or something. I didn't like being snapped at; I wasn't used to it and I wasn't good at answering back.

I like how you can lose yourself on the Net: one more click, and another, and another. I didn't notice how late I was till it was getting dark. The clocks hadn't gone back yet, so that was pretty late even in September. I had to log out and grab my jacket and run for home.

There was a tiny triangle of grass and scrub between our street and the main one. I always took a short cut across it, even when I wasn't several hours late, and that's where, that night, I ran into Jinn.

I didn't recognise her at first, aimless and crying and soaked through. Care in the Community, I thought, preparing to give the apparition a bodyswerve. Then I recognised the gleam of her hair, just as she stopped short and stared at me. And then she started yelling.

I just stood there, buffeted by her hysterical rage and a little bewildered too.

When she ran out of words and breath, she rubbed her eyes. 'I've been phoning you for *hours*!'

I tugged my phone out of my pocket, flipped it open, switched it back on. Oops.

It was too exhausting to explain. And of course it was far too complicated to explain to Jinn about the library and the dog and the vomit. So all I said, when she'd calmed down a bit, was, 'Sorry.'

'I tried everywhere! Bertha! Foley! You weren't anywhere!'

'Sorry,' I said again. 'I lost track of time. I didn't know you'd –'

'What?'

'I didn't know you'd miss me.' God, I hated the way that came out. 'I mean, I didn't know you were expecting me. I mean, I thought you'd be with – you know. I thought you . . . well. Did you have tea ready?'

'Like always!'

I opened my mouth but managed not to say it. Maybe she didn't realise tea had been a bit hit-and-miss lately. Maybe she'd lost count of the times I'd just gone for chips with Foley. It was the stupid phone, that was all. If I'd left it switched on it would have been fine. 'Sorry.'

She looked as if she was about to say something more, but just cracked her finger joints instead, and turned uncertainly, and walked beside me. Now that she'd run out of temper, her company was quite peaceable. We walked together under a swiftly dimming sky back towards the little grey house.

'Ruby,' she blurted as she opened the rusty gate. 'A girl got murdered.'

* * *

We sat on the doorstep, chilling our bums on the concrete and watching the street lights warm up in hazy orange auras. It seemed like the thing to do, madly enough: sit on the outside of our safe little house when a girl had washed up on the beach a mile north. Go figure. I think it was the coldness of the air, and the way it cleared our brains.

'How could somebody get killed here?' Jinn was hugging herself, as if she was trying to squeeze out tears of anxiety, but she was too hyper to cry.

Anyway, I think it was a rhetorical question, so I didn't answer it.

'You can't stay out late any more, Ruby. You've got to take care.'

'Course,' I said. 'Who was she?'

'Don't know. They just said on the news about the body.'

'So it's probably somebody she knew. Usually is, isn't it?'

'Yes.'

'I mean, it's not likely to be the Breakness Strangler, is it? I mean, can you see it?'

'I know, Ruby. It's just – it's *just*.'

OK. I could accept it was – just. I knew it couldn't happen to me, but getting oneself murdered by crazy strangers was the sort of things mothers fretted about, and so by extension Jinn.

'Sorry,' I said yet again.

'Oh, it's OK.' Jinn put an arm round me and jiggled my shoulders. 'I get worried, that's all.'

Which gave me a warm, reassuring sense of the-way-we-used-to-be. 'Is he back yet?'

She didn't have to ask who. Nathan had gone away south last night in somebody's borrowed car, which had made me wonder what he had on the Somebody. 'No. He decided to go and see his dad. He'll be another few days.'

Despite her wistful tone, I was glad. Not having Nathan was a treat.

'So we can go and see Lara tomorrow?' I suggested.

'Sure,' said Jinn.

Going to see Lara had never been morbid or depressing, except for the one time. The cemetery was like a park, with clipped lawns and rose beds and more-or-less unvandalised benches, and fairly unobtrusive CCTV cameras. It was a little oasis of municipal prettiness, though it overlooked the bypass and the industrial estate and even if there had been any birdsong you wouldn't have heard it, not with the constant roar of lorries. On the other side of the cemetery, overlooking it in turn, was a small estate of council flats, the kind with those inset balconies that must have been a charming idea at one time but which were now crammed with bikes and washing lines and washing machines. The yawning gaps gave the row of buildings a sort of Gaza-chic, like they were pockmarked with shell holes. Anyway, why would anybody waste their useful balcony space on flowers when they could look straight at everybody else's on the pristine graves beneath?

Jinn and I usually took a picnic with our garden flowers: ready-made sandwiches out of the mini-mart, cans of Coke, a giant pack of Maltesers. It was almost like a regular family picnic with Lara, except that she was under the neat green turf, peaceably decomposing.

I chewed on a cold BLT (tough bacon, not enough mayonnaise) and wrinkled my nose at the headstone: black granite, polished to a gloss except where it was etched with Lara's name and her dates and a pointlessly monochrome rainbow. I thought that headstone was a big mistake but it was something I could never say to Jinn, who had chosen it in a spasm of grief. It cost a fortune – demonstrably so, because that kind of ugliness doesn't come cheap.

Speaking of ugliness. 'He looks really rough,' I said.

Jinn looked up from the petunia-arranging, which was not going well. 'Who?'

Like she didn't know. 'Nathan.'

She contemplated me for a few moments, then seemed to come to a decision. 'I know.'

'Bertha says, is he on drugs?' I blurted.

Jinn stayed silent for a bit, but I saw the petunia petals tremble in her fingers, and one of the little stems broke. 'It's none of Bertha's business, is it?'

'It's mine.'

Quite violently she stuffed the fistful of petunias into their jar. 'That Foley's really bringing you out of yourself, isn't he?'

I didn't dignify that with an answer.

'He doesn't take it any more.'

It. I didn't ask what. 'Oh, right. Sure he doesn't. He could afford a bit of rent, then.'

'He's got his problems. He owes people money.' She didn't quite look at me. 'I wouldn't walk away from you and I'm not walking away from him.'

'He's not us.'

'Yes, Ruby. Yes, he bloody well *is*.' She was angry now; I could see the tears glitter in her eyes. 'I don't care what you think.'

'Yes, you do.' I could get angry too.

'Yes – uh-huh, *sure*. Ruby, I know you don't like him but *I do*. Does that matter to you?'

I shrugged. My turn to avoid her eyes.

'I can help him, Ruby.'

'Aye, right.' I couldn't help that one.

'I can *try*.'

'Not by nicking stuff to pay his debts.'

'Christ on a bike, Ruby. I LOVE him, right?'

I licked my lips.

'I bloody love him. I always loved him. He needs me, right?' She slapped the jar of abused petunias on to the ground, so hard I was amazed it didn't crack. 'He *needs me*.'

'Me too.'

'Yeah, well, my life doesn't revolve around you, Ruby! Not all the time, not for ever!'

Well, that took me aback, because I'd always kind of assumed it did. Jinn rubbed her eyes fiercely and it struck me for the first time (believe it or not) that she might need looking after too. And that if she did, old-fashioned girl that she was, she'd chosen the wrong kind of new-fashioned boy.

'We shouldn't be out late,' she said at last. 'Let's go home.'

Seven

Jinn was an old-fashioned girl and she liked her traditions. She liked Lara's old-fashioned holidays, which we always took somewhere on the west coast. If you asked me to point it out on a map, there's no way I could, though we must have gone to the same place six years in a row at least. It must have been somewhere between the Kintyre peninsula and Assynt, that's all I know. (There are some great words up that coast too but I've no idea what any of them mean.) That coast is longer than it looks because it dives in and out of sea lochs, it twists and jigs and doubles back. I used to imagine it was thousands of miles long, if you could only untwist it and lay it out in a straight line. It would circle the globe three times or something, like picturesque intestines.

The cottage itself was one of those ones that look lovely on the web page, white against a sky that's bluer than reality. Inside it had damp walls, paper that peeled in dark corners, awful kitchen cupboards where you kept everything towards the middle so your food wouldn't touch the mouldy sides, and crockery we'd wash before we used it.

The house was always cold, even on a blue and green summer day, and we had to pay for the electricity by shoving coins into an endlessly hungry meter. But there was a coal fire that filled the room with smoke and the smell of firelighters, so we could always huddle round that in the evenings, and at night I'd crawl into Jinn's bed so I could get warm enough to fall asleep. She'd tell me to go back to my own bed because I kicked in my sleep, but in the meantime she'd rub my back, her thumb bumping down my spine and up again, and when I was next aware of anything it would be morning and I'd still be cuddled against her, and her thumb would be motionless against my spine from when she'd finally dozed off.

Of course, the cottage's big advantage was that it didn't cost much. And the outside lived up to the promise, and when the weather was good it was true that the sky was unfeasibly blue.

The cottage was cheap because it involved pet-sitting two goats. I never saw a kid, and so far as I know Lara didn't have to milk them, so that's why I call them pets, though the cottage called itself a croft. The goats, like the ones in the petting zoo, were evil. The billy was marginally the better of the two, but the nanny swiftly learned to ambush Lara getting out of the car. Lara was scared of her, and the nanny knew it, so when the car pulled up she'd be waiting. She'd stand patiently beside the driver's door, watching Lara with her empty yellow devil-eyes. The first time, Lara thought this was adorable. As she climbed out of the car, cooing, and turned to pick up her groceries, the nanny put her head down and lunged, butting her violently in the bum. Lara and the groceries went everywhere.

After that, Lara was afraid to get out of the car. Jinn, who was not in the least afraid of the nanny goat (and the nanny goat knew that too), had to get out first and shoo her away. If Lara was on her own, she'd sit in the car tooting the horn, and depending on Jinn's mood either she'd rush out to do her duty, or she'd call me and we'd watch Lara through the flimsy net curtains, whispering and giggling and looking at our watches and taking bets on how long it would take our mother to lose her temper. Eventually Jinn would saunter out the front door and round to the back of the cottage, and pretend she'd been out playing and had only just realised.

Lara could never prove otherwise, though once or twice I could tell she was on the verge of furious tears. If she ever tried to cope on her own, the shopping ended up all over the garden, dropped in her panicked flight from the goat. So in the end she always waited for Jinn, for however long it took. It was Jinn's little game of control with our mother, but then it was the only one she really had. And sometimes she was just mad at Lara. Come to think of it, I don't think she ever stopped being mad at Lara.

It wasn't that Lara herself was over-controlling: quite the reverse. And it wasn't that she didn't care. Lara was just too fusionless. Her mind was on other things; either that, or it wasn't anywhere at all. Sometimes her mind went into hibernation, like a computer when you leave it sitting unused. You'd have to hit the space key – or butt Lara in the ribcage – to get it going again.

It was there at the cottage that Jinn first fell in love with goats. I think it was the whole set-up really, but the goats were a symbolic thing. Jinn wanted to live on a croft and keep chickens and perhaps a pig, but most especially goats.

I couldn't imagine Jinn coping with the winter cold, but she only knew the summers. Sometimes they were fabulously warm and we'd bask half-naked in the dunes, gently baking, letting ourselves get so hot we'd have to plunge into the sea to cool off. *That* hot. But sometimes, when the breeze stirred itself, you could feel how it might turn nasty in November. When the wind got stroppy and started to whip up little sandstorms, Jinn would hold her cardigan over the both of us, so we could still suck on ice lollies that were pebble-dashed with sand particles.

Jinn would sit up on the dunes with her arms round her knees, eyes half-shut, blonde sea-roughened hair breezing and flapping out behind her like the ragged mane of a pony, a perfect little happy smile on her face. Jinn's protective countrywear consisted of a useless lacy cardigan with no buttons, just a ribbon threaded round under the empire-line that she could tie at the front but never did, so it flapped loose, fluttering and shimmering in the breeze. The colour of the ribbon matched the river that wound down through the dunes and the rocks before spilling itself aimlessly over the beach. And the river was like scraps of ribbon cascading on to the sand, silver-blue and silky and rippling. I could look at Jinn, exactly matching the river, happy like a pony, and forget I'd rather be at Center Parcs.

Not that we could afford Center Parcs, but Lara wouldn't have gone there anyway. Lara had romantic dreams of being swept off her feet by a dour wild Highlander (which is proof that you should be careful what you wish for, because as it turned out, the driver of the fatal Vauxhall Astra came from Dingwall). But in the meantime she liked to hang out down at the harbour watching the boats come in and asking eager questions about the fish and the weather and the lobster pots. Every evening she'd be down to the Creel, having pints bought for her, chatting up drinkers who quite often turned out to be dour wild Londoners, but you couldn't have everything.

So Jinn and I more or less ran our own holidays, and very successfully. If we got bored of swimming, sunbathing, or nicking magazines out of the hotel, we'd go and annoy the little man who ran the shop. He did not think there was anything funny about life in a remote rural community, nothing AT ALL. He considered Jinn and me to be potential shoplifters and we'd play up to it even though there was nothing we wanted to steal. We'd huddle together over the shelves, picking up mosquito repellent and tinned hot dogs and baby shampoo, then putting them back again, while the little man glared and craned his

97

stubby neck. We'd go up and down the two little aisles, then just as he came out from behind his counter and started to follow to see what we were up to, we'd reverse annoyingly and go back the way we'd come.

If there was nobody in the shop and Jinn said solemnly, 'Busy day,' he'd glower as if he wanted to hang her from the strip light. The fact was he disliked tourists, and he liked children even less. But nothing he could say or do would stop Jinn buying stuff off him, though God knows he tried. We'd giggle our heads off afterwards, sitting in the dunes above the beach, eating our sandblasted lollies. For all his insular Highland pride, we knew fine he came from some grey town two miles west of Leeds.

So one day Jinn was standing in the aisle letting me read *Private Eye* over her shoulder – only the funny bits, we didn't have a lot of time before we got chased out – and she'd just snorted at a political cartoon that went straight over my head, when a voice at the end of the Pasta Sauce & Tacky Chinese Toys aisle said, 'Jinn?'

She was smiling even before she turned and looked. And this pleased me, because at the end of the aisle, his grin caught between chancy and shy, stood Tom Jerrold.

Alex was with him, of course, but we didn't take any notice of him. Not that Jinn rushed up and hugged Tom or anything stupid. She sauntered up to within millimetres and gave him her open sparky grin, but she didn't touch him. I just hovered behind her, making mental notes.

'Brilliant! Hi, Tom! Are you guys on holiday?'

Tom was clutching two litres of milk, an *Independent*, a *Daily Mail* and a box of frozen potato waffles, but he managed to look cool enough as he nodded. 'We're staycationing. Says Dad. So much for Cape Cod this year.' He rolled his eyes and made a face that made Jinn laugh.

'Oh, it's nearly the same.'

'You're so positive.'

'But we're annual visitors,' she said. I liked that term almost as much as Tom obviously did. The words put a new glamorous sheen on our crofty holidays. 'You've only just caught the trend, you sad latecomers.'

'Are the natives friendly?'

'No idea. Never met any. The candidate for Leeds West is a bit of a twat.'

And so they went on, giggling and flirting. I trailed them, and Alex trailed me. He didn't even get to carry the potato waffles; he got the air freshener and the midge killer, one canister in each hand. He traipsed along like fragrant pest control, trying not to look like he was trying to keep up. He fell so far behind, I occasionally forgot I was ignoring him.

Jinn and Tom found a bench outside the only hotel in the local planetary system, and lounged on it. Jinn sat up, arms round her knees, and I could see she was working the charm. Scottish geography and the summer holidays had distanced her from the Blessed Nathan Baird and she was ready for a holiday romance. I was delighted. When Alex shambled past me and tried to join them on the bench, I shot out my arm and stopped him in his tracks. He dropped the insecticide and it rolled noisily up and down on the tarmac.

I picked it up and stuck it back in his hand. He was eyeing me with suspicion.

I pointed at the square of lawn in front of the hotel. Obediently he plopped down on the grass, and I arranged myself, elegantly cross-legged, beside him.

We avoided looking at each other for five minutes, while we ostentatiously breathed west coast air and admired the view.

'You don't talk a lot,' said Alex after a bit.

'Do if I want to.'

'When's that?'

'When I've got anything to say. Worth saying. I mean. Like. You know.'

And there was me trying to be cool, and screwing up again. I thought he was a twat anyway, so I don't know why I wanted to look cool. I suppose I just wanted *somebody* to think I was cool. Even Alex Jerrold. Who was two years older than me, and a dick already. Irredeemable. By the time you were twelve you'd had your chance. I shivered and hoped I'd achieve effortless verbal elegance in the next twelve months or so.

'Do you not think it's easier to talk if you're walking?' he asked.

'Yeah . . . '

'Also, it's easier to not talk.'

'Yeah . . . '

'I just think it's easier when you're walking. Everything.'

'Uh-huh?'

'So do you not want to go for a walk?'

Which is how I ended up tramping around scrubby hills with Alex Jerrold for ten days, trying to give Jinn and Tom space while not giving Alex the wrong idea. I was so not Alex's girlfriend. For God's sake, I was still in Primary Seven. Which was no doubt why we got dragged around with Jinn and Tom anyway. They never left us to our own devices, so my devious matchmaking never had a chance of success.

Of course Tom and Alex were occasionally required to do family holiday stuff, parental bike rides, seal watching boat trips, that stuff. But when they were released from duty they'd come and find us – or rather, Tom would come and find Jinn and Alex would tag along – which was how they found us scoffing Magnums on the beach that day.

Jinn jumped down off her rock and smiled openly at Tom. 'We'll get you one.'

'We will?' I gave her a dark look. We were nearly out of cash.

'Yup. C'mon, Rubes. Watch this, boys.'

When we crossed the single-track road and went round the back of the cottage, the car was there, and so was Lara. Pretty obviously she was not expecting us. I was just about to kick open the back door and barge into the kitchen when Jinn grabbed me by the sleeve.

'Shush!' she told me, flapping her hand to keep back Tom and Alex. Tom ducked behind a big rock, dragging Alex with him.

Jinn had that secretive, sly look that promised fun, so I did what I was told. We crept round to the window of Lara's room and peered in, and sure enough, there on the sagging bed lay a butt-naked Highlander (maybe, or maybe he was from Bethnal Green or Croxteth). Something lay underneath him: something that on closer inspection proved to be our mother.

When I say 'lay', of course, it was not quite so passive; the pair of them were bouncing up and down in a unison of rhythm and creaking springs that nearly made us combust. At first I thought I'd die of shock, but Jinn was just about killing herself trying to laugh silently. She bit her lip so hard she made marks on it. When I tried to slink away, afraid we'd gone too far, Jinn seized me by the arm and dragged me back. We watched in awe as the rhythm grew faster and more violent, and I was so fascinated I even stopped nibbling slivers of chocolate off my melting choc ice.

Jinn could stay silent no longer. She nudged me. 'That's a very fine arse *indeed*.'

'Jinn!' I gasped.

'Very fine,' she murmured again. 'He's probably a mountaineer or something.' She paused, and there was choked hilarity in her throat. 'Or a caber t-t-tosser.'

This time we both exploded. Loudly. The putative

Highlander lost his rhythm, turned slightly to look over his shoulder, and leaped off Lara, starkers, with a scream that sounded like 'Fecking FECK!' It might have been Gaelic, but I don't think so.

Lara pulled an unfamiliar blue anorak across her front, stalked across to the window and opened it, wiggling it where it stuck in the frame.

Jinn smiled at her. 'We need more money. For the shop.'

Lara peered down at the pair of us. 'What's that you're eating, then? Looks like Magnums to me.'

'They're finished. They make Ruby thirsty.' That's right, Jinn, blame me. 'We need Coke. Lots of Coke.'

So Lara fumbled around in a pile of clothes and found her bag and scrabbled for coins and a tenner and pushed the lot into Jinn's expectant hand, and all the while I watched the Highlander with the nice arse. He was half-huddled behind a cane chair, desperately pulling clothes around his lower torso and goggling at me with mortified panic. Lara gave Jinn a slightly disapproving, tight-lipped smile and went back to him, but not before yanking down the blinds.

'That was excellent,' said Jinn, counting our haul. 'This could be a strategy.'

We stuffed ourselves on Magnums that holiday. It's possible to have too many. I haven't looked at one since.

My plans for Jinn and Tom were almost too successful; I was delighted with the romantic way things were going, but at the same time I was jealous, sulking at the loss of

Jinn's time and attention. The two of them went hunting in rock pools, scrambling on cliffs, drawing their names with sticks on the white sand beaches – all the Famous Five things Jinn and I used to do together. And all I had to compensate was bloody Alex.

It's not often it's me that has to start conversations. But we were crammed in the gash between rock faces one day, backs against one quartz-veined slab and feet propped up on the other, when I finally gave up. I sighed and said, 'So how's the high school?'

He shrugged, shifted his position, walked his feet along the opposite rock. 'You going next year?'

'Yeah.' I walked my feet towards his, just because it seemed like an entertaining diversion.

'I'm sure it's fine. It's probably fine.'

'What, you don't like it?'

'It's all right.' He walked his feet the other way.

Mine followed them. 'You don't like it.'

'It's not that I don't like it.'

'What, then?'

He picked lichen out of his fingernails. 'I don't like the people. I don't like the place.'

'Right. So you don't like it.'

'I like *school*. I just don't like . . . it. I don't want to go back. There's nobody like me there.'

I considered telling him to get his head out of his arse, but it would have involved some verbal bravery. 'Well, you've got to. Go back. What, are you scared of them?'

'Yes.'

'Oh.'

'It isn't any worse than being scared of talking.'

Even as I blushed, I was pleased with myself for getting an upfront normal human sneer out of him. But he'd pulled his head back into his shell, like a tortoise, except that a tortoise didn't have such delicate bones, such a sharp scared face.

'No, it's not,' I agreed. That was good politics. 'So what's scary?'

Obviously I had my own motives for asking this. I was kind of looking forward to high school, but I'd like to be forearmed. He didn't help a lot though.

'I'm just not very good at it.'

I sighed and took a stab in the dark. 'Maths?'

'Don't be stupid.'

'What then?'

He gave me a narrow-eyed glance, sizing me up. He must have decided I was the Girl Least Likely to Blab.

'Life. People and stuff. I'm just not good at it.'

'It's only a few years,' I said.

'No, it's school and then it's university and then I'll have to get a job and get married and have kids – all that. I can't do that, I know I can't.'

'Don't be mad. Everybody does.'

'I'm not everybody,' he said truculently.

'Yes, you are. You're just like everybody else. Get over yourself.'

'I'm not. I'm different.'

'That's your own fault.'

'Well, maybe it is. But I'm still not good at it. Being normal.'

'Being human,' I said.

I was annoyed with him, and we didn't speak for about half an hour, but then we did. I decided I just wouldn't get into the heavy stuff with him again. *Don't encourage him*, I told myself. *He does it for effect. Everybody knows that.*

Later, once we were back at school, I'd get his point a little better. Back at school Nathan mocked Alex and scoffed at Tom and enchanted Jinn back to himself with relative ease, and Tom didn't put up a fight: he just oozed 'Whatever.' (I was furious. All my scheming and sacrifice over the holidays had come to nothing.) So Tom retained his savoir-faire, but it didn't set Alex much of an example. If his cool brother couldn't keep Jinn, who clearly liked him a lot, what earthly chance did Alex have of getting the hang of Life?

Should have seen it coming, really.

After the drowned mermaid rolled up in the rock pools, I wasn't afraid, the way Jinn was. Like I said, I knew it wouldn't happen to me. I liked that Jinn was worried about me all over again, that she'd forgotten Nathan for a few days. It was like having my big sister again, all to myself: like when she'd go out of her way to offend the semi-locals, morally blackmail the biological mother, and get me ice lollies. There'd been a time lately when I found her maternal fussing a bit of a pain, but since she'd discovered Nathan and her own needs, I'd found I missed it. So I didn't even mind that she wouldn't let me walk over to Foley's on my own for a while, or stay out after dark. There was a frisson of fear across the town for a while, an electric crackle of risk, but I felt safe. I was Ruby, and immortal.

I wish it hadn't got personal, that's all. I wish I hadn't rapped on Jinn's bedroom door a few nights after they found the anonymous mermaid on the beach, and gone in to find her crying on her bed. I wish I'd never asked why, and what was wrong.

She rubbed her eyes on the corner of the duvet and said, 'The girl, the girl. The girl in the sea.'

And not being entirely obtuse all the time, I knew what she was on about, and I felt very bad very suddenly. I said, 'Was it somebody we know?'

'It's Marley,' said Jinn, and started sobbing again. 'It was Marley Ryan! Why would anybody want to kill Marley?'

Eight

I didn't really know Marley Ryan; I'd only met her the once. All I knew about Marley was that it wasn't her real name – her real name was Roberta, and what is it with all these people whose names won't stick to them? – and that she had my necklace. She didn't nick it or anything; Jinn gave it to her. Not that it was valuable, but I was upset because of what it represented.

Bear with me.

It was all down to Jinn being so responsible, so efficient. She'd been picking through Lara's few books, and she'd found this rather beautiful hardback that I doubt Lara had ever opened, but when Jinn did, it turned out to belong to the mother of one of Lara's old teachers. So of course we couldn't just give it to the Oxfam shop like anyone normal would; Jinn had to send me to the thirteenth floor of some tower block in Glassford to return it to the teacher who was the mother of a teacher who had taught someone who never seemed to learn.

Anyway, up I climbed (and that was no mean feat, because of course the lift was broken). The old dear hobbled to the door on her Zimmer frame and invited me in (she'd been warned so she knew I wasn't there to mug her) and I gave her back the book, and she was delighted about that, and terribly sorry about Lara, and far too polite to ask if she'd ever read the book. And she gave me a cup of tea and a Penguin I couldn't refuse, and we talked, except that talking isn't so much my thing, so she did all the talking.

She was incredibly interesting and smart for such a fossil. I liked her. And she must have thought I was great, nodding and smiling and being interested (which I *was*). She offered me a loan of a different book, and I very nearly took it. I must know myself too well, because I said no, maybe next time when I haven't got exams, and she must have thought that was as good a reason as any.

In lieu of the book, she gave me other things before I left: half a packet of Starburst and a little pendant. The pendant wasn't worth anything; she'd got it free out of a magazine, I think, but she said it was too young for her, so why didn't I have it? It was made of cheap metal: a little cat with an arched back and red glittery eyes. 'Ruby,' she said. 'Isn't that what you said your name was? Well, there you are, it has ruby eyes; it must be meant for you.'

I didn't much like the necklace, but I thought it would be rude to refuse. Besides, it was sweet of her and I didn't want to hurt her feelings. And she said, 'Come again! It's been lovely; we've had a nice chat.'

I lost the necklace almost as soon as I was down the

stairs. No idea what I did with it. Well, that's not quite true. I must have had it long enough to damage it, because when Jinn found it caught in the bathroom door jamb, it was missing one ruby eye and its paw was twisted.

As for going back to the old teacher lady in the tower block, the funny thing is that I meant to. At the time I really did. I said, 'Course, yeah, that'd be great,' and I thought I was telling the truth. Because I liked the old girl, and making her day made me feel kind of good.

But I never did go back. Life got in the way. Life, and going to the shops, and flirting with Foley, and watching TV. I never went back and it's too late now: maybe she's dead for all I know, and I'm afraid to find out. I'll never go back. I'll never know how well we might have got on or what might have happened. It's like Aslan in those Narnia books, who's so lovely in some ways and so bloody annoying in others. All his *nobody is ever told what would have happened*. Well, why not? What was such a big deal? What was it to him?

It seemed like nothing at the time and I didn't know how bad I'd feel later. But there's no atonement, ever. There's nothing you can do or undo once you've done it. It doesn't seem like such a demand but it's the most impossible thing in the world: going back even five minutes to change what's happened. Just not doing what you did. Even Doctor Who can't do that. If the old girl turned out to be dead I'd feel even worse; if she was alive I'd be mortified and what was worse I'd be *committed*. I'd be committed to her and no doubt doomed to make the same mistake again. So the best thing to do was stay in my antisocial limbo with my head down.

Jinn, of course, was better than Aslan; Jinn knew what would have happened and she bloody told me, too. I'd have been a better person, that's what. She was angry with me for not going back, she was angry that I hadn't taken care of the pendant, and she was even more furious when I mumbled that it wasn't worth anything. I glowered at the TV while she got out the pliers and twisted the cat's cheap metal paw back into place, and painstakingly untangled the knotted chain, and bitched at me about getting my head out of my own backside.

When she'd finished fixing the cat pendant I told her I still didn't want it, and she said that was fine, because she didn't have any plans to give it back to me, she was keeping it herself. God knows why. It can't have been that she liked it herself, or why would she give it away to Marley?

It was the same night I got vomiting drunk for the first and (so far) only time in my whole life. I got that way because I had no idea. It was an accident; it was one of those things I didn't think could happen to me. (I also did it because I was so hurt and angry. That's why I remember it was the same night she gave away the stupid cat.)

I'd just turned fourteen and Jinn and I were at a party down at the harbour, in somebody's sister's flat – embarrassingly, I don't even remember whose. Jinn was wearing the cat, its chain wrapped several times round her wrist; I remember being quite pleased, because it suited her and

I was glad she was treating it better than I had, glad that she was such a moral and ethical paragon compared to me. I had a vague unformed notion that this let me off the hook.

I didn't know Roberta Ryan from a slice of cheese at this point. I do remember her arriving at the party, mingled with a crowd of disreputable boys from Glassford Academy. You couldn't miss her, she had such a striking look. Her hair was in dreadlocks, pulled back into a ponytail – presumably that was why she called herself Marley; it was nothing to do with Labradors. One of the locks had escaped, and stuck out to the side. She wore baggy khakis and a combat jacket, a bright red T-shirt and a gleaming nose stud. Funnily enough, none of this was what you noticed first, because she had the most sweetly pretty face you could imagine. She looked like an angel.

She walked in with that kind of swagger that tells you instantly she was terrified. She kidded around with some of the boys and tossed back glasses of punch like a cowboy and didn't meet the eyes of anyone else, ever. Still, her eyes flickered across to people when they weren't looking at her, as if she wanted to make sure she wasn't making an arse of herself, that she was doing this right.

She must have set off my sister's maternal satnav, because Jinn went over to her after five minutes, and they hit it off straight away. I was hanging back at this point, dipping my lips in a plastic cup of punch, studying everyone else and hoping no one would try to talk to me. I'd have liked to go over and talk to the dreadlocked girl myself, but that was a ridiculous idea. Me! Introduce myself to a stranger!

Jinn and the girl weren't giggling away and swapping sweet nothings, the way you might expect. They talked very intently about something serious, and for nearly an hour. I hung about on the edge of conversations, nodding like I cared, practising for adult life. A few times I made like I was dancing, till I felt too daft moving my body self-consciously at the edge of what passed for a dance floor. When the heat in the flat got too much, I went downstairs and stood in the street, happily watching the moonlight glint on rocking yachts. I watched people go in and out of the Fu Ling takeaway a hundred metres up the road. I took lovely breaths of night air and listened to the party sounds from the open window above me. Eventually I wandered up to the takeaway myself, and coaxed a bag of oily chips out of Mr Fu Ling while his wife wasn't looking.

This was my kind of party. Nobody bothered me, and I liked to watch people, and I liked fresh air. A couple stumbled down the stairs behind me and lurched round the corner, her supporting him. Finding a quiet place, either for sex or for vomiting. The latter more likely, by the look of him. I tilted my head back and watched the orange glow of the sky, and the stars just visible over the skerries; I listened to the slap of the tide in the harbour and the

113

metal *ting* of masts, blending with the thud of music. Closing my eyes, I chewed the last of my chips and felt the breath of night air on my skin, and thought I should go back upstairs for a while.

Halfway up, I met Jinn and the dreadlocked girl sitting on the landing.

The girl had been crying, but she wasn't any more. Jinn had her arm round her; she was murmuring something comforting in her ear as she squeezed her shoulders. The girl was tucking the stray dreadlock behind her ear and sniffing and giggling.

She was also wearing my necklace.

There must have been thousands of the damn things sold. But no, even in the dimness of the stairwell I recognised the mutilated paw and the Cyclops eye. And Jinn's wrist was bare.

My sister gave me one of her Looks as I pushed past without a word. She didn't follow me immediately, though. I had time to squirm through the press of bodies to the punch bowl and slug a swift plastic-glassful.

Jinn was at my shoulder by now. 'What's wrong?'

'Why's she wearing my necklace?'

We were both shouting, only partly because of the music.

'It isn't yours. You didn't want it!'

'I gave it to you!'

'No you didn't, I took it because you *didn't want it*.'

Who'd have believed we were screaming at each other

over a cheap necklace neither of us had wanted? But I was so mad about her giving it away. Just giving it away!

She grabbed my arm and dragged me through to the quieter bedroom where several people were snogging, one couple was going a bit further than that, and at least one boy had lost consciousness. It was easier to talk in here with the human detritus.

'Marley's miserable. I gave it to her to cheer her up.'

'*Marley?* She's called after a dog?'

'Don't be stupid. She's had a fight with her mum and dad and then she had a fight with her boyfriend.'

'I'm not surprised, looking like that.'

'She looks lovely and you know it, Ruby. She was going to run away and sleep rough and I told her nah, if she promised not to, I'd give her the cat. My valuable jewel-encrusted cat. It was kind of a joke, right?'

'Yeah, I saw the pair of you sniggering. You gave away my necklace for a *joke*!'

'So what? YOU DIDN'T WANT IT!'

At which point I stormed off and got drunk.

I had a wonderful time. The combination of first being happy, and then being insanely, irrationally furious: that's what did it, I think. I actually talked, and talked a lot. I'd discovered the angel alcohol and it was good, it was the salvation of me, it taught me to speak and not just that: to make jokes. God, I was funny. I was witty like you wouldn't believe (I wish I could remember some of my lines). I didn't hesitate to say things and my tongue was not coated in Velcro, it was smooth and slippery and quick like a cobra. Thoughts bubbled up in my brain and they didn't go their usual roundabout way, they bypassed the barriers and fizzed right out. I was making people laugh, in a good way. They looked a bit startled and some of them took the piss, but I didn't even mind that. This was the new me and I was never going back. All I had to do was keep my punch levels topped up.

So one moment I was having a lovely time, necking punch after punch, not feeling remotely bad or odd, just high, high, high.

Then it happened. Something like a fingernail scratched at the back of my throat, and I hesitated. It scratched again. I stood up but the room did too. Astonishing. The room stood up and wheeled round me like a wonky Wall of Death and I had got halfway to the bathroom before Mount St Ruby erupted.

I knelt before the toilet like a worshipper, gripping its cold white rim, and barfed and barfed again. No question of making it downstairs like that other guy. I had the vaguest of memories of the Bathroom Dash, of seeing things through a great fan of vomit the colour of punch, so I guessed I'd made a bit of a mess. There were several varieties of Molotov in that punch along with vodka, rum and cider; I think that's when I first went off the Molotov magic rainbow.

Somebody must have summoned Jinn because she was kneeling at my side, making soothing noises and rubbing my back. I wanted to tell her to stop, because the gentle movement of her hand was making me throw up more and more and I wanted it to stop. But I couldn't speak, and anyway, stomach spasms or no stomach spasms, it was very comforting having her there. Through the fog in my brain I somehow knew this would be a matter for bitter regret in the morning – that yes, I'd know the true meaning of a Velcro tongue but that wouldn't be the worst of it – and I needed Jinn there to tell me it was fine, no worries, I'd feel better soon, and nobody was angry. I needed her there to swear loudly at the poor soul banging on the door, desperate to get in before her bladder imploded.

So, after all that, you'd think I'd be more sympathetic three months later when the exact same thing happened to Alex Jerrold.

I don't even know why Alex was invited to the next party, which was held in a nice old house in a good part of town, the parents in question having gone away for a week and trustingly left their daughter in charge. I suspect Alex was meant to be the light relief, kind of a jester. Either that or the hostess fancied Tom and thought she'd get brownie points with him for inviting Alex too.

As I've mentioned, Tom Jerrold was about three hundred per cent cooler than Alex. He was protective to a degree, but both for his own sake and for Alex's, there was a limit to how protective he could be. And he couldn't watch him all the time. That was how Alex, drunk to the eardrums, found himself a lair in the corner by the parents' CD collection and the amplifiers. Nobody paid him much attention until the amplifiers (which were huge, expensive, sophisticated and loud) suddenly let rip a solid pure blast of orchestral music.

Wagner, it was. *The Ride of the Valkyries*. Everybody turned round, stunned, to see Alex Jerrold standing in a small mountain of discarded CDs doing a Jesus Christ impersonation, eyes shut and arms spread wide like wings. And he was singing along, in pidgin made-up German, an expression of pissed ecstasy on his screwed-up face.

How could he have hoped to get away with it? Maybe he hadn't. It caused more stupefied hilarity than rage but he had to suffer for it anyway, so he was grabbed and hauled upstairs, then dangled over the top banister rail by his ankles. He endured it, silent and dignified as a painted martyr, his expression suffused with pained irritation like an inverted St Sebastian.

As for the perpetrators, it wasn't the best idea they ever had either. Holding a bladdered miserabilist upside down by his ankles is only ever going to have one outcome. The outcome was all over the hostess's mother's stair carpet, and because it came from a height, it splattered and sprayed a really long way.

The hostess was not drunk enough not to get hysterical about this, and it was mostly Alex who was blamed, then and later – which seemed less than fair to me, but after all, he had asked for it in a big way.

It was Jinn who cleared up the mess. She cleared up Alex's vomit and she cleaned up Alex too. She scolded the perpetrators, who were howling with laughter, dragged Alex to the nearest bathroom and ensured he'd emptied his heaving stomach. She rubbed his back and made soothing noises, just like she'd done for me.

Natural mother, that was Jinn. God knows where she got it.

Tom joined her after a while, silent as he watched his brother retch, passing Jinn a bottle of wine when she got a chance to take a swig. They kept one another company till Alex had curled up in a ball, fast asleep, a tiny vomit trail at the corner of his upcurled mouth. About an hour later, I found them snogging comfortably on a sofa.

This time, I thought. *This time!*

But yet again, it came to nothing. The following Monday, back at school, Jinn and Tom were mere friends once again, and she was the occasionally-favoured acolyte of Nathan Baird. He toyed with Jinn like he toyed with all the girls, flirting and scattering compliments, swaggering and showing off and sometimes kissing her like he meant it.

But he didn't need her in those days. Or now I think that he maybe did need her, and liked her more than he wanted to even then, but that he needed his reputation more. So Jinn went on lusting after him, and he went on encouraging her, and Tom and Jinn came to nothing.

Not then, anyway.

I remember the second girl because she made the news the morning after that party. The day after, rather, because I probably didn't see much of the morning. And the funny thing is, I remember thinking, Oh no, that's just like the other girl, the one with the stripy T-shirt and the big smile.

Didn't make a real, proper connection though.

Jinn was up already, of course, drifting elegantly around the house in a white waffle bathrobe and a hangover. Nothing like as bad as mine, which had had me up at four o'clock glugging pints of milk and water, but she was definitely a bit rough. She smiled at me, eyes all shadowy, our drunken squabble forgotten, and said she'd make a pot of tea and why didn't I go and sit down and watch TV.

A bit shamefaced from last night's scene, I curled my bare feet under me on the sofa and pillowed my aching head on lots of cushions. I was going to flip channels when I saw she'd left it on News 24, but then I saw the ticker rolling at the bottom of the screen, and I'm no different from anyone: I can't look away from a murder.

She was in a river, Girl 2; but they thought she hadn't died there, they thought she'd died somewhere else and probably with a punter, because she worked the red-light district. And there she was: she'd floated downstream, a naked Ophelia, surfing the current like a pale log till she bumped gently into the bank and tangled herself in branches with the crisp packets and the foamy river scum.

Her boyfriend said he hadn't seen her in two months. He said she was trying to get clean, but not like that. It was such an odd thing to say, even through his tears, they thought it was probably him.

Nine

I still hoped against hope that it might happen, Tom and Jinn. I fancied Tom myself, in an unattainable, worshipful, older-man kind of way, but I knew that wasn't a going concern, so I was wistfully thrilled rather than jealous that he fancied my sister. Anyway, the combined glamour of Tom and Jinn couldn't help but rub off on me.

I was doing my homework in the kitchen one night when there was a rap on the door, very peremptory, and I thought for the thousandth time that we ought to get a bell, it would be less unnerving. I was annoyed – I was concentrating, abnormally interested in social conditions in 1832 – but I wasn't so annoyed when I opened the door.

'Hello, Ruby,' said Tom.

I smiled at him, so that he had to smile back. He was shifting from foot to foot – a good sign, I decided. Romantic anxiety.

'She's not in.'

'Oh, OK. I'll –'

'Just come in. She'll be home from work soon.' Standing aside, I flung wide the door so that he had no option but to come in. If he'd had a flat cap to take off and wring as he sidled past, he'd have done it. Sweet.

'Do you want a coffee?'

'Yeah. Um. Thanks.'

Gotcha.

He couldn't do anything else but sit at the pine table as I bustled. He clasped his hands. Unclasped them. Glanced at his watch.

I set a mug of coffee down and gave him a dazzling smile. 'Five minutes. She'll be back in five.'

'Right. Thanks.'

Even I couldn't tolerate the awkward silence. 'How's Alex?'

'Uh? Alex is fine.'

'Recovered, then.'

'Oh. Yeah. Recovered.' He rolled his eyes in a *what-can-you-do* way. 'Sobered up, anyway.'

'It was a shame,' I said.

'It was his own fault, the wee tosser.'

'Biscuit?'

'No thanks.' He eyed the bright yellow clock on the wall. The second hand lumbered towards another half-minute. 'Well, OK. Yeah.'

I shoved a Breakaway across the table, wishing I could tie him to the chair or something.

It seemed I'd at last got him talking, though. 'He's a pain in the arse, my brother. But he's not normal. I hate it when he gets hurt.'

Oh yeah, everybody at school knew that. Everybody knew what had happened to the ringleader behind Alex's party humiliation. Damien Harris had been so proud of his long, artfully tousled hair, till it got mysteriously and incurably clotted with farty putty in the boys' toilets after school. His mother had to shave it all off that night. No complaint was made. Damien kept his shaved head down in shame and Tom remained inscrutably cool.

'He's eccentric,' he said now. 'He's not normal, is all. Alex doesn't think like other people think.'

I nodded, wishing Jinn would get her arse in gear and come home. I had a very bad feeling about this now and I didn't want Tom to go on talking. But it was too late.

'Listen, do me a favour,' said Tom. 'If Alex asks you to the Halloween dance. Gonnae say yes?'

And that's how I came to be on Alex Jerrold's arm at the Breakness High Halloween Horror. You'd think he'd be pleased with his remote-control conquest, but he didn't say a lot.

Alex had a startled crop of dark hair, a hint of bumfluff on his chin, and an expression of permanent astonishment. When I gave him a sidelong inspection, this close up, he had rather a beautiful face: long and pointed, with alarmingly sharp cheekbones and big eyes. The overall impression was not at all spoilt by his green complexion and the plastic bolt through his neck; he took very naturally to freakdom. My own hair was spiked up with the toughest gel I could find, with a sprayed white streak running from front to back; my eyes were sunk in smudged black eyeshadow and talking was even harder than usual through my plastic glow-in-the-dark fangs. I was very aware of the snorts and whispers. How well suited we were. How somebody had to have the pair of us and it might as well be each other.

I found I could be pretty relaxed about the whispers. Alex was silent, give or take an occasional sharp remark, but he wasn't nervous so much as distant. There was something just shockingly cool about him up close. Cool in an utterly nerdy and ridiculous way that shouldn't have been cool. I mean, we all liked to pretend we couldn't give a toss about anything. Alex Jerrold *really* didn't.

Or that's how it seemed at the time. Maybe he was just more convincing, or maybe I wanted to believe it in retrospect.

After one misguided attempt at the Time Warp, we didn't dance. We sat silently in a corner and then, by mutual unspoken agreement, we wandered out to a mild night and sat on the school steps, giggling quietly at the better-dressed, the more-popular and the altogether-less-chilled. He was funny when he loosened up. It was sweet.

After a while I turned towards him, thinking I might not mind at all if he kissed me. Nervously, like a heron darting for a fish, he took a stab at my lips but missed, because idiotically I'd jerked my head round towards a shriek from the Assembly Hall. Alex coughed, shuddered, turned away. He didn't try again.

He said, 'That new 3-D movie?'

'Yeah?'

'You want to go?'

I had to think for a minute. I wasn't much into animated films, and there was something I'd much rather see at Screen 5 that week, and I thought maybe Alex would like it too.

'I don't fancy that one,' I began.

I was about to follow that up with my alternative suggestion, but Alex readjusted the bolt in his neck and said, 'OK.'

He didn't quite look at me, didn't quite smile, just stood up and dusted down his backside.

'Better go back, I suppose.'

I thought of staying put till he sat down again, and trying to get back to the subject of Screen 5, and maybe doing some more intermittent talking. Instead, I stood up and dithered back into the hall with him to sit on the sidelines. I wish we'd done things differently, but then I wish that a lot.

Ten

The burly guy at the mini-mart counter did not look happy. He'd left his engine running – I could hear it through the open door – and he hadn't even paused to pick up a basket, so he was balancing his sandwich and his six-pack of beer and his wallet in his huge arms, while he eyed his watch and bounced on his heels and peered towards the back room, as if that would bring anyone running.

'This is ridiculous,' he said to thin air, or to me. 'Ridiculous.' He tutted for emphasis.

I shrugged, smiled, and muttered as I sidled past. I wasn't that worried about Burly Man and his petrol consumption, but if Bertha came in and found Jinn skiving off, she wouldn't be happy. It wasn't like last summer. Jinn had spent a lot of her credit with Bertha, some of it simply by being in love with Nathan.

I stuck my head into Bertha's cupboard-sized office, but there was no sign of Jinn. To be fair, she might have had to go to the loo suddenly. Still, the till could have been emptied by now, and it was pretty irresponsible of her to leave when she didn't have cover. Unless she'd emptied the till already. I wouldn't put it past her these days.

Oh, Ruby, don't be such a bitch.

I put my head round the door to the shop, but Burly Man was gone. So was the sandwich and the six-pack, and he hadn't left any money on the counter. I couldn't really blame him, but I was livid with Jinn.

I went through to the back again. The scruffy toilet was at the end of the squashed passageway, round a corner where the coats hung. I thought I'd knock on the door, hard, and give Jinn a fright, but she wasn't in the cubicle. She was standing beside the jackets, half-hidden, focused on one in her arms, going through its pockets.

'Jinn!'

I put my hand over my mouth. She jerked up like a startled rabbit, almost dropping the jacket. I saw her quickly stuff something into her pocket.

'What are you *doing*?'

'Nothing,' she hissed.

I stared at the jacket. It was Inflatable George's; I recognised it. 'What *are* you doing?' I repeated.

'Nothing,' she muttered again.

I didn't know what to say, and for once neither did she. I thought she'd brazen it out, but she must have known that this time she'd gone too far, because she looked pale as a spectre in the shadowy passage, and her hands shook as she hung the jacket back up.

'If you've taken money . . .' I was scared for her.

Twin points of colour reappeared in her cheeks. 'Of course I haven't!' she snapped. 'His wallet's not here, is it? He must've taken it. They must've gone to the pub for lunch.'

I turned and went back to the shop, planning to apologise to any waiting punters in a *really* loud voice. But Jinn was on my heels anyway. She tugged out her chair and perched on it, smiling blandly up at a mother with a child in her arms.

'Bless,' said Jinn. 'They're lovely at that age.'

All I could do was stalk out. I was too furious even to wait and buy a sandwich, so I had to settle for a cereal bar out of the newsagent's on the corner. I decided I'd take it up to the cliffs, because I had to think quite hard now.

Going north out of Breakness, beyond the harbour and the car showroom and out past the golf course, the long glittering beach broke very abruptly into more dunes and rocks and then sheered upwards into sandstone cliffs. It was a gorgeous walk on a bright day, if you could be bothered. I'd seen dolphins more than once, and more seals than you could shake a club at. I tried not to let it put me off that a drowned teenager had been scattered at sea there last year, out among the skerries, tipped out of a plastic canister from the harbour master's launch. It wasn't as if you could see him now, a slick of ash on fallow water.

Where would his family have their picnics? I wondered. Well, maybe they'd put up a bench, one with a little plaque. There were plenty of others; it seemed like a popular trend. This was a beautiful spot, looking out to sea and the skerries and the very, very distant hills across the firth. Patches of glitter and patches of shadow on the water. A sky bigger than anything you could imagine. You could fall through that sky and never touch ground.

The cliff path was high and narrow, and I kept my iPod clamped firmly to my ears because the diving gulls made me nervous. As soon as I got my own car I'd be taking the easy way to the cliffs, driving round the airbase and the hangars and up on to the flat field where you could park your car and watch the jets pierce the sky. A couple of miles' walk from the beach, it wasn't the most popular spot, but this was such a beautiful Sunday it was almost busy. I could see two four-by-fours, a dark blue Yaris, and one bright yellow sports car as shiny as a toy.

I tugged off my iPod and tucked it into my jeans pocket. Bertha's little Renault Clio was there too (never ceased to amaze me how she squeezed herself into it), and sure enough, when I walked a bit further, she and Inflatable George were crushed together on my favourite bench, twenty metres along and down, gazing out to the shining horizon. His arm was resting on the back of the bench and she was leaning into him, and I sucked in a happy little sigh and released it. Sitting down where I was, I decided I wouldn't disturb them. They looked so contented, it seemed like the world had it exactly right at exactly that moment.

And then the world blew it.

'Dead romantic, that.'

I froze to my patch of cliff, curling in on myself, keeping my mouth tight shut. Nathan, though, wasn't put off. He sat down beside me, leaning back against the slope with his hands behind his head. Down the slope, happy in their own little bench-world, Bertha and George hadn't even noticed us.

Lucky them. My day was ruined. He'd tugged a cloud across the sun again, even though the sea still glittered.

'Can we not, like, get along? I'm not leaving your sister anyway.' Sitting up straight, he leaned his elbows on his knees and turned his face towards me. He was grinning but it was a bit different to his usual smirk; it looked uncertain, a little nervous even. He looked a bit as if he was scared of me. I studied his face, less beautiful than it used to be. Or maybe just thinner and paler.

'Come on, Ruby Red. Mates? Just for show, at least? It would make her happy.'

'What would you know about her being happy?'

He didn't answer me at first, just counted on his long fingers. 'Eight words. Is that the most I've ever had out of you? It's a start.' He smiled.

I would not be charmed. I refused to be charmed. 'You don't make her happy.'

'Yes I do. Bloody should. She makes *me* happy.'

I couldn't go on watching his eyes, the only bit of him that was still really beautiful, golden eyes that had sunk into deeper shadow. I turned to stare out to sea.

'I love Jinn,' he said. 'I swear to God I love her.'

I still said nothing. It's not that I was being deliberately mean; it's only that I was giving it some thought, for the first time. But I must have thought about it too long.

'Can you not just accept it? Can you not just pretend to like me?' He swore under his breath. 'Jesus, Ruby, you don't deserve her.'

OK, he was doing fine till that point. 'Piss off, Nathan.'

'Rubes, we need to talk about it.'

I shook my head.

'Well, *I* do.' There was no trace of his sneer now. He was starting to be angry.

I scrambled to my feet. Nathan was between me and the car park, so I walked the other way, up the winding cliff path, fulmars tumbling round the sky below me. The breeze was stronger up here, stirring the dry gravelly path and blowing sand into my eyes, but I ducked my head into it and folded my arms, striding on. With the wind battering my ears and the sun's dazzle, I'd almost forgotten him scrambling along behind me.

'Ruby, listen!'

He grabbed my arm and pulled. I wobbled and slipped, and stumbled towards the edge.

I cried out, but not very loud: too busy panicking about the long plummet to my right, but I wasn't really off balance and I scuttled closer to the hillside. Nathan had skipped back a bit, his eyes wide and startled and possibly a bit remorseful, but as I recovered he grabbed for my arm again.

'Here, let me –'

Finish? Sod that. Viciously I kicked the dry path, sending up a shower of grit and sand; the breeze caught it and whipped it into his face. He gave a shout of surprise and covered his eyes with his hands.

'Ow! What'd you do that for?' He took down his hands, blinked, but his eyes were streaming and still full of grit, so he covered them again. '*Ow!*'

He jumped and danced, yelping at the pain. Big jessie. I looked at the drop.

I could have pushed him really easily. He was way off balance, thinking only about his stinging eyeballs. Honestly, I could have done it with one hand.

'I'm going home,' I said, pushing past him on the safe side. He was calming down now, blinking hard at the path and going 'Ow, ow! Feck, ow!'

It was another chance to shove him over, but of course I didn't.

I've done it in my daydreams, though. Many times, since that moment. What's that I said about wishing I'd done things differently? I could have stopped it all then, if I had pushed him.

If only.

The last time I saw Nathan Baird in our house, he was dancing the tango. At least, he was dancing a not-bad version of it, sliding his narrow hips against Jinn's in a way that made me blush. Her fingers slid down over his backside and they were gazing into one another's eyes.

A snake enchanting a mouse: that's what it made me think of. They were intense, hypnotised, the pair of them.

Jinn didn't giggle but she smiled as he pulled her face close to his. I'm sure it wasn't a proper tango, but what can I say? It was in the spirit of the thing. They were having sex with their clothes on. I almost didn't dare breathe but they wouldn't have heard me anyway. The Grumpy Old Bugger next door would be through soon to complain about the volume of Mary Coughlan singing 'Ain't Nobody's Business', all raw-Irish and passionate and tango-ey. Nathan Baird was gazing into my sister's eyes like he could eat her, but like it was all the same to him if she ate him instead. Like they could destroy each other, burn each other up, and neither of them would care. He slid his fingers under the chain of the amber drop and the dead mosquito and pulled her in so close I thought they'd fuse.

I look back on that tango and I wish he'd stayed.

Winter

Eleven

By November, the nights got dark really early. Winter was coming on in its usual dull snowless way and you almost couldn't believe the sun would ever reappear; you could understand why all those cavemen back in the day used to bribe it with blood sacrifices.

I thought I'd be late again but there was no smell of cooking when I got in from the salon, and there was no music. These days that usually meant Jinn was mad at me, but she didn't look too mad: she was peering into the toaster, pushing the lever down and down again. I picked up the disconnected plug and pushed it into the wall, and she turned to me and smiled, like she'd just noticed I was there.

Jinn was always the first one to speak. It was tradition. So it was beyond unsettling when she didn't.

I was scared, so I had to shield myself with high dudgeon.

'Where is he?'

She bit a nail. 'Who?'

'Nathan.'

She went on nibbling the nail, but sighed through her teeth at the same time. She looked more abstracted than upset.

'He's left,' she said.

She didn't look at me, which was just as well, because she didn't see me smile. I put my hand over my mouth and stopped myself, but I was wasting my time because she didn't notice.

'Why?' I said. Which was a pointless question, because I didn't care why. I wanted to drop the subject; I wanted never to mention him again and it would be as if he never existed. It would be Jinn and me again. Just us.

Jinn turned back to me. I was frightened by her expression because she didn't look happy, but then again, nor did she seem terribly upset. If Nathan had dumped her, she'd be devastated, so something wasn't right. The sun was streaming in the window and lighting her hair with a silver halo, and I had to peer quite hard to make out the look on her face. Her lips were tightly closed but she was smiling. Her expression was a bit judgemental. It wasn't Nathan she was angry with, I realised: it was me.

'He's got another place to stay. With friends.'

The implication of that was clear.

'What brought that on?'

'He said it wasn't really working. He said we'd all be happier. He said also you wouldn't end up killing him or blinding him if he just fecked off out of here.'

That took a bit of digesting, and Jinn obviously had no

intention of helping me out. She ripped off a square of kitchen roll and polished a butter-smear off the side of the kettle.

'So he's not coming back?' I said at last, hopefully.

She examined her reflection in the shining kettle. 'He's not coming back here.' She gave it a sliver of emphasis I didn't like.

Another awkward silence. I wanted to ask if she'd be seeing him again, but I didn't want to hear the inevitable answer out loud, so I left it.

I didn't have to ask again. Now I was sorry I'd driven him away, because at least I'd known where Jinn was and I knew what she was doing. Worrying about her was not something I was accustomed to; maternal fretting was Jinn's job. I didn't see so much of her but I didn't want to nag. She started coming home a lot later, sometimes when I was in bed, and there were times I was this close to snapping *Where have you been?* Or even *What time of night d'you call this?*

I was worse than Inflatable George, who fussed round Bertha like an obsessive sheepdog. It irritated her but she was pleased at the same time. He tutted about Jinn too, but that just caused me unmitigated annoyance. Jinn wasn't his business. I mean, strictly speaking even Bertha wasn't his business, given that she was married to somebody else. But that was up to Bertha. Jinn was up to me.

Work was going well. I loved it, I loved the salon and the training was good: one day a week for four days of work. The pay was pretty rubbish because all I was doing was washing hair and sweeping up clippings, but they were good about letting me watch the stylists. I loved the way their fingers smoothed out locks of wet hair like rivulets of water, I loved the sharp quick motion of the scissor blades, I loved the quiet buzz of shears and the high whirring blast of the hairdryers, the green and red foils decorating heads like Christmas, and the way the clients eyed themselves in the mirror, half vain and half apprehensive. I wanted to be let loose on them; I wanted to be the one making their eyes widen at the mirror with gratitude.

When I'd told Foley what I was doing, he thought it was the most ridiculous thing he'd ever heard.

'Hairdressing?' he yelped. 'You have to talk, Ruby.'

'You don't *have* to.'

'Bloody do. You have to ask them if they're going out at the weekend. If they've got any holidays planned. It's compulsory. It's in the job description.'

'Don't be stupid.'

'You, hairdressing! I mean, *you*.'

We fell out about it. I stormed off and he pretended he didn't care. We lasted about twelve hours, then our conciliatory texts crossed in mid-air. I fell out with Foley rather more often these days, which I looked on as proof that the relationship was going somewhere rather than fading out.

However, this new phase meant I wasn't paying such close attention to Jinn, and she must have seen it as a godsend. I'd stopped giving her grief about Nathan Baird, because he was out of sight and out of my mind as well as his own. I should have been wary, I should have been worried. All I could see was the surface and all I could feel was relief.

For months that's how I left it. Sleeping dogs and everything. It was only when she started staying away overnight that I got anxious again. Even then I thought: well, if the night was dark, if it was late, if it was cold, she wouldn't be wanting to trail home. She'd know I'd worry less about her staying over at Nathan's than walking home in the dark and the snow and the sleet.

That winter seemed to go on for ever. They always do, but that one especially. I saw less and less of Jinn. By February I was starting to wonder where she really, truly lived.

It was the beginning of May before I finally trailed her to Nathan's new place, and then it was kind of by accident. I didn't mean to follow her or spy, but I knew where it was and it was a spur-of-the-moment decision.

She hadn't been home for a couple of nights, and I was starting to be slightly worried. I thought: Friday afternoon. She'll be at work. So I nipped into the mini-mart, and she wasn't.

Wide Bertha wasn't around either; just Kim, sullenly swiping cans and cartons across the scanner as she chewed gum. I was taken aback because I knew Jinn always worked Friday afternoons. Wide Bertha wasn't around to ask, and I wasn't striking up a conversation with Kim of all people. There was only one thing for it and that was to check Nathan's place.

It was just a few streets away and the only reason I hadn't been near it earlier was I was trying to ignore the whole situation. I stopped on the opposite side of the street and stared.

I don't know why I'd expected nasturtiums. It wasn't the time of year. It wasn't like it was Jinn's home, and if she'd been treating it like her home I'd have been even more offended, so I don't know why I was surprised.

The name of the place was Dunedin, which sounds a lot nicer than it was. It was one of those quite stolid, respectable-looking houses that used to be the homes of middle-class merchants. These days, a lot of them had been split by landlords into flats. Outwardly Nathan Baird's new place looked a lot posher than our little grey sixties council house. But there weren't any nasturtiums.

I shifted from foot to foot, hesitant now, my hood up and my hands in my pockets. How I imagined this would make me invisible to Jinn, should she happen to glance out of a window, I do not know. But it wasn't the sort of house you'd look out of. The windows were grimy in a dirt-of-decades way, and one of them was cracked across a bottom corner. There weren't any proper curtains up, just lengths of faded patterned fabric. They were hooked back from the eyeless windows, so they can't have been strung up properly, just tacked above the windows with drawing pins. Up on the high point of the gable a seagull balanced, squealing over and over, plaintive and nagging, and all at the top of its voice. I squinted up at it, wishing I had Mallory's bread pellets and Mallory's aim.

Nathan's was a ground-floor flat, so it overlooked the tiny double-square of garden on either side of a short concrete path. I'd have thought the sight would have driven Jinn to gardening: the straggling grass, the dandelions, weeds twining through a single stunted rhododendron. It can't have bothered her. There was a tyre lying in one corner but Jinn certainly hadn't put it there. It was still stuck to a rusty wheel rim, almost swallowed by undergrowth. It had been there for ages. It wasn't a potential tyre garden, it was litter.

I found that garden beyond depressing; for some reason it made me feel slightly unwell. It was that uneasy nauseous feeling when you're faced with some danger you can't identify and can't avoid.

I knew three of them lived there, including Nathan. Not that I knew who 'they' were. I'd seen them hanging about with Nathan, coming out of the pub or propped against the wall by the newsagent: skinny wrecks with drained faces. Neither of them had Nathan's sleazy charisma, at least not at a distance. One was male and I think the other was female, but it was kind of hard to tell.

The almost-definitely-male one came out as I watched, caught nervous sight of me, then scuttled away down the road. Even from over the road I could smell the staleness oozing out when the door opened, a cankerous stink. Burnt candyfloss.

Five minutes later Jinn came out. I'd known she was in there, but it still jolted me, because she didn't fit. That's why I didn't turn quickly and walk away, just stood there staring as she marched across the road, arms folded, lips tight. I was scared, but not because she was going to tear a strip off me. I was scared because the house had started sucking the life out of her. The light and the sparkle had gone out of her hair and even though the sunlight was falling on both of us, it was like she was under a shadow. She didn't radiate light any more. I could see it and I was frightened to tell her. Even if I said it, I was afraid she wouldn't hear me, like she was already locked in an invisible shroud, like the house had dropped a clear glass bell jar over her. When she stopped right in front of me, and two fighter jets screamed overhead, the smothering noise just confirmed it. We couldn't even hear each other any more.

The jets roared into the horizon and she sighed out her impatience until the silence came back, heavier than before.

'Are you spying on me?' she snapped.

I shrugged. I was going to say 'No' but that would really have sounded mighty stupid.

'Leave us alone, Ruby. You kicked him out of our house. Isn't that enough?'

'I didn't!'

'You might as well have. Don't come round here.'

'I had something to tell you,' I blurted.

'What?'

Bugger. I'd been lying and now I couldn't even think of anything. The truth was hard enough to speak. Lies needed too quick a reflex.

'He doesn't love you,' I said.

'*What* did you say?'

I wished I hadn't, now, but I started again. 'He doesn't –'

'Yeah, I heard you! How dare you, Ruby. How dare you!'

I looked at the pavement, then at the view over her shoulder. The sea between the houses was blue and glittery. A white scrap of sail drifted behind the skerries on a May breeze. Idyllic. I was hoping that if I stayed silent long enough, she'd start to protest. She'd start shouting *He does love me! He does, he does!* And then I'd know she was protesting too much and I'd know it was all a fleeting lie and a whim and it wouldn't be for ever.

But she didn't do that. She didn't protest, and anyway she knew me too well and she was wise to my silent tactics. I'd lost and we both knew it.

'You don't even know him.' She said it with a tinge of disgust.

'I do,' I said. 'Sort of.' But I could feel the flutter of my heart in my throat and the tinge of heat in my face. I was embarrassed. I'd gone too far. I'd lost. Stop pushing it, Ruby.

'He needs me.'

'You can't help him. He's a useless jun –'

'And for your information,' she said loudly over me, 'he loves me. And even if he didn't, I love him anyway. So it's none of your *fecking* business, Ruby.'

There was nothing more I could say or do so I sloped home like a scolded puppy. I couldn't face going back to our empty little house, not yet, so I stopped by the mini-mart, and this time Wide Bertha was there. For the first time ever, she didn't look very pleased to see me.

Actually, that's an understatement. She tried to pretend she hadn't seen me, and if I hadn't shouted her name (just 'Bertha', obviously; I don't have a death wish), she would have slid into her tiny office cubicle and locked the door to avoid me.

I said, 'Why isn't Jinn at work?'

Bertha turned over a piece of paper and took a biro from behind her ear and scribbled down a random number. She stared up at the racks of cigarettes and nodded and scribbled again, and read what she'd written, and bit the end of her pen.

She said, 'I didn't know you could talk.'

And that's when I knew she'd sacked her.

Twelve

She had to let Jinn go, said Bertha. It wasn't that she didn't like her. It wasn't that she wanted to do it. It was just that she couldn't afford her any more.

I waited a week, counting to ten and biting my tongue, then went back to Dunedin. This time I didn't even get the chance to glower at the blank windows. Jinn came storming out, dragging on her thin cardigan as she crossed the road. She didn't look at me, just marched ahead of me and down through the town square to the playpark.

A haar lay over the town: had done for days, blurring the whole place. You couldn't see anything clearly, and even the jets weren't flying. There was still a smear of sunlight through the sea mist, there were half-shadows – shadows of shadows – and you could just make out the dunes across the river mouth, glowing pearly-pale-gold. There's something oppressive about that haar, something that smells of mystery, and not a nice one: a Fog out of Stephen King or Bram Stoker.

The frog rubbish bin at the playpark entrance loomed, lime-green and gape-mouthed. Jinn stopped right beside it, so that I almost tripped, and turned on me.

I said, 'You lost your job.'

'Tell me something I don't know.'

'You didn't tell me ...'

'No indeed.'

'Bertha's upset. She didn't want –'

'Bertha's a bitch. She won't even give me a reference.'

'She's not a bitch.'

'What are we going to do for money?'

'*We?* You work, don't you?' She gave me a filthy glare. 'Me, I get benefits. When do you think I got sacked?'

I opened my mouth, shut it again.

'She kicked me out three weeks ago, Rubes. Social's paying the rent.'

'She says she wants you back.'

'She doesn't want me back any more than you do. She wants Jinn Carmichael, goody-two-shoes. *You* want your mammy. Well, I'm not your frigging mammy. I've got a life of my own.'

I bristled. 'Bertha just doesn't want you nicking the profits. What's *he* gonnae live off?'

Jinn swatted a couple of early wasps away from the giant frog. 'None of your business, Ruby. You had to get rid of him, didn't you?'

'I don't want to be around drugs.' Miss Prim. What did I sound like?

'And I don't want you around drugs. So we're fine then, aren't we?'

'The house stank.'

'Sure did. Well, it doesn't any more, does it?'

'Are you coming back, Jinn?'

She just smiled at me.

'I miss you,' I mumbled.

'I don't want you around drugs,' she mimicked.

Cold nitrogen running down my backbone. 'What about you?'

'Oh, piss off, Ruby. You know I wouldn't take that stuff. Nathan's his own person. He's been in trouble. He's trying to get clean and they won't leave him alone. He's in trouble and he needs me and I want to be with him. Help him get free of those people. That's all.'

I thought: she's addicted, just like he is. But she's addicted to Nathan. I felt like I wanted to cry but I didn't want to do it in front of Jinn.

She licked her lips and looked out to sea: the sea that was invisible, smeared out of sight by the mist. She frowned, pushed a twist of hair out of her eyes.

'That bloody smell,' she said. 'It sticks to my clothes.'

When late spring turned to summer, Jinn got another job to go with her benefits. Cash in hand, I think, and not a lot of it, but summer jobs weren't so easy to come by as they'd once been. She'd stopped even pretending to live with me; hadn't been home for weeks. That's why I didn't

151

recognise her at first: that, and the fact she was dressed up like an idiot.

The house was lonely without Jinn, but I was damned if I was telling her so. We were still pretending to the housing authority that the two of us were living there. Nobody checked. We'd always paid the rent on time and now the social werc doing it. There were nasturtiums and Livingstone daisies outside, seeded from last year, and I kept them going, and bought a few more sickly plants on a three-for-two special. I kept the blanket tucked tight round the tyres too, weighted down with stones. I didn't want the tyres to get in a mess but I didn't want to get rid of them either. One day Jinn was going to want them for her tyre garden, and she'd do something with the mush and pustules that were the old potatoes. I took to looking in the garden tent in Tesco's car park every time I went in, thinking about herbs. I wondered if Jinn would want basil or dill or parsley, and I wondered if it was worth trying tomatoes. I didn't buy anything, because there wasn't any point till Jinn came home. I'd only kill them; even the nasturtiums were on borrowed time.

It was on the way home from Tesco one day that I saw Jinn, looking windblown outside the Folk Museum. I'd just got off the Glassford bus with a bag in each hand and I did a double take. The Museum was holding a Witch Month to commemorate the burning of four witches in the town square in sixteen-whatever, which was more reasonable than it sounds because the witches had done something sinister with eggshells and milk, and sunk a fishing boat. The Museum said the townsfolk had been very credulous. I reckoned they were smart and entrepreneurial and not a little far-sighted. The witch trial may not have done a lot for the witches, but its magic spell on the Breakness tourists had only just worn off.

So there was Jinn, handing out leaflets that fluttered in the breeze. I'm sure the witches themselves didn't dress like that because it would have been a bit of a giveaway, but then I suspect the costume was a Halloween leftover. Her black dress came nearly to her ankles, layers and layers of lace and tulle, with a glimpse of buttoned-up black boots beneath. It was an off-the-shoulder number, and her pale shoulders were pink with the sea breeze. Fingerless black lace gloves didn't help much, but her head was probably quite warm under the wild black wig. Her lips were scarlet, her eyes black-lined, her face death-pale. She wasn't striking sparks today, not even in the breezy sunshine. I couldn't see a single strand of silver-blonde hair. She must have been taking her work very seriously: a Stanislavski witch. When I got closer to her I saw fake black pearls wound into the wig.

'What if the social sees you?' I said. 'That's benefit fraud.'

'Piss off, Ruby. I'm ghostly and aloof.'

I swear she winked at me though. I couldn't help smiling.

'I'm not getting paid anyway,' she went on. 'Much. I'll

get a commission if anybody turns up with a discount leaflet. Doubt anybody will.' Sure enough there were tattered leaflets stuck to the mud in the gutter where they'd been dropped. 'Don't suppose you want twenty per cent off a Witch Tour?'

I shook my head, annoyed with her for trying to change the subject. I tried again. 'What if somebody sees you, though?'

'They won't, and if they do they won't recognise me.' She tugged at a coarse black strand of fake hair. That drew my attention to her white throat. The amber drop wasn't there. It had been replaced with a cheap Germanic cross strung on a black leather thong. Noticing my stare, Jinn put her fingers up to her throat and clasped the cross in her fist.

I decided I wouldn't mention the amber. Why would I care anyway? It was a gift from *him*. And he'd nicked it in the first place.

'Are you coming back to the house some time?' I asked.

'Maybe at the weekend.'

'I'm sorry,' I blurted.

Jinn thrust a leaflet at two tourists. 'S'OK.'

'I mean he could come –'

'No,' said Jinn. 'No. I don't want him to. I don't want his stuff in the house.'

She didn't say 'our house'. I noticed that.

'But he's still –'

'Yes,' she said. 'But not around you, he's not.'

'Jinn,' I said. 'Jinn, are you OK?'

'Ruby, Ruby, I'm fine,' she mocked. 'Do feck off. Say what you've got to say and get it over with and feck off.' She wiggled a thumb under her armpit. 'This corset's killing me.'

'Not the corset,' I muttered.

Which was when she stopped talking to me.

Summer

The third time it happened, I saw it in the newspaper racks in the big supermarket. I picked up the *Mirror* and the *Sun* and I read the story in both of them, and then I folded those ones up and tucked them back in the rack, and moved on to the *Record* and the *Glassford-Breakness Courier*. That's why I remember the third girl so well, because the security guard gave me a row for reading all the papers and not buying them and then she chucked me out.

They'd realised there was a connection by now, but it didn't do them any good. There was no CCTV footage; he'd been careful or lucky again. There wasn't any DNA that wasn't their own to connect the girls. He left nothing of himself. He left nothing of them either but a pale shadow in water that might have been a discarded doll or a reflection.

That was what the ghillie at the trout farm thought. Standing on the little bridge over the weir, looking down into the nursery pond, he thought she was reflected sky: so white, shining there a metre or so below the surface. That's what he thought till she moved, till the current from the diverted stream shifted a little and rolled her to face him.

He'd have liked to take her hand and pull her out, he said; she didn't look bloated or badly nibbled, she couldn't have been there for long, she looked like a nymph asleep under the weir with her dark hair drifting. But he wasn't a superstitious man, and he knew she couldn't be sleeping, not now; so he left her there and took his phone from his jacket and went back to the hut to find a signal.

Thirteen

Having Foley around was like picking a scab. I veered wildly between fancying the pants off him and being thrown by his very existence. Without Foley to impress that day, I wouldn't have showed off, and I wouldn't have told Alex to take a running jump. Foley was half boyfriend, half reproachful ghost; I would have liked to sleep with him, but Alex Jerrold kept getting in the way. I'd be sleepily cuddling up to Foley on the sofa, and his hands would be exploring one breast while he kissed me, and *ker-plunk* Alex would land like a bag of meat in my imagination.

Foley was getting tired of me turning him down, but not quite tired enough to finish with me. Besides, I think he loved me, in a Foley kind of way, and he didn't want to dump me. I got the impression he was willing to wait, which made me fabulously complacent about keeping him in line. *And* he was at school. Still! I'd be shagging a schoolboy, for crying out loud.

I thought it was high time I slept with him. I'd have *liked* to sleep with him and I might have done it by now, but I had to consider Mallory the Walking Contraceptive.

Mallory's bedtime was the boundary between indentured servitude to a six-year-old and freedom, but Mallory's bedtime was a very flexible thing, and quite a lot of the time Foley was a twenty-four-hour childminder anyway. Ma and Pa Foley took Apache and Mojave to an awful lot of dog shows, and even when they were home they were making the brutes roast dinners, or bathing and brushing them like gigantic My Little Ponies.

Very occasionally we got shot of Mallory early enough to watch a DVD at my place. Our place, I mean. Jinn's and mine. Our place.

'There's a Foley in every movie,' he told me once as we huddled on the sofa. 'You watch the credits.'

'That's nice. What's wrong with Brad?' I asked. 'Matt? Ben? You could change your first name.'

'Nah.' He nudged me. 'Foley Operator – you just watch.'

'Oh yeah. What does Foley Operator do, anyway?'

He shrugged. 'Operates the Foley.'

'Cameron's a lovely name,' I said. 'Nothing wrong with it.'

'Bloody is when you're named after Cameron Diaz.'

'Oh.'

'Ma liked the name cos of Cameron Diaz. She told me that. I mean, Jesus. It's like being called Paris. Or Beyoncé.'

'Coulda been worse,' I said. 'She could have called you Cherokee to match the dogs.'

He sniggered. 'Dances With Alsatians.'

He got up and put another packet of popcorn in the

microwave. I could hear him messing about in my kitchen. Slamming cupboard doors. Rattling bottles in the fridge. Fizzing the top off another Molotov, and another. Pinging the microwave, and deciding the popcorn needed longer, and clanging the microwave shut again. I could smell something acrid and I decided he was going to burn it, but I didn't shout through. I was drowsy and cosy lying on the sofa and I liked listening to him. I could be quite a domesticated creature, I thought. I quite fancied having Foley around all the time. I wondered if he'd be able to shack up with me next year. I wondered if he'd get to leave Mallory behind. Fat chance.

I heard him hiss and swear because he'd burnt his fingers on the popcorn bag; then I heard the soft rustle of the popcorn being shaken into a Pyrex bowl.

He came back through. I didn't look at him, just shut my eyes and smiled and enjoyed the way the sofa sagged and my body lurched into him when he sat down. He lifted my head like it was a cushion, and dumped it on his lap, and put a nugget of popcorn between my teeth. I wrinkled my nose. It was singed. Thought so.

I ate it anyway. As I chewed I heard him suck in a breath. I wriggled my head, like I was trying to get comfier, and he actually squeaked like a mouse.

I was being an insufferable tease and I knew it, but I liked having Foley physically close, I liked curling up against him. Sometimes I was tempted to shag him, just to keep him till morning, because I did get lonely. However well you know them, however long you've lived there, houses are bad about going all Stephen King when you're on your own. But he couldn't have stayed all night anyway. I couldn't keep him there, so it wasn't worth it. He got frustrated and impatient and who could blame him? But it wasn't worth it.

I heaved a sigh. *Spider-Man 3* was OK but I'd seen it twice before. I heaved another sigh.

'Are you bored?' asked Foley.

Well spotted. Ever sensitive to my moods.

'The popcorn's burnt,' I said.

'I abase myself,' he yawned.

I giggled.

He squirmed and wriggled till he was lying behind me on the sofa and I was curled comfortably into him. I could smell his jumper and boy, was it good. I didn't feel sleepy, but what was hypnotic was Foley stroking my spine with his thumb. After a moment of surprise, I let him get on with it. I rolled slightly on to my tummy to give him a better angle. Couldn't see Spider-Man now and didn't care. Bump, bump up my vertebrae. Bump, bump down again.

After that I'm hard-pressed to remember anything, because I fell asleep.

Fourteen

He can't have minded the endless frustration, because he kept coming back for more. We were still dancing round the issue in early September, on a lazy afternoon in the Provost Reid Park, when the trees weren't even beginning to turn after the long warm summer. Cut N'Dried was shut on a Sunday and I deserved a break. I deserved to be where I was, curled up in the broad basket swing, lying half across Foley's chest, absorbing sun-rays like a gecko as we swung back and forth. We were putting no effort into this. Mallory was pushing us, and she was already getting fed up, moaning that her arms were tired.

'You better give me that fiver, Cameron,' she whinged.

'Yeah, yeah. Course I will. Keep pushing.'

His arm was round my neck, and he was holding my *Cosmo* up against the sun, shading his face and reading the sex advice at the same time.

'Jaysus,' he kept muttering, and 'Feck,' and 'Holy shit. Is this for real?'

'For heaven's sake,' I murmured, bored and superior. He was only making things worse for himself. If he was frustrated he had nothing to blame but his prurient curiosity.

Mallory gave us a violent shove, so that we almost decapitated a toddler running in front of us. Its mother gave us a foul glare and swept it up. By the time we'd finished muttering apologies, the swinging basket had slowed almost to a standstill.

'Oi, Mallory!' barked Foley.

We could see her skinny rear view in the distance, running in the direction of the petting zoo in the company of an unsuspecting boy. As Foley yelled her name again she flicked him the finger.

'*Jay*sus. I hope the gerbils eat her.'

'She'll probably eat them.'

'Oh well.' He shrugged. 'Suppose we can't stay here anyway.'

It was true that we were getting the evil eye from a growing posse of toddlers, not to mention their parents. We clambered down from the swing and wandered after Mallory.

'Oh. Got you something on holiday,' said Foley. He rummaged in his jeans pocket like he'd only just remembered, but I think he'd been picking his moment.

He handed me a tiny tartan bag made of stiff paper, and I opened it nervously. The Foleys' annual holiday revolved round dog shows like everything else did, and I didn't know what he could have found in Ingliston or wherever that was worth having. A collar and lead set?

Silver tick remover? I was already psyching myself up to look thrilled.

From folded tissue paper I drew out a thin silver chain. I had to stop and peer at the little silver-and-enamel figure hanging on it. I laughed.

'Were these being traded illegally or what?'

'Aye. I had to meet a shifty guy round the back of the chemical toilets and pass him unmarked notes in a plain envelope.'

'It's very nice,' I said. 'Thanks.'

I wasn't lying. It can't have been expensive but it looked kind of good. The cat was stretched in a frozen pounce, the slender chain threaded through a little loop on its collar.

'Yeah, I liked it,' he said.

'You big rebel. Bet you didn't show it to your parents.'

'Too bloody right I didn't. It's real silver,' he added anxiously.

I slipped it round my neck as we walked. The catch worked smoothly, thank goodness. I didn't want Foley to start helping me with it, because I'd remembered that moment when Nathan Baird fiddled with the catch of Jinn's amber pendant. That was when it had all started. I shivered.

'You cold?' He sounded surprised, as well he might. It was baking hot.

'Nah.' I took his hand.

Making my brain change the subject, I wondered if I

should now return Foley's scarf, the one he'd left at my house last January. Now I had a real proper gift to remember him by: a piece of jewellery, no less. Why, it was practically a ring. So I should let him know where his scarf was.

Or maybe not. I liked that scarf: it smelled good. It smelled of Foley, and I liked that smell. I took it to bed with me if I couldn't sleep, which was a teeny bit pathetic, but even after all these months it could make me forget the stink of burnt sugar in the small hours.

'I didn't get you anything,' I said apologetically.

'You didn't go on holiday.'

'Neither did you, really.'

He made a sound between a proper laugh and a snigger. 'True.'

'Ever considered poisoning those dogs?'

'Oh, *yeah*!' he said, and we both giggled.

I touched the little cat, which felt bumpy against my collarbone. It reminded me sharply of that other cat necklace, and Marley Ryan who'd had it and was dead now. See the way memories come back and ambush you when you least expect them? I hate that.

'Awfurfecksake,' said Foley.

We could see Mallory and her new pal inside the petting zoo gates – hadn't paid, of course; she'd pulled her usual trick of sneaking in under cover of someone else's chaotic family – and now they were perched on the rail of the pigpen. The pigs were short, hairy and unfeasibly disgusting: blotchy charcoal and pink. Mallory and the boyfriend were burping at them, violently and deliberately, the families around them shocked into awed silence. It had turned into a contest between Mallory, the boy and the pigs. Mallory was winning. Her belches were loud and happy and triumphant.

'She starts a farting contest,' said Foley, 'I'm bloody selling her.'

'She can't do that. She can't fart on demand.'

Foley gave me a look that was nine parts pity, one part scorn. 'I'm away to kill her. Talk amongst yourself for a mo.' He marched through the entrance gate.

I so did not want to get involved. I didn't even want to go into the petting zoo. Relieved, I turned away and pottered as I waited, picking dead heads off a scarlet rhododendron.

I heard somebody on the radio the other day saying your mind isn't bounded by your brain, that it can kind of reach out beyond you, further than sight and smell. It *feels*. Your mind can reach out and touch, and it knows things that aren't physical, it knows when it's being touched by another mind.

'That's why,' said the man on the radio, 'we know when we're being watched.'

I could feel watching eyes right now, burrowing into my skin. I didn't want to turn, not at all, but the sensation went on and on, tiny insects digging into my epidermis, and I knew fine that there was only one way to make it stop, and that was to turn round so that whoever it was would look away, embarrassed.

The man did not look away. Our eyes met. It must have taken a huge amount of willpower not to flick his gaze away from mine, just by reflex, but he must have had it. Either that or he simply didn't care. I held his stare for as long as I could, but in the end, I was the one who looked away.

I had no idea what to do now. When I risked another glance at him, he was walking away, and Foley was emerging from the petting zoo, dragging Mallory by the sleeve.

'I saw Tom Jerrold,' I blurted.

'Oh?' Foley was still working at hanging on to Mallory. 'Well, he lives in Glassford now.'

'I know. But he was –' I hesitated. What was he doing? Looking at me? Oh, call the armed response unit. 'He didn't say hi.'

'You didn't seriously think he would?'

'No,' I admitted. 'Think Alex told him? What I said?'

Foley didn't say anything for a minute. He rubbed his nose and scratched the back of his neck. 'Yeah. I think it was, like . . . I think it was, like, common knowledge.'

Yeah. Of course it was. Enough people heard me. I forgot that sometimes. I even forgot Alex now and again, forgot he'd ever existed or that he still did. I forgot that for minutes at a time.

I don't suppose Tom Jerrold ever did.

Fifteen

Just as well Folcy wasn't staying the night; I'd have been mortified. It was so long since I'd seen Jinn at our house, I'd forgotten she still had her own key. I didn't hear the door open because I was brushing my teeth, but I heard it do its delayed-slam thing, and nearly impaled my brain on an Oral-B.

I stuck my head out of the bathroom door, my brush at my side dripping blue toothpaste-foam on the carpet.

She still looked a bit huffy, and let's face it, she had me at a disadvantage. I grabbed a towel and wiped my foaming mouth. 'Hi.'

We watched each other, half embarrassed and half wary. At last she smiled.

'I'm just picking up some stuff. OK?'

'Yeah. Yes. Um. You want a coffee?'

She glanced at her watch, like she had forty appointments that day or something. 'I can't, Ruby. I got to go.' She tossed back her hair and smiled properly. 'Next time.'

'Uh-huh,' I said, but she was already sidling into her old room.

I'd have loved to know what she was hunting for,

slamming drawers and creaking open cupboard doors, but I didn't want to hover in the hall and be too blatantly nosy. I went to the kitchen and made a coffee I didn't want, then leaned against the cabinet and waited. I could have gone out. I could have left her to it, let her lock up, but that felt sort of . . . inhospitable. Which was wrong and stupid when it was meant to be her house too.

When she came to the kitchen she was carrying a plastic Tesco bag stuffed with clothes. 'You haven't messed with my stuff, Ruby, have you?'

I felt my face go hot at the injustice. 'No!'

'OK.' She half turned away, then. 'You wouldn't, would you?'

'No, I *wouldn't*.' I could get angry if she went on like that.

She didn't, though. She smiled with one corner of her mouth. 'Good!'

I glared.

'So don't!' she warned me. 'And I wasn't here, OK?'

My glare became a frown.

'I wasn't here, and you never touch my stuff.'

She went out the front door and tried to slam it, except of course it wouldn't slam, not on demand. As she tugged on it I giggled.

It was nearly shut, but she stuck her head back round, and winked at me, and giggled in turn.

'But you still don't touch my stuff.'

And then she was gone.

*   *   *

Jinn's new job, of course, didn't last longer than the summer. They had a bonfire in September in the Dot Cumming Memorial Park, by the sea, where they burned fake witches made of mouldy pillows and the clothes even the charity shop couldn't sell. That was the climax of the witch festivities and the end of Jinn's job, though I saw her making the most of it, dancing round the blaze in her witch get-up, clapping her hands and scaring small children, feeling guilty and hugging them if they started to cry. She must have enjoyed it, even if the money was crap, because she looked high as a weather balloon, her eyes brilliant with the fun of it.

Foley was busy that evening making sure Mallory didn't immolate herself or any one of her pack of small boyfriends. Thank God fireworks weren't in the shops yet; the little brute would have been throwing them at the witches both on the bonfire and off. I was bored with the whole thing, or pretending I was. Unaccustomed alcohol had made me melancholy. I'd had a few drinks – Molotovs, as it happens, but with vodka in – and I had a hankering to talk to Jinn. When words want out of me, boy, do they want out. If I didn't corner Jinn and bend her ear, I was going to combust.

She'd disappeared. I circled the bonfire three times (which in Breakness mythology probably means the Devil will appear in a puff of smoke and eat me) but could see no sign of her. I swear, in an instant of irrational terror I even checked the smouldering lumps of pillow on the bonfire, screwing up my eyes through the smoke to identify cheap clothing and green raffia wigs, but the burning witches were damp and mouldy, and not far gone enough to be unrecognisable. Jinn had not through some bizarre accident been mistaken for a witch-guy and thrown on the fire.

I bought a poke of chips and nibbled on them as I edged through the crowd. It was quite a warm night and she should have been incredibly conspicuous in her get-up, but there was no sign of her. I backed away from the crowds and wandered back towards the edge of the park and the river where it spilled into the sea. There was a big wall there with a mural on it: witches (of course), and garish mermaids with fat lips, and skinny dolphins with heads way out of proportion to their tails. Mallory's school had done it as part of a civic arts project, and I suppose it was better than blank concrete – just. The evening air was cool in its shadow, so I strolled out past it into the slanting evening sun. The mural wall screened this part of the river from the park and the bonfire, and it screened the rickety bridge too. That troll could be up to anything.

Beyond the wall I sat down, dangling my legs over a high stone dyke that jutted over the river. From here I could see the rickety bridge, anchored in hard sand. With the tide out, its first two stanchions were on dry land, dry sand. In the furthest deepest shadows, where the tide would come last and the sand would be softest and driest, I saw a haphazard pile of black. You'd think it was a pile

of black bin bags if you didn't know what you were looking for, but it was most unlikely you'd look at all. It was
only that I was searching for her, only that my eyes were
peeled.

Tulle and taffeta and lace, all bunched up and messy.
Black hair askew, silver strands escaping like ribbons to
match the river. White limbs all exposed.

I thought she was dead. Then I thought, no, not yet, but
he was killing her.

That's what I thought before age and experience and my
brain kicked in. They were only twenty metres away but
the sun was lowering and the shadows were deepening
and it was so hard to see; and I was on my own, and angry,
and afraid, and I thought she wouldn't do what she was
doing, so I that's why I thought he must be killing her. My
legs wouldn't work for a little while – and I was too busy
staring – and then I stood up so fast, she saw my
movement.

Jinn didn't stop straight away. I saw her head turn, and
her eyes darken, but they didn't spark with rage, they
didn't spark with anything. You know, I can't really have
seen all that, can I? Not at that distance. I suppose I only
felt it, her dull resentment battering at me.

She didn't let on to the man grunting and bumping on
top of her. When I realised she wasn't going to stop, and
he wasn't killing her, I put my hands over my eyes so I
wouldn't see. When I dared to look again, she was standing up and dusting off the sand, and straightening her

black tulle skirts and tucking something into her bodice; and the man was hunching his shoulders and walking away.

It wasn't Nathan Baird. That's why I lost my temper. She'd given me up for him, and now she was shagging someone who wasn't him at all.

She caught up with me at the mural wall as I clambered up the rocks. Everybody in the whole town was watching the bonfire. Nobody was interested in a catfight.

'It's none of your business, Ruby!'

'Where's Nathan?' I yelled. 'Doesn't he mind?'

She took a step back then. At first I thought she was angry, then I realised it wasn't that. She was confused, that was all. Like she'd thought I was on to her, and abruptly realised I wasn't.

I blinked.

She said, 'Listen. You wouldn't understand.'

Then we stared at one another again, for quite a silent while. I could hear myself breathing but I couldn't hear Jinn.

'I love him,' she said.

'So why . . . are . . . you . . .'

My voice trailed into nothingness because my slow old brain had finally answered my own question. A pair of fighter jets screamed past, then faded into a sonic boom. And silence.

'I love him,' said Jinn. 'You don't love him.'

'If you loved him,' I said, 'you wouldn't help him . . .
get . . .'

God, my brain was doing some catching up.

'What happened to your pendant?' I said.

She touched the black leather thong, stroked a fingertip
across the gothic cross.

'It's at home,' she said.

'You can come home,' I said. 'Please come home, Jinn.'

'No.'

'You can bring him.' There was a hideous edge of desperation in my voice.

'I won't,' she said. 'I won't have him round you. Him
and his shit. And the guys, his old friends. He still owes
them. I don't want them coming to the house and I don't
want you having to deal with them. When we pay them
off, then we might come back.'

I blinked my blurring eyes. 'You love him more than
you love me.'

'No. I love him as much as I love you and I won't have
you around those people.'

'Stop him *doing* it,' I said, like a petulant toddler.

Jinn just laughed.

I begged, 'Just bring him home and stay home.'

She laughed again. 'I'll be fine.' She sucked her lip and
shut one eye. 'Look, Ruby, it's cool. It's not a problem.'

'It's a problem, it is, it is.' Tears pricked like needles
under my eyelids. 'Jinn, why are you doing this?'

'Ruby, shush. I didn't get in his car. See, if you don't get in a car, it's safe. It's easy money and it's safe. I'll – look, I'm in control.'

I stared at her. I couldn't speak. What's new?

'I'm sorry, Ruby. I'm sorry. It's just the way things are.'

And then she fell silent. There's an irony, because for once I went the opposite way. Actually I couldn't shut up, not once I started.

I don't even remember what I screamed at her. It wasn't anything sisterly. I couldn't stand the way she was standing there taking it. I didn't think she should. I wanted her to howl at me, scream back. I wanted her to hit me. I wanted her to slap my silly face and bring me to my senses and tell me it was an optical illusion, a hallucination, a dream. Instead she just watched me, her face a pallid mask of remorse and guilt. I had never seen that expression on her face, never, and I decided it was something to do with the crappy foundation and the God-awful scarlet lipstick, so I flew at her and tried to wipe them off. I tried to wipe off the make-up, and her grim miserable expression, and her whole face.

I hit her till my arms were tired. Thank heavens we were below the mural wall and nobody could see us. I don't think there was much to be heard, though I can't be sure of that. I think she didn't cry out and I'm pretty sure I didn't scream at her any more, not after I started clawing at her face and hitting and punching. She tried to defend herself a little, but not enough. There was red lipstick smeared across her cheeks and my fists, I had fistfuls of fake black hair where I'd torn at her stupid wig, and the wig itself, when I came to my senses, lay on the tarmac like a crow that had crashed and burned. Jinn was blonde again, but her hair didn't have silver sparks; it was dull and lank and squashed flat by the wig.

She blinked at me, her lipstick all smudged across her chin and her mascara running with her tears and her ear red and sore where I'd whacked it. I think I might have bruised her jaw.

'It's cool, Ruby,' she said, and wiped her face with the back of her hand. She was crying, hard, quietly. 'It's fine.'

I didn't have a single word left in my head. My palms hurt from slapping and my knuckles from punching and my lungs from crying.

'And it's only for a bit, you see. It's only till Nathan gets sorted.'

I wanted to call her what she was but I could no more get that word out than any others. She was going to end up like those other girls, those other girls who worked for a living. Those working girls, like the one they'd found in that trout pond, sleeping with the fishes. That's what happened to those kind of girls, wasn't it? In cheap crime novels with lurid covers, in gritty mini-series, in real life. They knew that when they started out but I expect they only did it for a bit, too. Just till they got themselves sorted. Just till they got themselves killed.

'I'll be fine, Ruby. Nothing's going to happen. I don't get in cars. I don't go to their houses. I'm really careful.'

You can't be sure of that, I wanted to say, but I'd have been wasting my breath. I think she was sure of everything, and she was most sure of the stupidest thing of all.

'I don't have a choice, see.' And she smiled like a fallen angel, and her red bruised mouth was a knife slash. 'I love him, Ruby.'

Sixteen

I had to have it out with her. I had to try one more time. I was working that Saturday but I slogged back to Dunedin on the Sunday, and this time I didn't stand on the pavement opposite; this time I opened the gate – I had to jerk it hard and my hand came away orange with rust – and walked up the path. My heart was banging so hard I thought it was trying to escape out of my throat. I pressed the doorbell.

I had plenty of time to look at the house. Dunedin: it sounded like a medieval fortress, or something out of Middle Earth. Dunedin: Last Homely House of the Crack Elves. Foursquare and granite, the name was printed in gold letters on the semicircle of glass above the panelled front door. The grass was straggling up and over the steps; now that it had overgrown the cracks in the paving it was empire-building and if it ran on unchecked it would probably smother the house. I pictured Dunedin with a shaggy wig of yellowing grass. A magic house. If I broke off a piece of the crumbling window ledge, maybe it would taste of coconut ice.

God's sake, listen to me. I didn't need drugs.

I pressed the doorbell again, leaning closer this time and frowning. A tiny frisson ran along the nape of my neck. Perhaps they were all dead. That didn't seem a possibility, not all at once, so maybe they were just coming back from some parallel world. I had to give them a minute to get through the portal.

Something more prosaic occurred to me, so I made a fist and hesitated just once. I could turn and walk away now. My thundering heart was urging me to do just that. The non-working doorbell might be an omen.

I made my fist even tighter, took a breath, and thumped twice on the door.

It didn't fly open like I thought it would. After about thirty seconds it creaked ajar, then swung wider.

Nathan Baird didn't say anything. He just watched me while I watched him. He was biting on his lip, which looked raw from the habit. He looked so pale, an underground elf who never saw the sun, or possibly a Ringwraith. He should be wearing a hooded cloak. Instead he wore a T-shirt loose over black jeans, and he was barefoot. It was that T-shirt with the Batman logo, now even more cracked and faded from age. I guess it hadn't been washed for a while, because it clung to his thin muscles and I could smell his sweat, all mixed up with that crack smell I didn't use to recognise. His hair straggled into his eyes like the grass outside. Lifting a hand, he shoved it back. That made me look at his sharp cheekbones and the brilliant golden eyes above them, and because I didn't want to stare, I looked back at his feet, long-toed and elegant.

I felt that little shiver of something. I wasn't lusting after him – God almighty, no, but I could see so very clearly why Jinn did. He just smelt of sex. Sweat and crack and tobacco smoke, but mostly sex. I was glad it wasn't me that had fallen for him. In the exact same moment I wished it had been, because then it wouldn't have been Jinn.

He gave me a hostile smile, his eyes crinkling slightly. 'Ruby Red.'

'Is Jinn in?' I snapped.

'Nope.'

I rubbed my arms, then straightened them at my sides, annoyed with myself. 'When's she back?'

He lifted one shoulder. His eyes were bronze now and shadowy. 'Want to come in? You can wait.'

I shook my head.

'We won't eat you, Ruby Red.'

Oh yeah? I thought. You ate her.

I bit back my hatred, choked it down my throat, and said, 'You want to come back?'

What made me say that? It just kind of came out, like Mount St Ruby erupting all over again. Maybe I contain my words so tightly, they burst out whenever they get a chance. I need to consider that.

Nathan Baird was just watching me, smiling a little bit. No teeth were involved in his smile, just his twitching lips. He pushed his fingers through his hair again, and shook it back out of his eyes. I had the craziest urge to take his hand. Take him and Jinn home and tuck them up.

'I think it's a bit late for that, Ruby Red. And you don't really mean it, eh?'

I shrugged.

He propped his shoulder against the door jamb. 'Things are complicated just now.'

'You owe some guys money, you mean,' I said.

His turn to shrug.

I peered over his shoulder at Dunedin, the Elvensquat.

'I'm sorry you left.' My words came out on a snarl.

His eyes crinkled more but his mouth tightened and he said nothing. He looked kind of hurt.

'I want Jinn to come home,' I said, still staring at the coconut-ice window ledge and the crackled toffee varnish.

'You'd better ask her then.'

He wasn't making it easy, but who could blame him? 'Where is she?'

'I dunno. Maybe she's with people she likes.'

I didn't want to turn my back on Nathan, not straight away. I took a couple of backward steps, eyeing him for any sign of lies, any complacent smirk. He just watched me back, expressionless, but then he lifted his gaze and his wide pupils dilated a little more and he stared over my shoulder.

Oldest one in the book, I thought, narrowing my eyes suspiciously, but then I twisted round.

Inflatable George was on the other side of the road, right where I'd stood before. He didn't duck or hide, and he didn't even look at me; he just stood there with his hands in his pockets and glared at Nathan. The look Nathan gave him back was rank with loathing.

The face-off seemed to last for ages, and I'm not sure who won it. At last George smiled right at me, and gave me a small friendly wave, as if Nathan didn't even exist. I heard the door slam shut, and even that sound was full of hate.

I crossed the road. 'Hi.'

'Hi, Ruby. I came to talk to Jinn. She's not in, then?'

I shook my head.

'Bertha's that upset about her. She doesn't show it, but she is.'

'I know,' I said.

'She pretends she doesn't care and she gets all uppity, but you shouldn't take any notice.'

'I know. I don't.'

'She's that fond of Jinn. I wish Jinn would come to her senses.'

'Yeah.' I shrugged uncomfortably. 'I don't know what to do either.'

'Well, don't be a stranger. Bertha wouldn't want you to stay away cos you're, like, embarrassed or something. OK? You're kind of on the same side. You know? She doesn't blame you for Jinn swiping stuff. Course she doesn't.'

Jesus, how did people get all those words out in one breath? I appreciated it though. I smiled at him. 'OK.'

He smiled back. 'No point me hanging around, then. I'll maybe try another time. Or maybe she'd just kick me out.' He patted my arm, then stuck his hands back in his pockets and walked away back towards the mini-mart.

It was nice of him, but it made me feel kind of guilty. Here were all these people looking out for Jinn, worrying about her, and I hadn't really been keeping up, I'd been too busy feeling sorry for myself and missing my mother-substitute. I had to find the silly bitch, make sure she was OK. What had Nathan said again?

Maybe she's with people she likes.

Well, the people she liked best, apart from me, were Wide Bertha and Inflatable George, and she was hardly going to go running to them right now. I had to think about it harder.

Maybe she's with people she likes.

Or maybe it wasn't people.

I caught a bus up to Glassford and picked my ticket into so many tiny bits, I'd have been fined if a ticket inspector had got on. I had to hold my breath every time the bus halted, every time a little old lady had to manoeuvre herself and her pull-along trolley down the steps, every time a mother had to manhandle a buggy. We didn't miss out a single stop; there was someone waiting at every one and the bus had to stop for them, as if I was under some evil bus enchantment and I was never, ever going to reach the Provost Reid Park.

A wee man got on just as we hit the Glassford outskirts, sat down on the seat opposite mine and got going on his phone. I thought he was never going to shut up about his big night out. After a bit he lifted up one bum cheek and let loose a loud fart, and I couldn't do anything but stare. He smiled and gave me an amiable nod.

The boys in front of him exploded into giggles. Usually I would have too, but he'd distracted me so much I'd missed the stop for the park. I wanted to light a match and incinerate him with his own outgoings but I didn't have time; I flew to the door just as it hissed shut, shouting at the driver and ringing the bell over and over to make him stop again ten metres on. Somebody behind me tutted and the wee man said, 'Nae hurry, hen, nae hurry, it wis just wind;' and the driver shouted at me, but I didn't hear what he said. At least he opened the door. I jumped out and bolted back down the road and through the park gates.

The petting zoo wasn't as busy as it had been in the summer, but it was a weekend and there were still people around. I had to pay to get in; I hadn't had a freebie visit since Jinn stopped working for Wide Bertha and wasn't bringing free treats for the animals.

The place was buzzing – obviously something was happening, so I didn't hang around paying my respects to the guinea pigs. I ran straight to the goats, and that was where I found Jinn, right inside the pen. She'd opened the gate wide and the nanny goat was wandering out and nibbling the grass at the edge of the tarmac path, and a few children were laughing and taunting the creature, and a few more were squealing with fright as she took trotting steps towards them.

Jinn was still in the pen, her arms around the billy goat's neck, trying to drag him to freedom. He didn't seem to want to shift but he seemed content to have her wrapped round him. In turn a park official in a green shirt had his arms round Jinn's shoulders, trying to pull her off the goat. A group of boys on the other side of the fence was in fits of hysteria, and so would I have been. But because I was her sister, I felt tears sting my eyes and I ran into the pen and pulled at the ranger's arm (yes, they called them rangers, like they were on the African savannah tranquillising lions, not in a squashed corner of the municipal park with a few guinea pigs). Now we were starting to look like something out of *The Enormous Turnip*, Jinn holding the goat and the ranger clinging on to Jinn and me grabbing the ranger. The boys at the fence were just about peeing themselves.

At last the ranger got his senses back in gear and let go of Jinn, then turned and disengaged me.

'Get her out of here!' he yelled at me.

'I'm trying!' I was furious. Being furious stopped me crying.

Between us, the ranger and I got Jinn off the goat and manhandled her out of the pen, just as the boy from the entry kiosk shut the gate. That was a waste of time, since the billy goat wasn't trying to escape and the nanny goat was still outside, clearing great swathes of the path by her mere presence. I made a hesitant approach, but the ranger seized my arm and turned me and shoved me towards the gate.

'Just get out!' he shouted. 'And take *her* with you.'

Jinn wasn't in a state to argue by this point. She was just standing there weeping over her failed rescue attempt, like the most incompetent animal liberationist in the world. The kiosk attendant gave her a sorrowful glance, but he was too scared to come near her – more frightened of me than of the ranger, I think. I left him and the ranger trying to round up a bolshie nanny goat, and I took Jinn home.

I didn't take her to the little grey house. I thought she'd want to go home-home, to the home where she was loved, so I took her to Dunedin.

She was still crying when we got there, still mumbling about the imprisoned goats. I'm not sure she was stoned but she was certainly a bit pissed.

Nathan didn't really look at me when he opened the door. He took Jinn by the hand and I followed them into the sitting room, where the carpet felt sticky underfoot and plaster was crumbling from the ornate cornices. Out of the greasy back window I could see their overgrown square of weeds and paving stones, and a whirligig draped with limp grubby dishtowels. It wasn't crisp flapping laundry like at our house, like when Jinn was with me, but she was trying. She was trying.

Nathan pulled her down into his arms on the sofa and cuddled her and kissed the top of her head. Instead of raking through his own lank hair, his fingers were combing through hers. I didn't want to sit down on any of the chairs and I didn't know where to look, so I examined my feet, and the remains of Chinese takeaways, and the paraphernalia I didn't use to recognise any more than I did the smell: bottles and dismantled biros and tinfoil rolls with little squares cut out.

After a while I heard a faint snore and I saw that Jinn had fallen asleep with her face crammed into Nathan's neck, and his head had drooped over hers too. I swallowed and hesitated, and then I just left the house and closed the door quietly and walked home.

Seventeen

What with my minimum-wage job and my part-time cowboy efforts at other people's hair, I was going along quite nicely, financially. I let things like the landline fall into arrears and then it got cut off, but I had my pay-as-you-go mobile. I kept that topped up and I paid the electricity bill and the TV licence – that sort of thing. And the rent was covered, though I dreaded the day the social would find out Jinn wasn't actually living in our house. I should have gone and confessed and made other arrangements, but I was scared to disturb the arrangements that were already in place.

Another thing I should have done was buy proper flowers for Lara. You can get a bunch for £1.99 in Tesco, for heaven's sake. But I thought Lara might actually prefer something out of her garden (not Livingstone daisies; they were long over, and anyway they just close up when you pick them). So I'd picked snapdragons and wrapped a rubber band round them and on the way to the cemetery I stopped by the Last Homely Crack House.

Jinn was back to her old self. She looked quite bright when she opened the door to me, if a little wary.

'Do you want to come and see Lara?' I said.

She hesitated. She glanced down at the phone in her hand, lit up with a message.

'I can't.'

'Oh,' I said.

'Work.'

'Oh,' I said again.

'It's not what you think.'

If I didn't know by now when Jinn was lying, I wouldn't have been much of a sister.

'Does he – does Nathan –'

Quickly she flicked the snib and shut the door behind her. 'Listen. He doesn't ask me to work. He doesn't ask me to do it.'

'I meant, does he *mind*?'

'Of course he minds. He'd mind more if I didn't have any money. He has his problems.'

So I kept hearing. 'Yeah. So do you want to come and see Lara?'

'I don't. Really. Want to.' She didn't quite look at me.

She thought she'd failed Lara. I realised that quite suddenly. She didn't want to go and look our mother in the face, loosely speaking, because she'd failed and she felt guilty about that. And anyway, I guess she was working.

'I've got Maltesers.' A tinge of desperation there.

She gave me a sort of pitying look.

'I've kind of gone off Maltesers, Ruby.'

Sitting alone at Lara's grave, I was angrier with Jinn than I'd ever been. Guilt was my department; Jinn's was to be reassuring and loving-me-whether-or-not-I-deserved-it. That made me remember the one time it had been horrible coming to Lara's grave, when Jinn had burst into tears because she was so tired from working (respectably) and looking after me and just missing Lara. I remember her flapping my awkward consoling hand away and shouting at me, '*Ruby, I love you but that can't be all I do!*'

I didn't see why not. It seemed a noble calling to me.

I tried to be Jinn. I wanted to be more like her, I did. Once I'd even tried to emulate her, sentimentally and pointlessly. I found a baby starling. I know now, of course, that you're supposed to leave them where they are, like baby seals. Starlings and seals do not get bladdered and walk in front of Vauxhall Astras, so there is a good chance the mother will return to its baby and look after it.

But with only Lara for a model, I thought the mother had probably come to grief, so I rescued this pathetically ugly creature and took him to the kitchen, where I created a shoebox nest for him, lined with the local free advertising rag. I fed him bugs and bread and milky cornflake dregs; I named him Ozzy, though I don't know to this day what sex he was, and I nursed him proudly. I fancied myself the Saba Douglas-Hamilton of suburban Scotland, reintroducing native species to the wild. I encouraged Ozzy to totter around on his little legs, and at last there came a time when I felt I should let him socialise (this entire episode only lasted about forty-eight hours, by the way. I had little patience). So when a flock of grown-up startings clustered in the trees, yelling at each other like fishwives, I let young Ozzy flap out to the grass, in his sweet ungainly way. Whereupon the flock of grown-ups swooped down and pecked the little bastard to death.

I kept quiet about this. I was ashamed, and starlings being starlings the same way scorpions are scorpions, I couldn't blame them. The death of ugly little Ozzy was entirely on my conscience.

There were starlings in the cemetery when I got there, and gulls fighting over a leftover sandwich they'd fished out of the bin. Ozzy and his tragic fate cured me of being sentimental about birds. If those starlings and gulls could have robbed a few graves, they would have; they'd have hauled up the corpses and had a go. They'd strip poor Lara down to the bones.

I emptied dead petunias out of the jam jar (it had been a while) and tried to arrange my snapdragons artistically. Some of the graves never had any flowers; they looked sad and bare and lonely. Some of them were practically smothered in carnations and cellophane and broad garish ribbons. I reckoned Lara enjoyed a happy medium. Nicer than Tesco's £1.99 bunch. Though I should get her some of those too, some time. For a change.

'I'm not sure what to do about Jinn,' I said.

No answer.

I felt like an idiot. I couldn't open my mouth and speak to the living, so I don't know why I was trying it on with the dead. The wind stirred a sickly birch tree, and a few dry leaves drifted down. I shivered. When you speak out loud like that, it's as if you break something. I felt they'd all been chatting up till then, all the dead people under the ground, and I'd walked in like an eejit and interrupted an interesting conversation. I felt as if they'd all fallen silent and now they were listening and waiting for what I was going to say next.

I thought about Alex Jerrold, and wondered if he thought he'd be in here by now, but he'd blown it and caught himself on that truck. Safety-netted like a fly on a web. No wings though.

I stood up sharply. I looked out past the headstones to the industrial estate and the bypass. I could hear cars on the bypass, and the sudden blare of a lorry horn, out there where I wouldn't have to listen to the soft rustle of the birch or the murmur of the dead.

I picked up my bag and took my Maltesers somewhere else.

Eighteen

Cut N'Dried had big plate-glass windows facing on to a narrow one-way street. That meant you could all too easily see passers-by, if there was a moment's peace. It was always hot in the salon, with the dryers going constantly, and today was a mild day, so I edged across to the open door when I got the chance, just to catch a breath of the outside air. It wasn't busy anyway; it was one of those quiet days and I was only sweeping clippings.

I opened my mouth to suck in air that didn't taste of coconut shampoo and conditioner. It stayed open, and my eyes goggled. Nathan Baird had just come out of the surf shop opposite (like Glassford was a small town in California or something), and he was looking happy. Too happy, I mean. Happy like Lara: bad-happy.

I mumbled something just low enough for the boss to miss it, and headed outside.

'That your coffee break, Ruby?' Clarissa's sharp voice floated after me.

She could assume so. Fine with me.

'Nathan!' I yelled.

He semi-glanced over his shoulder, then mockingly walked on.

I came to a halt, undecided. But I knew the reputation of that surf shop; hair salons are good for gossip. And Nathan hadn't emerged with a shiny new surfboard. I ran after him, dodging two old women, jumping on and off the kerb to avoid a pushchair and getting blared at by a souped-up boy racer.

Nathan kept walking. He knew I was there; he was just taking the mickey. Pausing teasingly, then walking on when I called his name. I hated him. I wanted to shove him under a bus. Sod all that, I just wanted to *catch up.*

At last he swung open the door of the staidest tearoom in town, where the waitresses were more than a hundred and eighty years old and wore white aprons. In here they'd never heard of a hazelnut latte. Nathan sat at a lace-frothed table in the window, ordered a pot of Darjeeling and grinned at me.

I yanked out a chair opposite him and sat down. I wanted to shout, hit him, but I couldn't make a scene in here of all places. There'd be multiple cardiac arrests. Nathan 1, Ruby 0.

'Have a scone,' he suggested. To rhyme with 'bone'.

'Leave her alone!' I blurted.

Quizzically he studied the old dear behind the counter, placidly rearranging day-old pancakes. 'I'm sure she won't mind. It's her job.'

'Stop it. I mean *Jinn*.'

He leaned forward, smile gone. 'It's not your business, Ruby Red.'

'Just leave my sister alone. Please leave her.'

'I can't do that.' For an instant he looked perfectly serious. Sad, almost.

'You know what she does for you,' I hissed.

A pause, a sip of Darjeeling. He was mocking me again. 'What she does for me?'

'Stop that! If you just –'

He was eyeing me over the rim of his cup, lasering resentment. That was funny.

'You've gotta do what you've gotta do.' He shrugged, all indifferent again, the shutters down over his eyes.

I wondered, suddenly, if he'd known at all, or if I'd just blown it wide open.

Whether by bad luck or good luck, Jinn picked that exact moment to swan into the tearoom, all smiles and glitter. It was her nail varnish that had sparkles though. Not her skin.

'Hey, babe.'

'Hi, Jinn.'

'Ruby!' She blew me a kiss.

Nathan was perfectly cool as she half-sat on his lap and smiled at me, pushing a strand of hair behind her ear.

'How's things, Ruby sweetie? How's the job?'

'Fine . . .' So how was I meant to ask about hers?

As if she understood, she turned away to put her arm round Nathan's neck and delicately kiss his ear.

He seemed very easy still. He laid his hand lightly on her bare forearm, his forefinger stroking her skin. His Batman T-shirt was really loose and misshapen now; I could see his prominent collarbone. Jinn kissed it, still smiling. I hated him, I hated her. I wanted him to be using her, I wanted him to be a loveless bastard. He wasn't obliging me.

Nathan was watching me, and I wondered if he could make out the green veil of jealousy across my eyes. I didn't even know who I was jealous of. Him? *Her?* Their whole insane, enviable, rare-as-rockinghorse-shit love affair?

His lips brushed her throat; she giggled and arched her neck. It was worse than the tango and it earned them a disapproving glare from the old waitress, muttering behind the Victoria sponges and the Empire biscuits. While Jinn laughed at the ceiling, he smiled directly at me. He didn't have to open his mouth.

She loves me.

I love her.

I win.

I stood, scraping my chair back. Under Nathan's victorious stare I stalked out of the tearoom and back to the salon, beaten and seething and hateful, and wanting more than anything a lover like him; a lover who'd one day shock a waitress by loving me in public.

I couldn't imagine her with another man. I knew fine she was, frequently; I just couldn't imagine it. As for the man I saw her *with* . . .

When I saw Jinn with Tom Jerrold that same night, to say I was surprised would be putting it mildly. It was dark, the clocks had gone back a week earlier, and if I'd turned the corner a minute later I'd have missed her. But I saw her.

I stood stock-still, shocked by what she was doing, slouched against the wall between the harbour master's office and the marina. Her skirt was too short for the cold of the November night, and her boot heels were too high for the cobbles. Her hair glittered, though. She stood in the white light of a cast-iron retro-Victorian streetlight. They'd put those there just a few months ago for the heritage tourism. Not many tourists around at this time of year, so Jinn was making the most of it, the white light striking sparks off her hair. Which was lanker and yellower than it used to be, but not in this light. In this light she was magical, a white witch, an elven queen in trashy boots. She leaned down to the car, talked for a while to the driver and then – oh my God – she got in. I had to stop my jaw hitting the cobbles.

See, if you don't get in a car, it's safe. It's easy money and it's safe.

So much for that, then. I scuttled back into the shadows as the car went past. It was a very distinctive car, bright yellow with a soft top, and it was driven slowly, so I saw his face; I saw Tom Jerrold. He wasn't smiling but Jinn was; she'd turned to him and was touching his face and she was actually laughing, like she was his prom date or something. So Jinn didn't see me.

Tom Jerrold did. Tom Jerrold saw me, but he still didn't smile. He let his eyes rest on mine, then steered the car up the bumpy lane behind the harbour master's office, and I stood for twenty minutes or more, trying to breathe right, trying to think what to do.

There was nothing, really. So I went home and watched *CSI*, so that I wouldn't worry.

I'd always wanted them to get together, of course, but not like that. And suddenly I was seeing Tom Jerrold all the time.

Saturday morning was very cold but it was brisk and blue and sunny, and as I opened the door into Cut N'Dried I was in an excellent mood. I even smiled at Mrs Bolland, who had a head full of foils and a face that could melt bricks. She shook out her magazine and gave me a scowl that was slightly more like a smile than usual. You wouldn't want to look at her for terribly long, so I looked in the mirror next to hers. And there was a reflected Tom.

Leanne was just brushing the clippings off his neck, and as he stood up, shaking hair off his jumper, he spotted me. Making a slight face – either friendly or sort of facetious, I'm not sure which – he walked to the counter to pay.

Still no hello, then.

I understood why he'd come back, but I wished he hadn't. I saw him in Glassford; I saw him in Breakness. I saw him unpacking his clubs in the golf club car park;

I saw him walking briskly between his office and, I don't know, some other office.

He was something hot with a firm of surveyors. His job must have been pretty high-powered, because that glossy yellow car was brand new and fully loaded and top of the range, all those things that I don't understand because I've never had a car of any description. It wasn't a Porsche or anything – it was a Toyota, but it was a sporty, fast, beautiful Toyota. He seemed truly to love it, caring for it the way he might care for a racehorse. I wasn't likely to forget it even if I hadn't seen Jinn step into it smiling, skirt up to her arse.

I saw Tom Jerrold in the big Glassford Tesco, I saw him going into the nicer Breakness pub with his suited mates, I saw him eating his lunch alone on a bench by the river in the Dot Cumming Memorial Park. That was the time I glanced up and he was there, seven or eight metres away. I was sitting on the high river wall, dangling my legs over the side, eating a rice salad with a plastic fork and trying not to spill anything out of the flimsy bowl. I was concentrating so hard I was amazed anything could make me look up, but I must have felt Tom Jerrold's stare again, because there he was. There he was, making me nervous.

The river was a different beast altogether in the winter. It was opaque and cold, rushing down to the sea in a brown flurry, no summer meandering and no glittery sparkle. I still liked to sit on the wall and look at it but I'd hate to fall in, and I didn't like the way Tom Jerrold was walking so purposefully towards me. All my muscles tensed, and I forgot to eat.

He didn't shove me though. He hesitated, then sat down at my side, but not close enough to touch. Neither of us spoke. I thought: if he seriously thinks I'm going to open my mouth to him of all people ...

He leaned forward, studying the rush of water beneath us.

'You'd never jump, would you, Ruby?'

I couldn't speak. Too scared. I shook my head.

'Didn't think so. You never know, of course, but I didn't think so.'

I licked my lips. I picked up a last grain of rice with my fingertip and put it in my mouth. 'I saw you with my sister.'

I am not sure what I was hoping to achieve there. It sounded vaguely like a threat but I hadn't meant it to. At least, I don't think so.

'Uh-huh.' He was still staring down at the river. 'I like her. Always liked her.'

Be careful what you wish for, Ruby.

Tom looked a good bit older, but not in a bad way. He had the same solemn look as Alex, but without the gawky geekiness. He looked self-contained, another guy who didn't give a damn. He had sad and handsome eyes and a straight mouth but he looked like that didn't matter, that it was fine to be sad and handsome, no big deal. Happy and ugly would have been just as acceptable.

I felt even worse now about not visiting Alex. I'd have liked to be able to say, 'I saw your brother,' or 'He's looking better,' or heck, even 'He isn't looking so good.' Any of it would prove I cared enough to call on him. Unfortunately, I didn't.

Well, I did. I cared hugely, enormously, violently. It was just that my shame (and my sheer embarrassment) overwhelmed the caring part. Go and see Alex? Oh, just no *way*.

I shook that thought off, and told Tom, 'Jinn kind of liked you too.'

'*Jinn* liked me.' He shrugged. 'Jinx couldn't give a toss either way but I still like her.'

'Who's Jinx?' I don't know why I asked. The way the name landed hard in my stomach, I knew fine who it belonged to.

'That's what she calls herself.'

'She's got another name?' My throat was all dry. I didn't want to hear about Jinx. This person *Jinx*.

'Nice name,' he said, with an edge of viciousness. 'Not much of a camouflage, but it's got a ring to it.'

'Shut up!' I snapped.

'Yeah, right. 'Kay.' He got up and walked away.

'Her name isn't Jinx,' I shouted after him.

'No, it isn't.'

'I mean it!'

He turned on his heel. 'So do I.'

'Tom! Did you – did you –'

He waited: he stood there and waited for me to finish the sentence. He *made* me finish the sentence because, though it was clearly none of my business, I felt like I had to know, and I was pretty certain he'd tell me. So I took a deep breath, and I asked.

He smiled. It wasn't a nice smile. It was a sad and bitter one but still I got the funny impression he enjoyed it, he enjoyed baiting me, he'd enjoy lying awake thinking of me lying awake. A little revenge. He hadn't turned my sister into a prostitute, but he'd paid to have her. I hadn't pushed his brother, but I'd told him to jump. Was that us quits? I hoped so.

'No,' he said. 'I didn't. Not with Jinx.'

I glared at him, sure he was lying.

'With Jinn,' he said. 'Sure. But not Jinx.'

And you know, that made me feel even worse.

So there was this girl called Jinx, and there was my sister, whose name was Jinn. They were not the same person; they lived in different worlds, different dimensions. Jinx was the elf queen in tarty boots who lived in the Last Homely House of Dunedin. Jinn was the lost girl, the girl with no existence on our plane. She was trapped between the worlds, trapped in a bubble in the past, trapped till the magic was broken and the ending was happy and the talisman was found. And then, only then, could she finally have her name back.

Nineteen

The irony is that I thought at first, on that fateful day, I was helping Alex Jerrold. I was actually concerned for him. It was the way he was crouched over the river under the iron bridge, like a predatory bird but without the attitude. I saw him as I walked back from the library through the park, and I wouldn't have seen him if he hadn't moved, wriggling something out of his jeans pocket so awkwardly he nearly fell over into the muddy grass. Then he crouched again, staring at whatever it was.

I hesitated. I didn't really want to get involved. But there was something about his posture I didn't like, and I felt I had a duty to go and ask him what was wrong. I'd once been his nearly-girlfriend after all, even if it was in my prepubescent days and even if it was a kind of mutant holiday romance. And last year, I'd just avoided kissing him at the Halloween Horror. That had to count for something.

So I left the path and swung down under the iron bridge, and said, 'Hi, Alex.'

He jerked his head up, more like a nervous bird than ever. Was that what gave him the notion he could fly?

He blinked. 'Hello.'

I wanted to ask him what he was doing, but it seemed presumptuous. I just sat down beside him – not too close, though – and rested my arms on my knees and looked at the thing he was looking at. I shuffled a bit closer and looked harder. It was one of those knives that folds back into the handle.

'You're not meant to have that,' I said, shocked.

'Oh, it's not like I'm going to use it.' He could do scorn, he really could.

I hugged my knees and rocked back and forward a bit. 'What are you doing?'

'I'm thinking.'

I wondered why he had to think in the slimy air beneath the bridge, or why he needed a knife to do it. Then I realised his sleeves were rolled up. My eyes widened.

'You're not cutting yourself?'

He gave me an acid look. 'Don't be stupid.'

Sure enough, his arms were smooth and unscarred. I licked my lips, wondering why my heart was thumping. I wanted to make a joke and say, *There's always a first time*, but I didn't want to because I had a horrible feeling about this. Instead I said, 'Are we going to stay here, then?'

His eyes went wary and wide all at once. 'We?'

'Yeah,' I said. 'We could go and get a coffee or something.'

'I'm not really in the mood . . .'

All the same, I wanted him out from under that bridge. 'You like walking, don't you?'

'Um,' he said. 'Um. I guess.'

He snapped the knife shut and put it in his pocket.

It was kind of like our impromptu west coast holiday, only more so. Maybe we were both just older and less hung up. I don't think he was seriously considering slitting his wrists, but let's just say I was happy to have moved him on from under that bridge. Alex himself seemed to float at my side like a helium balloon. I actually heard him laugh, more than once, rather than snort and put his hand to his mouth.

Since he wasn't in the mood for coffee, we stayed in the park. We bought ice creams, we harassed the seagulls, we fooled around on the swings and slides. I can't remember what he talked about, but that boy certainly could talk. I didn't, much, but I liked his company. He had some interesting thoughts about things: books, life, the world. I thought again about how I'd been his nearly-girlfriend, and wondered if it would be so bad, or maybe kind of good. There didn't seem a lot of point pining for Foley, not when he was snacking habitually on Annette Norton's ear.

We shouldn't have left the park. If we hadn't left the park and walked up to the community centre, leaning in to each other and having a bit of a laugh, we wouldn't have seen the other kids from school, we wouldn't have seen Foley. We'd have walked on up to Starbucks and had a coffee and eventually we'd have said goodbye and gone safely home. Our parting gazes might even have lingered an extra second.

Except we did go out of the park towards town. And we did slow and stop as we saw people we knew – or rather, people I knew and people Alex occasionally passed in the corridor.

'Hi,' said Foley, and smiled.

He drew out of his little group, and turned a bit towards us. Except he didn't turn towards *us*, he turned to me.

And Annette Norton nowhere in sight. Hallelujah.

'Hi!' I said. I smiled. Smiling I could do.

I don't remember what we talked about (or let's face it: mostly what he talked about). I remember Foley was really funny; he didn't say anything earth-crackingly philosophical but somehow everything he said was interesting, half of everything he said made me smile, and altogether it seemed like the best time I'd had in ages.

I thought we were including Alex. I thought he was in on the joke. But maybe in hindsight we weren't at all. Maybe that's why, when I finally turned to him and frowned, he had stepped back a few paces, breaking the circle of laughter.

'Come on then,' he said.

'Come on what?'

I was genuinely bewildered. I didn't have a clue what he was on about.

'Starbucks. We're going up to Starbucks.'

'I thought you didn't want coffee.'

'Yeah, but we were going up that way.'

I frowned at him, annoyance rising. 'Yeah, well, no hurry. Right?'

'No hurry,' he said. 'Right.'

I wanted to stamp my foot with impatience. Foley had drifted back to his little group, and though there were a few girls there, they didn't include Annette Norton, and I wanted to affix myself to his side while I had the chance. He was interested; even I could see that. If Alex hadn't been there I'd have had a clear run at Foley, and the worst of it was, it was *my own stupid fault*. If I hadn't taken pity on Alex, there under the bridge ...

'Come on then,' he said.

'In a minute.' I returned his scowl.

'Not in a minute. Let's go now.'

I stared at him, nonplussed. I wasn't that assertive myself, but to be over-asserted by Alex Jerrold of all people ... God's sake, I'd only talked to him out of pity.

'So,' he said. 'Are we going then?'

'No we bloody aren't,' I said.

'Oh, right?' The beginnings of hurt, and that was what I couldn't stand.

'Oh, Alex,' I said. All grown-up and withering. 'Take a running jump.'

'So,' said Bertha. 'This is the part where you ask me if I'm going somewhere nice at the weekend.'

I grinned and rolled my eyes. I was looking at the back of Bertha's head and she was looking at *Coronation Street*, and I'd been kind of hoping I'd get away with it. Unfortunately not a lot was happening in Coronation Street tonight.

'Oh, leave her alone,' said Mr Bertha.

That wasn't his name, of course. I suppose he was Mr Turnbull, but I always thought of him as Mr Bertha, especially as he never came out of the house. We were in their hot little lounge and the TV was too loud, at his request. Mr Bertha's theory was that he was ill, so everything had to be very loud – even though he wasn't remotely deaf – and *very* hot. I think that was why Wide Bertha loved the open air so much. This was why she liked to be outside at lunchtime, even in the middle of winter, or up on the cliffs, jacketless on the coldest days, letting the wind blow her hopeless hair into an even more hopeless tangle. (And it was nice and private up on the cliffs when Inflatable

George was in town, so why would she mind a bit of a breeze?) I'd seen her sitting on the river wall in a T-shirt and sandals in January, smoking her head off. In between drags she'd breathe in a huge lungful of frosty sea air, as if compensating for the nicotine. No wonder she liked the outdoors. No wonder she liked Inflatable George and his outside life and their secret cliff walks.

'You need a bit of looking after yourself,' George would say. 'You need somebody looking after you, Bertha.'

Wide Bertha would eat that stuff up. 'Oh, for any's sake,' she'd sigh, 'what a load of nonsense,' but she'd be lapping it up all the same, trying not to smile too obviously. I think she did wonder wistfully how it would be, being flirted with and appreciated and coddled 24–7 instead of once a fortnight on delivery day.

I was barefoot as I cut her hair, because it was the best way to keep cool, and I'd stripped down to my strappy top. I wiggled my toes in the deep pile of the beige carpet. The room was crammed. Besides a television and two leather sofas, there was a tiled fire surround with leaping flames, a sideboard and a glass cabinet stuffed with ornaments, as well as a tall dresser crowded with the decorative plates Bertha liked to collect and which were rotated weekly. Today's favourite, brought proudly into pole position, showed the head of a golden Labrador, grinning manically like something out of *The Omen*. Despite all the clutter the room had a thick atmosphere of homeliness which I liked. It had its very own atmosphere, dense with the smell of burnt dust, but warm and breatheable. It was Mr Bertha who took up most of the room, parked firmly in his chair with his feet up on a stool and under a rug. A rug!

'I tried to phone you today, Ruby,' said Bertha. 'I was going to say, come a bit early. You could have got home a bit sooner.'

'Sorry,' I said. 'I lost my phone.'

'Oh, for goodness' sake, Ruby. How did you lose your phone?'

I shrugged, drew a lock of wet hair straight and trimmed it. Snip snip snip. 'I don't mind, anyway. I haven't got anything else to do.'

'Aye, right. So how did you lose your phone?'

I hesitated and drew another thin lock of hair between my fingers.

OK, Bertha, here's how it was. Foley and I were at the little playpark, the one by the river wall on the furthest side of the Dot Cumming Memorial Park. We were watching Mallory scramble up the rope rocket. That girl was going to go far; she was completely ruthless. She shimmied up those ropes, overtaking toddlers and teenagers alike, standing on anyone her own age till they shrieked. She was a spider on her own web, fast and sure and pitiless. At the top she hung triumphant, gloating at the rest.

I envied her the certainty that she wasn't going to fall. She'd never jump either, not Mallory. If you shouted at

Mallory to Take a Running Jump, she'd tap her temple and stick out her tongue and swear at you. Mallory had the sense and survival instincts of a six-year-old and they may not have been perfectly honed to the ways of the world, but at least she wasn't old enough to be stupid.

Foley and I were sitting on the river wall, backs to the river. Because we were high up, we could see straight through the playpark to the road beyond, so when Jinn came out of the pub in the middle of the day I was looking straight at her.

She was with a bloke I'd never seen before, fat and beery, and she had that fixed but empty look on her face. Any minute now she was going to raise her head and look across the road and see me. And in a sort of perfect storm of buttock-clenching coincidences, Tom Jerrold's car was slewing in to park at the side of the road, right opposite the building site where new flats were going up. He hadn't seen Jinn yet, but I knew he was going to. Jinn's head was coming up towards me and the light of recognition was starting to warm her dead eyes. So I swung round quickly, a hundred and eighty degrees, almost unbalancing, and dangled my legs over the other side of the wall towards the river.

Foley leaned back a little, and tilted his body so that his shoulder knocked into mine. Languidly he said, 'Will I tell you when she's gone?'

I was mortified. 'Yeah.'

After a few moments he said, 'She's away.'

I shivered. 'I'm not ashamed of her or anything.'

'Sure.'

I bowed my head and stared at the brown rushing river. It was maybe four metres below us, but the tide was high and the river was full and the water came right up to the wall, mounting up against the stones with its force and leaving foaming eddies of beige scum. The wall was black up to the high waterline and there was dark green weed growing off it that streamed out horizontally towards the sea. It was hard to remember paddling across to the dunes in summer, when the river was silver and gentle.

Foley pushed himself off the wall, jumped down and walked away, but I didn't turn to see where he was going. Anyway, I knew, because I could hear him shouting up at Mallory.

'Would you let him go, ya wee MINX? Put him DOWN.'

I was too used to Mallory's evil schemes to bother to turn and see which child she was torturing. Instead I narrowed my eyes and peered down at the water through my lashes. It wasn't so far below, but you could pretend it was; you could pretend it was hundreds of metres below. But if I sat on a wall just this way, but the wall was fifty times higher, it wouldn't feel the same. It *would* be the same, strictly speaking, but I'd probably fall because I'd *know* I could fall.

It works the other way, I'm sure. You see pictures of climbers standing casually on the edge of insane corries. Climbers must have brains that know there isn't any difference between five feet and fifteen hundred feet, that you're standing on the same square metreage, that the air isn't any heavier higher up, that the hill can't tilt you forward and knock you off.

On the other hand, some of them do fall off.

Anyway, I don't have a rational brain like that. I could sit on this wall, close to the river – that was easy enough. I probably couldn't sit on the edge of the rickety bridge over there. It was only a few metres higher than this one, but that was too high.

I wondered if Alex Jerrold had a rational brain. I wondered if he'd stood up there on the community centre roof and known he was just as safe as he would have been on a low garden wall. His feet were taking up the exact same space. It wasn't any different than it would have been if the ground was two metres below. I wondered if he'd got confused, and forgotten he was up so high, and thought maybe he'd just step off and go and get a fish supper.

Making excuses again.

I jumped when my phone vibrated in my pocket, and then shrilled its ringtone. My fingers were shaking when I pulled it out and flipped it open. It was from Jinn.

U ignorin me?;–)

I peered at that, a horrible feeling in my stomach. Partly the message itself and the implication that I was ashamed of her, partly that the Jinn I knew would never have bothered with winky smiley faces. Before, she'd have asked me straight out and po-faced, because she wasn't scared of rejection. She was sending me winky smiley faces because she wasn't a hundred per cent certain of me any more.

'Hello,' said Tom Jerrold.

That was when my phone took a flying leap out of my fingers. A life of its own, I always said, and now it was committing suicide. I watched in horror as it arced through the air, and snatched once at it, uselessly. It hit the water with barely a splash and was swallowed. I swore.

'Oh,' said Tom. 'Sorry. Did I give you a fright?'

I swore again, scrambling down off the wall so I could lean over it and peer down, but the phone was gone. If it ever surfaced again it'd be in Norway.

'I'll get you a new one,' he said.

I shook my head. I didn't want him to buy me a new one. I didn't want to be any deeper in debt to Tom Jerrold. I'd buy it myself; I could afford it, just. But it was starting to sink in, what I'd lost: numbers, ringtones, photos. Shit.

'What d'you want?' I snapped. I didn't mean to, but I was furious about that phone.

'I was going to ask you for Jinn's number.'

'Hah!' I glanced at the river again.

'I wanted to talk to her.' He reached into his pocket and brought out a pen, waiting expectantly.

Something, oddly, made me want him not to.

'I'm really sorry.' I licked my lips and lied. 'I don't actually know her number.'

'Oh.' He twitched an eyebrow.

'It was on my phone. Quick-dial. Just pushed a button. Sorry.'

'OK. My fault then.'

'I'm the one that dropped it.'

'Yeah, but – never mind.' He shrugged. I'd thought he had a grown-up face but the way he looked now, he was like a schoolboy again. 'Well. I can get hold of her, I suppose.'

That made me want to snigger, in a very juvenile and schoolgirlish way. I managed not to, but he blushed and turned even younger.

'Sorry,' he said. 'About the phone, I mean.'

I lifted a shoulder. I wondered where, in the weird power play between us, he'd suddenly become the supplicant. And I wondered how long it would last.

'You'll just have to go and look for Jinx,' I said.

'Well?' said Wide Bertha.

I shook myself. 'I lost it,' I said again.

She tutted. 'That's not what I asked. The phone was five minutes ago. You're a hairdresser, Ruby. If you can't be a good talker you'll need to be a good listener.'

'Sorry.'

Bertha's fingers fluttered through her hair. 'Can you make it a bit pink next time?'

I stepped back and examined her head. 'Yeah. Could do.'

'I think it would look nice.'

'Bloody nonsense,' said Mr Bertha over the racket of his TV. '*I* think it would look ridiculous.'

'Aye, but nobody's asking you,' retorted Bertha.

'It'd look good,' I said, partly to annoy Mr Bertha, who was getting on my nerves. 'I'll put in some highlights. Really funky.'

'Uh-huh. That's what I thought.' Her face pinked with pleasure.

'Rubbish,' growled Jabba the Hutt in the corner.

I handed Bertha her own little mirror and she admired herself. She was in her forties but she still had lovely skin. Her pale mousy hair would take colour well. Almost too well. Maybe she'd need something more subtle.

'You don't want lilac,' I thought aloud. 'I could do lilac but it'd be like a blue rinse.'

She nodded happily. 'That's what I thought. Can you do it on Thursday evening?'

'Yeah.'

I caught her smile in the mirror and returned it. Inflatable George delivered on Fridays. As if on cue, the phone beside her buzzed and tinkled.

She lifted it, made a face, showed me the text message. George.

'He does fuss a bit,' she whispered as I leaned down to peer at it.

She didn't seem displeased though. With one shifty glance at Mr Bertha, she tapped out a quick reply with her thumbnail.

'How's Jinn doing?' she asked loudly.

'She's OK,' I lied. 'She was working at the Folk Museum.'

'Aye, two months ago. What's she doing now?'

'She's signing on. She's looking for a job.'

Bertha put down the phone, tilted the mirror higher. Gave me what the books call a gimlet look.

'Nathan Baird?'

I hesitated, picked at a nail. 'Still going out with him. Loves him, unfortunately.'

Bertha snorted. 'Each to his own.'

'She'll get over it,' I said.

'Sooner the better.'

My fingers trembled as I put away my scissors and my combs and my razors. I needed to breathe clean air; I needed to get out of this house. It wasn't cosy any more, it was suffocating. I felt like throwing the hairdryer through that bloody TV screen, just to shut it up.

'I'd like to have her back,' said Bertha.

'She'd like to come back.' I don't know why I said that. How would I know?

'What's she living on?'

I shrugged. 'Benefits.'

'Ruby.' She hesitated. 'Is she really OK? I mean, she's had her problems, Jinn, but she's a good girl. She doesn't deserve her troubles.'

'She's fine.' I hadn't seen her for weeks, so I didn't know how she was, but I wanted to make Bertha feel better. I wouldn't want her feeling guilty, because after all she hadn't had much of a choice. Even Jinn said that once. She said she'd have sacked herself if she was Bertha. 'She's getting herself together.'

'Oh, I'm glad to hear that. Is it Tom?'

My fingers froze. 'What?'

'Tom Jerrold. I've seen her with him. He was a good boy. I was hoping she'd left Nathan for him. He'd be better for her.'

'You've seen them? Together? A lot?'

'Well, a few times. In his car and that. By the marina once.'

I didn't know what to say. I was scared and I didn't know why. 'Yes, it's maybe – it's maybe Tom then. She's getting herself together.' A flash of loyalty came out of nowhere. 'She's getting *both* of them sorted. Her and Nathan.'

Why did I not just stop there?

'She's talked to her GP. She's trying to get Nathan to go to rehab. They have that – there's a clinic up in Glassford. They've got an appointment.'

And that's one more reason I don't overdo the talking. Because when I do I overcompensate, and all that comes out is lies.

Twenty-one

I didn't know where she'd been for the last few weeks, but she couldn't have been far away. Glassford's one of those towns that isn't huge, it's just big enough to lose yourself. Small enough to let you reappear though. Jinn cornered me in the Tesco car park two days later.

I was so glad to see her, despite the way she looked. And I was glad she was stealing from a bigger company these days, and it was a massive relief to know she wasn't going near the mini-mart. I was guiltily glad to know that she was as ashamed as I was. Jinn didn't hang around Breakness so much; she was always up in Glassford. This didn't worry me too much and it saved me from embarrassing moments like that one by the river. Life without Jinn was becoming normal life, easier life. To reassure myself I walked by Dunedin sometimes, but even though it was dark and silent I knew she'd be all right; Jinn always was. Somewhere nearby, Jinn was all right.

Richer pickings in Glassford, I told myself: more clients, a bit more anonymity. I suppose she worked in

Breakness too, but if she met a punter at the pub by the marina, she'd get in his car (because I knew she'd lied about that) and they'd go into the countryside, and then he'd drop her off in Glassford.

Even that thought didn't upset me too much any more. I was getting so used to the notion of what Jinn did – what Jinx did – I was inured to the fear. The thing is, I knew it wasn't for ever. What I'd told Bertha wasn't so much a lie, really. It was by way of foretelling the future. It was a prediction. It was wishful thinking.

In the meantime, I bought her a coffee. Should have gone to Starbucks in Glassford, for the anonymity, or stayed at the Tesco cafe, but we took the bus home – well, to my home – and went to the Mermaid Cafe in Breakness instead. It had always been Jinn's favourite, and Lara's before her.

We didn't say a word to each other until the sullen waitress had delivered the coffee. I'd asked for some toast too, so some warm singed bread had appeared with a tiny plastic tub of Flora. I'd ordered it for Jinn, but she showed no intention of eating it. She prodded it with her thumb. It was squishy. Wrinkling her nose, she wiped her fingertip on the paper tablecloth.

'Have some?' I tried.

'Not hungry.' She smiled, but with an edge of desperation.

The Mermaid Cafe was as quaint, but not as nice, as it sounds. The painted chipboard mermaid outside was grotesque enough to put off a few potential customers even if they hadn't tasted the toast yet. She was more like a sea-witch: ogreish, with glaring eyes and lips that were too red, and she didn't have any eyebrows, and her forehead was the wrong shape. The incompetent artist had covered that up with curls of blindingly yellow hair.

But the cafe itself was popular with locals for cheapness, and with tourists for character. It was crammed full of old trinkets and photos, far too many ever to be dusted. The walls and the ceiling were swagged with old netting and rope, and tucked into that were glass buoys thick with dust, driftwood and old bottles. Every other inch of wall space was covered with monochrome postcards and seashells and bad paintings. The whole place smelt funny. It smelt of all the years trapped in those trinkets and photos and postcards. I think it was the smell of all the sepia people, surly and poker-faced. It was the smell of their surly sepia lives.

Though it was brightly sunny outside, indoors was a puddle of dark. That made it a little harder to see properly, but I could see well enough. Jinn looked terrible. There seemed to be a layer of grime on her, too, like she hadn't been dusted for a long time. So thin, so fragile, she could give you a paper cut. I shivered. Somebody kept dancing over my grave and I wished they'd stop it.

'I'm kind of stuck for money, Ruby.' Jinn smiled into

the dusty air. She smiled at a stiffly-posed thirties tourist by a motionless sea, like she had more in common with dead people than she did with me.

A shaft of sunlight angled in, but it didn't light her hair: all it lit was the floating dust motes. It cast her face into beige shadow.

'Are you really stuck?' I swallowed and hesitated. 'I thought you were OK.'

'Well,' she said.

'You know,' she said.

'Things are a bit complicated just now,' she said. 'We've got something coming off but there's a delay. You see? I just need something to tide me over.'

'Tide you over?' I repeated.

'Till we're sorted. Till we can pay these guys what they're owed. Then we'll be fine.'

'Till *youse* are sorted.' I licked my lips. 'You and Nathan?'

I couldn't leave it there. Oh, if I just had, but I opened my mouth again.

You see? You see what happens? I opened my mouth and said the one word I should never have said, the word I wish more than any I could take back. I parted my lips and detached my tongue from the roof of my mouth and out it came.

'Jinx,' I said.

Her face didn't move, or not much; her determined smile might have twitched a bit. 'You shouldn't call me that, Ruby. Don't. Nobody calls me that. Nobody but Them. OK?'

'OK,' I said.

'It's not my name. Tom doesn't call me that and neither should you.'

'You're still –?'

'I've seen him a few times. I like him. Not like Nathan,' she added belligerently, 'but I like him so I don't –'

Charge him. It hung in the air like a dusty net.

Jinn ran a finger round her cup's chipped rim. Inside it was stained pale brown, in rings, like a tree. She poured new tea in to cover the stains and then she poured for me.

Shall I be Mother?

Oh yes, please, Jinn. Yes, do.

I watched the flow of tea. The pot was a bad pourer. Tea dribbled out of the spout and spotted the paper tablecloth with a spreading brown stain. Every damn thing in here was sepia.

'Jinx is *her* name. Not mine.'

I tapped my teaspoon against my cup, dipped it in the tea, but I didn't take sugar and I didn't take milk: there was nothing to stir. I wanted to say *So get rid of her, Jinn. Leave her behind*. I wanted to say *Get a life* and mean it in the best way. *Get a life without Jinx. Get your old life back*.

But I'd already said enough and there was guilt blocking my throat. I should have said any one of those things but I didn't. Things might have happened differently if I had.

226

But I didn't, and so it's like with Alex: I'll never know. I'll never know what *would* have happened.

After all, I never said anything to Alex. I didn't shout *Stop* or *I didn't mean it* or *Do you want to go to a film after all?* I didn't shout *Get a life, Alex!* and mean it in a good way. All I said, the last thing I said, was *Take a running jump.*

And I hadn't learned my lesson, because I didn't say the right words to Jinn either. All I said to her, all that she heard, was *Jinx*. I didn't say the words that mattered and it's just like Alex: I'll never know what would have happened.

I pulled out my bag and gave her some money, and she crumpled it in her fist, eyes bright and grateful and loving. 'I love you,' she said. 'When we've paid them, I'll stop. I love you.'

I tried to say it, but it got stuck. Instead I said, 'Call me, Jinn? If you need more. If you need me.'

As I stood up and left, I took one look back at her. I couldn't help myself. The shaft of sunlight had migrated across the dusty space and her head was turned a little away as she pocketed the money. The dust motes looked like they were dancing in her hair, and they turned it silver like before, like a Molotov girl, all life and sun and beaches. She felt me looking and turned and smiled, the motes sparkling round her head like stardust. She was very beautiful, that time.

And I try very hard to keep that tarty stardust elf-queen

in my head, smiling like she'd just remembered she loved me. Sometimes I like to bring the memory out and dust it off, and set the silver motes dancing again in my head, because I never saw Jinn alive again.

Winter

Twenty-two

I'm very possessive about my name now. I don't like being called 'Rubes' any more. I've hung on to my name this long and I'm kind of proud of it, the more so since Jinn lost hers. Jinn was two names away from herself by the time she died.

I didn't know for á long time that she was dead. Nobody did. She wasn't around any more, but then she hadn't been around for a while. Wide Bertha said she'd maybe gone to Glasgow or Edinburgh or even London. Maybe Jinn wanted to be somewhere anonymous, she suggested. Bright lights, big city. A place where nobody knows your name, and nobody knows or cares if it's the one you were born with.

I woke up at three o'clock one morning, in my quiet house that seemed to belong exclusively to me now, and had a sick feeling in my stomach. The silence was so heavy against my chest and face I could hardly breathe, and I was afraid to anyway, afraid that if I breathed out someone would hear it. When I had to breathe at last, it sounded loud, like a cry. I'd just remembered something.

Call me, I'd said. *Call me if you need me.*

If she called me, she wouldn't get me. The phone she called would ring underwater, or in Norway, or wherever the hell it had ended up. Some ugly mermaid with red lips and bilious yellow hair was using my phone. I snatched my new one off the bedside table and texted Jinn that minute, not caring if I woke her up. My God, I'd forgotten it for this long; how could I trust myself to remember in the morning?

That was when I started to wonder if I'd done it on purpose: forgotten to give her my new number.

I didn't wake her up. I know that now, because by that time it was already too late. There's another thing I'll never know, and that's if she tried to call me. I'll never know if she did need me. Maybe she tried to call and ask for some more money; for all I know she called me while she ran, or while she fought or hid or whatever it was she did with her last minutes. Maybe she cried because I didn't answer her. But like so much else, I'll never know.

When I went back to sleep, I dreamed I was under the bedclothes again. I saw Jinn's face, haloed in the torch-light like a hollow-eyed angel. She was smiling at me, pricking her finger, pricking mine, swearing me to honour her choice. Overdoing the pricking thing, like Sleeping Beauty going to extremes. Blood getting on the sheets, Jinn giggling, our thumbprints smearing the polycotton as we tried to wipe it off, just making it worse. Jinn taking hold of my hand to try to clean up my bloody thumb. But it was all wrong. My hand got tangled in the duvet cover, and my arm, and I couldn't move. Jinn's hand slipped out of mine and I couldn't find her; she bobbed away from me like a green-and-white striped ball, the sheets and the duvet settling over my face like smothering waves. I struggled to surface, woke, tore myself out of tangled bedclothes and took a breath with a high squeal in my throat.

I'm wondering now if that's when it happened.

It snowed that winter more than it had for years. Every night it snowed more, and in the morning there would be a new thick crust of it. Everybody marvelled at it, except Mr Bertha, who grumbled even though he never went out of doors. It was the kind of snow you think can never end; you can't imagine the world being green again. Like Narnia. The world became silent and beautiful and perfectly clean each night, laundered by cold.

In the morning, the schools being closed, the kids would tear out to sully it the best way they knew how. The play-park and the golf course and the hilly field just outside town were pocked with angels and blistered with snow-men and scored with sledge tracks, the slopes ironed into smooth and superfast chutes like the finest ski piste in Austria. Mallory's preferred spot was the Tesco car park in Glassford, where she would cycle round and round like a suicidal maniac, scaring the motorists, doing stunts off icy lumps of shovelled snow that were blackened with dirt and exhaust fumes, but Foley spat out the taste of the air and put his foot down. While real life and real winter were on hold, we'd take our snow in the fields on the edge of town and the country beyond.

I wasn't too old for it, I discovered, and neither was Foley. Mallory fell out with us both because we monopolised her plastic sledge, which could go like a bobsleigh when you picked the right track. She screamed abuse at us, hurling viciously packed snowballs as we threw ourselves on to our bellies for the umpteenth time and hurtled down. Eventually, when we started to feel sorry for her, we let her have the sledge back. She was in a murderous mood by then, and her gang of small henchmen suffered for it.

Between Foley's ongoing school career and my job there weren't a lot of daylight hours to spare, but there's something about snow: you just make the most of the hours you've got. To avoid the spontaneous combustion of Mallory, or maybe just because we tired of sledges faster than she did, we took the chance to go for walks.

So we'd leave Mallory with the sledgers (she was safe in a crowd; it was everyone else who needed protection) and we'd walk through the woods where sledging was impossible and where it was lonely except for dog walkers, feeling more benevolent than usual towards them, since dog shit is easier to see in the snow and the old stuff was buried. The field up beyond the woods – flat, and therefore a fat lot of use as a sledging arena – was untouched, the sheep who were there earlier having been slaughtered. Foley wanted to run on to the field and spoil the snow, but I wouldn't let him. It was perfectly smooth, perfectly pure, like a linen sheet, except that it had a crust of ice that glittered like crystals in the sun. The tree shadows that lengthened too quickly across it were blue, nearly as blue as the sky. When you pushed your fist into snow piled against the fence, it glowed like aquamarine.

We'd walk as far as the distillery, and then Foley would get guilty and roll his eyes and we'd go back to find that no, Mallory hadn't been abducted, but arrest was a real possibility. I wouldn't let us turn round before the distillery though. It was a tourist attraction as well as a working distillery, which meant the grounds were groomed and landscaped and pretty even in the summer, with wooden benches and flags and beautifully painted signs. In winter it was magical: young trees and ancient stone, and snow. It even had a mill wheel.

The burn that turned the wheel flowed out of a small loch where in summer small boys sailed boats and older ones fished for trout. That was a pretty place too, wood-fenced and idyllic; choppy and windswept on some days and millpond-flat (naturally enough) on others, the reeds at its edges mirrored so perfectly, you could have turned the picture upside down. There was an overflow where a burn ran through a metal grille and then vanished under the road, but it was a quiet trickle in the still freezing air, even though the loch was brimming. In the snow the loch had frozen over, opaque and misty and flat as a curling rink. It would have been stupid to skate, but it was tempting. As the winter days went on with no change, snow settled on the ice in a soft shroud, and no one walked on it.

In the snow even Dunedin was beautiful. I made a detour to pass the house on my way to the Glassford bus stop every morning, pausing to try and make out any signs of life. A forlorn string of Christmas lights hung over the window, but they hadn't been switched on for weeks. I wasn't sure if anyone was there or not, and I didn't dare look through the letterbox to see if my Christmas card lay on the mat unopened. The slate roof was blanketed in snow, and that could have been because of excellent roof insulation or because no one was trying to heat the place. I suspected the latter.

Nathan's friends might still have been in residence but I didn't think Nathan was. I don't think Jinn had been there for a long time either. Perhaps the pair of them had moved on. It should have chilled me that I didn't know, but I could only feel numb about it. I didn't have any feelings, I didn't have any opinions. It was an interlude, this thing with Jinx. It was a warp in the space–time continuum. The portal was jammed. One day the spell of Dunedin would break and the portal would open and Jinn would find her name, and then she'd be back, tumbling into the light, laughing as the credits rolled. *Jinx* was an interlude.

I still think that would have happened. I do believe she'd have found her name and come back through the portal; it's just that she never got the chance.

I should have known that, looking at Dunedin, frozen in the snow. The place was dead and the inhabitants were lost and the portal was closed for ever. I just didn't know it at the time.

Foley and I walked through those woods again a week later, when neither of us was working. It was too pretty to stay away, too pretty to miss the transient snow. A path had been crushed into the snow but it was still hard going, except under the trees, because the flakes couldn't fall so heavily there. Under the thick pincs there was only a crusty skin of snow, and when I looked up, the lumps on the branches were turning translucent in the winter sunlight.

The silence was cracked. There was a sound I didn't recognise at first. It wasn't water really. It wasn't a drip-drip-drip sound, it was a gritty click-click-click, like tiny beads of ice pittering down.

That's when I knew it was thawing. It was the slow reluctant end of winter. Aslan had come back to Narnia, just like in the books, but too soon: we weren't ready for him, we'd all been enjoying the fun and beautiful company of the White Witch, and hoping deep down that he'd never come back.

They found the fifth girl in the distillery pond when the ice melted.

She'd been under the ice, under the snow, trapped against the grille where the burn ran out to the underground culvert. The water was deep at the edge there, and the bank sloped under itself, and the slow flow of the water had caught her like a small thing in amber.

The man from the distillery could tell there was something there, so though he'd come only to brush the cement paths clear of thick frost-dust, he lowered his broom into the water to shift the obstruction. That's when she was dislodged, that's when he saw her hand drift to the surface. He saw it bob there, pale against the peaty water, and when he peered closer, fumbling for his phone with one hand, he saw the rest of her: a white slender ghost lost for ever in the portal.

Twenty-three

Not lost for ever, of course. Not really. They pulled Jinn out and put her in a plastic bag and zipped her up, and then they unwrapped her on the mortuary slab. There they unwrapped her again, right out of her skin, to find what had happened to her.

She hadn't drowned, they said. She was dead before she went into the water. There were marks on her neck. There was a good chance she was unconscious, they said; she didn't have any defensive wounds. But unconscious wasn't good enough, and he'd throttled her, partly with the cord of her gothic necklace and partly with his bare hands.

I didn't get to see the marks on her neck, with the sheet pulled up so high. There was a bruise beside her eye socket, that was all. I tried to look at her and see only Jinx, but it was no use. Lying there pale and waxy, no breath at all, she was back to just Jinn. She was very well-preserved: she'd been in a frozen pond. She looked as if she was smiling a little, but that was only the shape of her mouth; her mouth had always curved upwards that way. Her hair in the white glare of light was pale and lifeless, but if I narrowed my eyes and blinked some of the blur away I could make myself imagine the sheen of stardust again, and the Molotov beach girl.

All my grief was in my head at that point. I'm not being facetious or saying I imagined it – I mean literally. I could only feel it in my head, throbbing behind my eyes and filling my throat and my nasal passages and my sinuses. I couldn't feel it in my stomach and chest; they seemed to be numb. I thought my head might explode messily, and if I'd thought speaking was hard before, I hadn't realised the half of it. I physically couldn't get any words out, not without my skull collapsing in on itself, so all I could do was nod.

A journalist came to the house to see me the next day, to see if I wanted to talk about it. I didn't, but he made me take his number anyway, 'for later'. Then a kirk minister turned up. She put an unasked arm around my shoulder and said that thing on the slab wasn't really Jinn, I mustn't think of it like that, it was only an empty shell.

I wanted to slap her but I couldn't be bothered; I couldn't even be bothered arguing. It wasn't a shell, it was Jinn. Jinn had hair that glittered in sunlight, and hands that fitted snugly round mine, and skin that smelt vaguely like Red Bull mixed with mown grass. Jinn had a tiny X-shaped scar on her chin where she'd fallen off her bike when she was seven. Jinn had warm breath; she could run her thumb up and down your spine to make you go to sleep. Jinn had this physical existence, and it was still there even if it had gone cold, and I'd seriously let her down, because I'd gone and left it lying on a slab.

'Have you heard from Nathan Baird?'

They both looked at me, the young policeman and the policewoman. They wore professional faces, the kind that make you think they get polished and put away in a cupboard at the end of their shift.

'Has Nathan tried to get in touch with you?' he tried again.

What, so I could stab him with a kitchen knife?

I didn't say that – as if! me! – but I must have telegraphed it somehow because he looked down at his notebook and cleared his throat. It was really a formality, this.

'No,' was all I could say.

They exchanged a look. I wondered if they were sleeping together. In their cupboard.

Ever so tactfully and ever so gently, they asked me when Nathan had been away. Could I recall the exact dates? Had Jinn said where he was going?

I looked out of the window while I tried to remember through the thick wet fog of grief in my brain. Jinn's windmills were spinning in the breeze, flashing and glittering, and the wind chimes clinked, too tangled to ring properly. The sun was very bright and there were snowdrops pushing up through the hard earth already. The ugly gargoyle looked somehow more lonely than ever, as if his mask of cross-eyed aggression had begun to slip. Staring at him, I realised it had. The frost had split his head in two diagonally, and the top part had slipped a few millimetres. It kind of suited him, but he looked terribly miserable, the poor little sod. I'd have to try and fix him.

'I'll have to move,' I said suddenly.

Why hadn't that thought struck me before? This was a two-bedroom house, I could hardly expect to be allowed to stay.

Wide Bertha chose that moment to shuffle through from the kitchen, bearing a tray of mugs. 'You will not.' She glared at the police, as if it was somehow up to them.

'I don't think the council are going to be in any hurry,' soothed the woman.

'They better not be,' said Bertha threateningly.

I thought I might want to move out anyway, but I wasn't about to say so and betray Bertha's fierce loyalty. The two cops asked a few more questions about Jinn's 'lifestyle', and her friends, and her clients. They knew about Jinx. They hadn't found her phone, despite picking through every inch of mud at the bottom of the distillery pond, but I think that was no more than irritating to them. It seemed pretty clear-cut. But they asked questions anyway.

They probably thought my monosyllabic answers were me being truculent rather than me being normal, but I couldn't think. The only 'client' I knew was Tom, and he wasn't even a paying customer.

'Is there anything else you can think of, Ruby? Anything you can tell us?'

I licked my lips. I didn't suppose it was relevant, but I didn't want to leave anything out. 'I saw them fighting,' I said.

Both of them raised their eyebrows expectantly, deliberately not looking at one another.

'Who, Ruby?'

'Jinn and – him. Nathan.'

When I thought about it, I'd never seen them fighting. Why hadn't the strangeness of it hit me before? But there they'd been, in broad daylight, having a fight on the glass-speckled track behind the playpark. I was well back from them, and I'd come to a halt in shock, and they were too busy shouting at each other to notice me.

Or rather, Nathan was shouting. That's why I heard what he said. Jinn's hands were fisted at her sides and she'd just snapped at him, and he must have lost it then.

'You're the one that says we need the money! You are!'

I'd swallowed, backed off, gone the other way. I remember thinking that if he was angry about the prostitution thing, it wasn't very grateful of him. But no way did I want to get involved.

When she'd scribbled down the story, the woman officer put her notebook away. 'If Nathan tries to contact you, call us straight away.'

Bertha sat down and put an arm round my shoulder. I wished she wouldn't; it felt smothering, like a gigantic tentacle, but I didn't have the heart to shove her off. When the police stood up to go, I took the chance to stand up too and dislodge her. That made me feel guilty all over again.

'We'll be in touch again,' said the woman. 'We'll keep you informed of developments.'

Maybe I was overly pessimistic, but I doubted there would be developments. Not unless Nathan showed up, and even then he'd have to confess. Jinn had been in that water for too long. She was preserved but his DNA wasn't. She'd been trapped in cold amber but this wasn't Jurassic Park and they couldn't rebuild her.

Bertha stayed around to make sure I was OK. I didn't really want her to, but it was sweet of her. She seemed terribly unsure about what to say. God, was I this aggravating when I couldn't talk? I got so irritated with her, I found myself saying things just to provoke a conversation. I could see where Foley was coming from now.

'They think he's killed other girls, don't they?' I said.

Bertha nodded and put too much sugar in my tea. 'Sounds like it.'

'All those girls in water. I remember them.'

She patted my hand. 'At least they know now. They know who they're looking for.'

'Yes.'

Except for that tango, and that look, the I-love-you look. When I remembered, I still couldn't quite believe it.

But maybe the tango and the look had a lot to do with it.

I remembered Nathan's teaspoon clinking against a delicate china cup. *You know what she does for you*, I'd snapped at him.

And to her I'd said, *Doesn't he mind?*

God, I was a stupid mouthy bitch.

'They'll find him soon,' said Bertha.

'I guess.'

'He's panicked, he's run away, but they'll find him. You don't need to be scared. He won't come back till they drag him back.'

It hadn't occurred to me to be scared till she said that. Cheers, Bertha.

We wandered out to the garden, clutching cups of tea. It was cold, in that still, windless way that bites your bones. I felt about sixty years old. Here's dear old Ruby, inspecting her dahlias. Her sister died, you know. Jinn never got old like Ruby did. Age did not wither Jinn. Even if she'd have liked the chance to wither, she didn't get it.

Anyway, I didn't have dahlias, only dead Livingstone daisies and leafless stalks. Would I still be living here in a few months, so I could colour the garden in again, in Jinn's bright crayon colours? Who knew? I hoped summer would be a long time coming.

Somebody coughed. I glanced up, never in my life so glad of an interruption. Inflatable George pushed open the gate, all diffident, not wanting to intrude. It's awful when people do that; you feel you have to be kind and encourage them.

I didn't though. I just smiled, which visibly threw him. But in his presence Bertha grew confident again, as if she'd needed the validation. She almost swelled with it, with his adoring attention. It didn't annoy me, even though she hugged me. I was happy for her.

I poured the dregs of my tea on to the stone gargoyle, like a benediction. (I swear he winced and grimaced and shook it off.) 'You can go, it's OK.'

'Oh, Ruby. Are you sure?'

'Are you sure, love?' echoed George. He frowned and raised his eyebrows at the same time, giving him an odd and rather startled expression.

'Sure. Honest. I'm fine. Right?' I gave the last word a touch of belligerence, because otherwise I'd be stuck with Bertha for a fortnight.

'You'll be fine on your own?'

'I'll be fine. Fine.'

'Well,' she said, shaking her head, 'if you're fine.'

'If you're fine.' There was that echo again from George. I made myself not roll my eyes.

'I'm on the other end of the phone, Ruby. Just call if you need me.'

'Yes. Course. Sure.'

She took a breath to do a bit more protesting, but Inflatable George grasped her elbow. 'I'll get you home,

Bertha.' He turned his sad, Clooney-in-pastry eyes on her. 'You've had a shock too.'

'Oh. Yes. Well, thanks, George.'

Despite the distractions I liked the way Bertha's eyes lit up, and I had to turn away to hide my smile. It wouldn't do to be seen smiling so soon and I felt bad about doing it at all.

Twenty-four

I'd thought I wanted to be alone. I was surprised how the emptiness of thc house weighed on me, and by the loudness of the silence. I couldn't sit down, not till I'd pulled an armchair over to a corner so that my back was to the wall and I could see the whole room. It wasn't fear; it felt more like anticipation, like I was waiting for Jinn to come in the front door. So the hesitant rap, when it came, was not as terrifying as you might imagine.

I knew it couldn't be her. I knew that in the front part of my brain, so I was fine about opening the door. When I saw Foley standing there like an awkward bollard, I was shocked by relief and even more by inappropriate happiness. I threw myself into his arms.

'Bloody cold out there,' he said.

He wasn't much of a cook – he could make dog food, of course, which now I think about it probably means he could handle a three-course roast dinner – but he dumped his jacket and a DVD on the sofa and kissed me again and went off to microwave some popcorn. His lips were cold from the outside air. I licked my own.

'I was going to get a takeaway,' he called from the kitchen as I surreptitiously sniffed his jacket lining, 'but I didn't think you'd be hungry.'

Which was precisely right. I liked a boy with good sense in place of sympathy. I picked up the DVD and examined the back cover. 'Did you get shot of her?'

No names, no pack drill.

'Uh-huh. Mum's *actually* picking her up. After Brownies.'

'Brow –' I began, then shrugged and shut my jaw. I turned the DVD over again. The plastic case was mauled and punctured by teethmarks. Sometimes I was surprised that Foley and Mallory weren't more chewed themselves. 'I haven't seen this.'

'It's a laugh.'

There was silence for long seconds. Smugly I let it hang there, till his sheepish head appeared round the sitting-room door.

'Sorry,' he said.

I smiled at him. The things people think will upset you! My sister just got strangled and left in a pond, so Foley's bad movie choices weren't going to make things critically worse. Anyway, I needed something stupid and meaningless. I certainly didn't need *Saw III*, I needed this lame, straight-to-DVD flick that had got such terrible reviews last summer.

I heard the *pof-pof-pif-pof* of popcorn hitting the sides of the bag, and thirty seconds later Foley was back with me.

I was using his jacket as a cushion for my head, but he didn't move it, just smiled knowingly and shoved a cold vodka-and-Molotov at me. When he'd started the DVD and flicked through the trailers, he relaxed with a noisy sigh and put an arm round me. At that point I could detach my head from his jacket lining and snuggle it into his armpit. Boys' armpits can be a thing of nightmares or they can be pheromone heaven. I was more than happy with Foley's place on the spectrum.

The movie was even worse than its reputation. Its only redeeming feature was the constant farcical stunts, which were so noisy and extreme, with such over-the-top acting, there was no brain space left to brood. I felt as if my cerebellum had switched to standby, and that was strangely soothing. I couldn't think, could barely picture Jinn. I fell asleep, and when I woke up there was no plot worth Foley reiterating for me.

'You're not enjoying this,' he said.

'Yes, I am.'

'You were snoring.'

'Oh.'

His fingers ran across my scalp. 'Nice snoring.'

'Oh. Fine.'

'As snoring goes.'

I stretched out a hand to the Pyrex bowl but all that was left were tiny bullets of unpopped corn.

'I'll make some more,' said Foley apologetically. Pausing the film, he started to stretch and rise.

My hand shot out to hold him in place. It landed on his inner thigh. At his squeak, I uncurled my fingers reluctantly and loosened my hold on his flesh. He replaced my hand where it was and held it there with his own.

The character on screen, frozen in mid-air at an hour and twenty minutes and sixteen seconds, goggled at us.

'I'm not sure we –'

Just in case *should do this* was following when he got his breath back, I moved my hand. That shut him up. I blinked at the on-screen guy. Foley clicked the remote with his free hand, and the irritating gurner vanished.

I glanced up through narrowed eyelids. I expected to see the relevant pages of *Cosmo* and *Bliss* scrolling down Foley's hungry eyes, but it wasn't like that at all. I could hardly read his expression, or maybe it was so intense I didn't want to. A lurch of lust hit me. Suddenly I wanted him ferociously, desperately, like I'd die if I couldn't have him now. *Now*.

Reaching up, I pulled him down and kissed him. He wriggled back, mumbled something like 'Ruby', and 'Ruby' again. And 'Ow', because the phone in my pocket had jabbed him in the groin.

I jiggled it out and let it fall between the sofa cushions. Foley seized my hands and said, 'Can we move?'

So this is the part where you're meant to be swept into his arms and borne regally to the four-poster. Instead Foley and I stumbled up, still attached at the lips and the hips. Mobility was difficult but detachment didn't seem a possibility. I tugged his T-shirt over his head in a move that must have nearly dislocated his neck, as we did our clumsy crabwise dance towards the bedroom. He was having no end of trouble with my bra clasp, so I reached back with one hand and undid it for him. He banged into the doorway, almost fell, then both of us collapsed on to the bed.

With my face between his hands he gasped, 'Sure?'

'Nah,' I gasped back. 'Changed my mind. Let's go back to the movie.' I tugged at his belt. 'Got a condom?'

'Uh-huh-uhhh.'

'Good-oh,' I said, and wrigged our tangled bodies under the duvet, where we could strip off one another's remaining clothes, away from the ghostly watching eyes.

Twenty-five

Foley wasn't quite looking at me any more. He was looking at my right shoulder, and stroking it over and over again with one finger. I curled my toes into his, and they tightened round mine. I took a strand of his hair and pushed it behind his ear, and it fell forward again. Which gave me an excuse to touch his ear again. He gave a tiny shiver.

'I feel a bit bad leaving you alone,' he said.

A *bit* bad? That wasn't bad enough, not by a long way.

'Cold outside,' I said.

'I know, but I've got to go.'

'It's OK.'

'On your own? Sure?'

Why did people feel the need to rub that in? The truth was that I was being haunted by Jinn, but that would be fine if people didn't go on and on about not being scared. It wasn't like I was afraid of Jinn. That would just be stupid.

'It's just, I've got to take Mallory to school in the morning.'

'Yeah, that's fine.'

'Mum and Dad, they're going to a show. Early, like. Mallory won't even be up when they leave. I've got to be there.'

'Do shut up,' I said. 'I'm fine.'

He disengaged from me and the duvet, rolled off the bed, hunted for his clothes. My toes flexed and curled, empty and cool. I'd been alone for ages in this house. This wasn't any different, it wasn't. Jinn hadn't been dead before, that was all. I wriggled under the duvet and somehow found my top and pants and squirmed into them. Nothing to do with modesty. I felt less vulnerable, that was all.

'Are you really OK?'

I pulled the duvet off my face and opened my eyes. He stood there, awkward again.

Was I? Yes, I was OK. The dislocated grief had seeped down to my chest and stomach, but it was a diffuse pain, nothing I could cut open and cry over.

Sighing, I clambered out of bed and kissed Foley brusquely. That changed my mind. Reeling him back in, I kissed him slowly.

'I've really got to go.' He sounded as if he was in an agony of guilt. Good-oh.

'Piss off out of here.' I shoved him gently doorwards. 'Bye.'

Opening the door let in a wall of cold night. Foley hesitated, turning to watch me while I leaned on the door to heave it shut. I smiled at his remorseful face the whole time. It wasn't me leaving, it was him, and may he suffer for it, I thought cheerfully.

When the door finally slammed shut, I was shocked once more by emptiness and silence. The ache in my body had coalesced, in an instant, and at the same time it had filled every bit of me. My skin felt electric and I couldn't shut my eyes. I felt as if I should cry, as if I very much wanted to cry, but it was still impossible. Something inside me clawed to get out but there was nothing I could do to release it; it would just have to dig. And despite that I was inside out, raw and exposed to the night. Cry? Sleep? You're joking.

The house was a vacuum. Of course Jinn wasn't here: there was no spirit in it at all, barely even my own. That was an even scarier thought, as if I might evaporate without her ghost to hold me here, so I went in search of her.

I hadn't disturbed her room at all since she died. I'd disturbed it plenty before then, despite my promise, borrowing her stuff and occasionally stuffing mine into her unoccupied space. But I'd left it pretty much as it was, seeing as she'd be coming back and all.

Now I felt the need to open her wardrobe doors and plunge my hands into her clothes, to bury my face in her old gardening shirt, which had sparkly bits – what shirt of Jinn's didn't? She'd been gone a long time and gone from that shirt longest of all, but it still smelt of her: of Jinn and earth and weeds and Miracle-Gro. I pulled open her drawers, rummaged in lipsticks and combs and broken hairclips, half-empty bottles of yellowed perfume the colour of pee, and twists of sweet wrappers around leftover Love Hearts or Chewits. There were some bits of underwear, too: scrumpled tights, sports socks, a few pairs of pants. I felt like a grave robber.

Blushing, I slammed the drawer shut, then rubbed at my fingerprints on the melamine as if the police were going to be checking it later. Talk about a guilty conscience.

I couldn't quite bring myself to leave her room; my skin felt less raw in here. Stuff on the surface was fair game, wasn't it? Her jewellery box, her old hairbrush with gleaming strands still in it. The shoebox on the windowsill that she'd covered in an old cut-up shirt. How did she ever have time to do that stuff? I recognised the fabric: a satiny red shirt of Lara's. I'd never looked in the box before but now the curiosity was intolerable.

I picked it up, sat down on Jinn's bed cross-legged, the box in my lap. On one side, the window side, the red satin had faded to pink in the sunlight. Easing off the ribboned and sequinned lid, I half expected the plagues and pestilences of all mankind. But they were loose already and running free, and Hope had left with them.

Bloody hell, I was hallucinating again.

I reminded myself there was no life to intrude on, it was dead and gone. All the same, my fingers trembled as I touched the things in the box.

Shells and pebbles. I swear I could remember her picking them up, and I thought I remembered that they'd meant as much to me at the time as they had to Jinn. Now I didn't recognise their shapes or mottled patterns; nothing sparked a flare of nostalgia. The traces of sand that stuck to them were bone dry, and they didn't smell of the sea any more.

I picked them out one by one, set them out on the bed beside me in a neat row, then dug further down into the box. More scraps of fabric. Bits cut off a scarf of Lara's. An old hair tie I used to wear, when my hair was mousy and long and I wore it in bunches. I rubbed my itchy nose with my fist. There was a fold of silver-blue ribbon, river-coloured, neatly wrapped, but inside it was something hard: another beach stone maybe. When I unwound it, the pebble of amber fell into my hand, and the thick silver chain trickled through my fingers.

Oh.

I remembered Jinn coming home that day. The awkward silence as she rummaged in her room, the offer of tea refused. *I'm just going to pick up a few things. Have you been messing with my stuff, Ruby? Good. So don't.*

She left it here that day, because she was less likely to sell it if she couldn't lay her hands on it. I rubbed the amber with my thumb, feeling the warm texture. She hadn't sold it. She'd left it here. In my unknowing care. Shutting the door of her room with a warning glare at me.

Don't mess with my stuff.

I stared down at the amber in my lap. I wondered if it would have been harder to strangle her with this chain, if she'd have had more of a chance had she not chosen that leather thong.

Probably not.

The last thing in the corner of the box was a square of folded tissue. I nearly didn't look inside, thinking it was only there to cushion the amber, but when I unfolded it I drew out a thin cheap chain, carefully wound in a circle so it wouldn't get knotted. On the end of it dangled a tiny cat, winking at me with its one ruby-red eye.

Nestling it in my palm, I touched it with a fingertip. I couldn't breathe. Guilt and remorse washed over me like a big wave. Marley had returned it, and Jinn hadn't told me because she was angry about how I behaved. Or maybe Jinn had asked for it back. Maybe she'd been waiting for the right moment to give it back to me, waiting for things to be all right between us, or waiting till she wasn't so mad at me. Things hadn't been right enough that day. Blinking, I let the chain trickle off my palm and fall with a tinny click on to the shells and pebbles.

I thought of the old lady waiting in her locked tower for my return visit, gazing out of the window over Glassford. Sighing, deciding I wasn't coming back, hauling herself on to her Zimmer to make another cup of tea. Violently I shoved the image away.

I put the amber pebble back in the bottom of the box, coiling its chain round and round it. The mosquito no longer looked unhappy. It was just fixed. Just dead. I laid the blue ribbon over it and piled on the other rubbish, and finally I put the little cat pendant on top. Changing my mind, I hooked it round my finger and lifted it out again.

The clasp was a bitch, cheap and awkward and stiff, but I finally closed it at the back of my neck. The Cyclops cat hung with Foley's silver cat, a little lower because the cheap chain was just a bit longer. They kind of matched.

I shut the door on Jinn's room and the box, and began to pace. I walked from room to room of the little house, staring out of each window in turn. I went back to the bed I'd shared with Foley, but I couldn't sleep. My blood was still electric. I got up again, paced the house again. I tried lying on the sofa, staring at the television's standby light, at the DVD timer that still read 01:20:16.

And then I must have slept. Not well. I kept half-waking, seeing that number and the little red standby light. I heard cars go by outside, distant shouting revellers coming from the pub. I heard knocking, urgent and getting sharper, and I thought, *Foley*. And it was for that reason, drugged on half-sleep and confusion and remorse and longing, that I rolled off the sofa, blundered to the door and opened it.

I think Nathan Baird was as shocked as I was. That was how I got my chance. Against the frosty wall of night, and in the half-glow of next door's security light, I saw the haggard bones of a face. Pale skin, caramel eyes set in shadow. I smelt sweat, and alcohol, and crack and, unexpectedly, fear.

I didn't scream. I tried to slam the door that wouldn't slam. His foot was in the gap, his fingers holding the edge of the door, and he was shouting something. I leaned and heaved, and he must have been weakened by his lifestyle because I was winning, and his fight was oddly pathetic. I shoved, I stamped on his foot, I head-butted his fingers and cracked my own temple on the edge of the door. He yelped, protested. This time I bit his fingers, and he snatched them back, and I stamped on his foot again, hard as I could, till it shot back and at last, at last, the door slammed shut and the lock clicked.

I shot the bolt.

I stepped back.

His fist battered the door again. 'Ruby!'

One more step back.

'*Ruby!*'

'What?' Why was I talking to him?

'Please, Ruby. Please. Open the door.'

'No.'

'Ruby!'

I pressed my lips together to stop my heart escaping. My throat being blocked, it tried to hammer through my ribcage.

His breathing was rapid and desperate and far too loud. Or maybe that was mine.

'Ruby. I just want to get something. Please.'

I didn't answer.

'Something of hers. That – that necklace, remember? I want it back. Please.'

'Why?'

'Because it was hers and I want it, Ruby. I really want it.'

To sell it? To keep for a souvenir? 'Go away.'

'Ruby, let me in.'

Little pig, little pig. 'No.'

The door shuddered under his fist. I couldn't take my eyes off it. I wanted to turn my back on it but then his fist might come through. Like in *The Shining*.

The thudding stopped at last. Silence, except for my breathing. And his. I slumped down with my back against the wall, but I couldn't take my eyes off that door.

'Ruby, I'm sorry. I just –'

'No.'

'Please open the door. Please.'

'No.'

'I didn't mean to scare you. I just want the – I just miss her. Ruby.'

'Go away.'

'I didn't mean to scare you.'

Too frigging late, mate. What was I doing? Why was I just sitting here? My phone. My phone. I was sitting here in my underpants and a T-shirt and I didn't have my phone.

I glanced at the living room but just that instant of

looking away from the door struck me rigid with terror. My phone was stuck between the sofa cushions.

I could get up. I could run and get it in a matter of seconds.

I wasn't getting up.

It wouldn't kill me. He wouldn't get through the door in the time it took to fetch my phone.

It might kill me.

I could take my eyes off that door for five *seconds*, goddamit.

No. Couldn't.

I pressed my body harder against the wall, wanting to weep at my own cowardice. I couldn't turn my back on the door. What if the phone had got lost? Fallen right down the back? What if I had to pull all the cushions off the sofa? How long would that take?

'Ruby, I need a place to stay. Please.'

Oh, as *if*.

'It's cold. Just one night. I'll pick up her necklace and I'll go in the morning. Please. I'm sorry, Ruby. I'm sorry about everything. I'm sorry I didn't look after her. I loved her and you know it. Please, Ruby. I'm sorry but let me in.'

He had to be kidding. Right?

'Ruby! Ruby!' His cries were turning to angry sobs.

I didn't want his voice to get quieter. I wanted the Grumpy Old Bugger next door to hear him, to come and see what all the fuss was about. Call the council. Call the cops.

No chance. A huge shudder went through my guts.

Please, I thought. Please make it morning. My skin, my heart, my guts were so cold.

I looked at my watch. Three o'clock? It wouldn't be morning for five hours. G.O.B. might be up in four. Nathan could be through the door. I could be dead in four hours.

'Ruby, it's so cold out here. Please. I just need a place.'

I put my hands over my ears.

'Ruby? I'm cold.'

Her too.

His voice was a lot quieter now. He must have been sitting down, curled up, pressed right against the door hinge, because I could feel his voice almost in my ear.

'Ruby. Why won't you let me in?'

I'll huff and I'll puff.

'Ruby. It's cold. I'm so cold.'

Very, very tentatively, I laid my head against the door. Our skulls must have been almost touching. If he banged on the door again I might die of fright, but he didn't. He was whimpering. I stared and stared at the painted plywood, wishing I could see through it, glad I couldn't.

'I'm sorry, Ruby.'

I angled my head. His voice was a pitiful mumble.

'I'm so sorry. I'm sorry I didn't look after her. Just let me in. I haven't got anywhere else to go. I'm so cold. Please.'

'No,' I said, quite softly this time. My lips were almost at his ear, after all. And I decided I wasn't going to speak to him again.

'Cold, Ruby.'

'Please, Ruby.'

'Let me in. Ruby?'

The demands were growing less frequent, but I still heard them. I heard them like in a dream, and maybe they were, because exhaustion was overwhelming me now, stifling even the fear. I drifted in and out of sleep, there in the hallway, pressed to the door, close enough for Nathan to murder me.

Except for the door.

'Oh, Ruby. Open the door, Ruby.'

I think that was the last one. I didn't hear any more, unless I heard them in my sleep. When I next woke I was curled on the floor, the crown of my head pressed against the door, and I was chilled to the bone.

Violent shivers racked me straight away. I forgot about Nathan long enough to crawl through to my bedroom and drag on jeans and a thin jumper and a thick jumper, and woolly socks. Even when I'd done that and let myself remember him, I wasn't afraid because I knew he must be gone. The door hadn't been opened. And filtering through the thin curtains was a gauzy winter light. Death didn't stalk in the daylight. He was gone.

Just as I thought it, I heard the storage heating click on. I curled into my bed, hugging my knees under the duvet, waiting for the house to warm up fast as it always did. Eventually I stopped shivering, and after an eternity, I was hot enough to throw off the duvet and sit up.

I fetched my phone. It was half-sticking out of the space between the seat cushions; last night I could have snatched it up and called the police in a few seconds. Idiot.

Anyway. It was fine. Nothing had happened. I was fine.

I turned the phone in my hands. I should call the police now anyway. Nathan Baird had come back. He'd reappeared and now they would find him quickly.

I stared at the door. After last night it looked as menacing as a tombstone.

My hand trembled as I reached out, gently unsliding the bolt. Just as carefully, I turned the Yale lock, reached for the handle and turned that too. I wasn't breathing as I pulled it silently open.

Nothing. Not even a dent on the frayed rope matting, not even a smell of sweat and crack. Maybe I'd dreamed him. The air on my lips and nostrils was bitterly cold but I drew in a huge breath and stepped outside. Through my socks, the doorstep and the paving slabs chilled the soles of my feet, but I went on taking steps, one foot in front of the other. My phone was in my freezing fingers but I'd almost forgotten it. I reached the corner of the house, where the stone gargoyle gazed reproachfully up at me. I almost raised a finger to my lips. One hand on the grey roughcast wall, I stepped round.

Nothing to see, at first. Nothing but a pile of tyres and an old blanket. Not weighted down with bricks any more, it was wrapped tight round something. Wondering why I wasn't afraid, I stepped close, touched the blanket. It was stiff with frost as heavy as snow, and whitest and iciest where I lifted a corner of it. Nathan looked back at me, eyes half-closed, lips blue. His lank hair was stardusty with ice.

I folded back the cardboard-crisp blanket, tucked it round his neck and throat as best I could. Then I sat down on the plastic bench and watched him.

Was I expecting him to move? Like a bad horror movie? He looked asleep, all tucked up in his blanket, except that his breath didn't cloud the cold air, and his ribs didn't rise and fall, and his skin was so very waxy, so very blue. And he didn't blink those half-closed eyes, and those amber pupils went on gazing into the middle distance.

Still, I didn't want to turn my back on him. It was like last night, but a little bit different. As I hesitated, and shivered, I thought about what people say: that it's not so bad, freezing. That once the cold bites deep enough, you only feel warm. You only want to sleep.

I thought about other things too. I thought of flies preserved in amber, in blue ribbon, in a shoebox, in a safe house.

I thought about dogs that didn't bark. I couldn't remember why, for a moment, the famous dog was silent; and then of course it came to me, the whole story, and I remembered why the dog didn't bark in the night.

I flipped my phone open and scrolled down the contact list, frowning and biting the corner of my lip. I let my forefinger hover for a moment.

And then I called Foley, to let him know I was fine, that it was OK and I wasn't scared, and that Nathan Baird lay dead in my garden.

Twenty-six

'I don't know what you're on about,' said Foley. 'It was him that killed her.'

'No,' I said. 'He couldn't have killed that second girl. He was in Manchester.'

'Doesn't mean he didn't – doesn't mean he didn't kill Jinn,' he said softly, as if to a hyper-sensitive idiot.

I licked my lips. I cleared my throat. 'He didn't. I know he didn't.'

'How?'

'I just do. And anyway.' I had to swallow and frown, because I still didn't quite believe it myself. 'They arrested Tom Jerrold.'

'You're kidding!'

I gave him a Ruby look.

He blushed. 'Sorry.'

'You'll see on the news tonight. They found her DNA all over his car. Hairs and that.'

We walked on. I stared at the ground, trying hard not to think.

'Ruby . . .'

'You know those other girls? They were killed when Tom was living down south. He was in all the right places. And Jinn – I saw Jinn in his car. He acted so odd. He was obsessed with Jinn, and he was always so jealous of Nathan. It all makes sense.' My brain was dizzy with the amount of sense it made. I felt high, and angry, and righteous, and wildly sad. But mostly high.

'I thought you said Tom was cool about Nathan.'

'He pretended to be cool. That's different. Probably worse.'

Foley fell silent again, and he didn't say any more for a while. We walked as far along the bay as we could, and then some. My heart was racing and my breath came fast and shallow, and not because of the walk. The sea was a shining sheet of metal, but alive and moving. We walked to the end of the tarmac track and struck out into the wilderness of seagrass and sand by the golf course, where there were still tracks of people who walked their dogs through the roughest of rough. I wore jeans but I could feel the prick of salty stalks through the denim, and my trainers felt gritty from sinking in dry sand. I had to concentrate, and I was glad.

Also, round this headland Breakness was out of sight, and that was an advantage too.

Foley didn't hold my hand, didn't need to. When the lacework of paths started climbing the cliffs the way was narrower, more of a scramble, though we didn't want to climb right up to the car-park field at the top. We wanted the beach, and cold silence, and being alone.

We didn't speak as we negotiated the path, hugging the jutting lumps of headland and clambering across the rocks that spilled towards the sea. We scrambled down at last on to a flat and pebbled shoreline, hidden and private. There were dry flat rocks to sit on, even though they were rimed with ice and the seagrass at our backs was frosted. That's how cold it was: ice and frost on the sea edge, holding salt spray and the Gulf stream in contempt.

Poor Nathan.

Foley was reading my thoughts. 'What made you realise it wasn't him?'

I opened my mouth, then chewed on a fingernail instead of talking. I released the fingernail, seized my knuckle in my teeth, chewed hard on that. It was going to take a bit of explaining and I had to take a few deep breaths.

'He never once said he didn't kill her. All that night. He sat outside my door and tried everything to get me to let him in. But he never once said he didn't kill her.'

'So?'

'It never even occurred to him. It wouldn't cross his mind. He didn't have anything to protest about. See? He ran away because he'd lost her. Not because he was guilty. He didn't once think *anyone* could think it was him.'

Foley didn't look convinced.

'Doesn't matter what you think. Or me, even. It was Tom.'

I locked my arms round my knees, barely able to contain my raging elation. Such a weird, disorienting feeling. I was stunned by Tom's arrest and his guilt, and yet I wasn't. He'd come back and hung round Breakness and made me feel even worse than I did before, and I realised that for quite a long time I'd wanted to hate him. Now I could, and with a ferocious justice. In some barmy way, everything had come right.

Foley wrung his gloved hands, slapped them together as if he was trying to get warm. Coward. His cheeks were pink with the effort of the walk. He just didn't want to talk about this any more.

Obviously, that was fine with me.

Twenty-Seven

The Fu Ling sign had been vandalised again. That was the first thing I noticed as I came out of the Co-op with my newspaper and a bag of crisps. A metal paint-spattered stepladder was in my way and Mr Fu Ling was at the top of it with a bucket and a brush. Seeing me, he gave me a smile and a silent nod.

I paused for a second to smile back. And then I started to walk past his doorway, but I had to stop because someone was coming out.

Tom Jerrold let the door swing shut on Mrs Fu Ling's screech of farewell. He was carrying his takeaway in a paper bag, which smelt familiarly of Szechuan chicken and egg fried rice. It was such a regular smell, and such a regular sight, I didn't even react for a while. 'A while' felt like an hour, but really it was only a few seconds.

I stopped. I didn't have any option because my legs wouldn't move.

Staring at Tom Jerrold, I felt blood rise in my face as he watched me. He'd stopped too, of course. But after a moment he simply walked on, shifting his takeaway into the other hand and tucking his wallet into the back pocket of his jeans. He didn't nod or smile. He cut me dead.

He cut me dead.

Mr Fu Ling, unaware of the operatic drama unfolding beneath his feet, went on scrubbing at his sign. After a while of listening to the rasp of his brush and the tune-free whistle hissing between his teeth, my limbs jerked back into motion and I walked on as if I'd never stopped. Like a real-life CCTV image, like I'd just been on pause. Like I was a ghost.

You never see CCTV images unless somebody's dead. I've noticed that. If your CCTV image is played you're already a ghost, jumping forward in time in jerky incre-ments, forever on repeat on the ten o'clock news. It's not the privacy thing that bothers me with those cameras, it's the way they foretell your violent death. They're record-ing you in case you're never seen again. It's those cameras I can feel walking over my grave; little Terminator machines. It's that shutter I can hear: Click. Click. Click. And you're gone.

The police had let him go.

How had he got away with it?

The cameras lost me at the corner of the road and I felt as if I was dead. I don't remember unlocking the house and going in, but I do recall locking the door behind me and crawling fully clothed under the duvet, and wanting to cry, and not being able to.

I didn't sleep much. I didn't answer my phone any of the

times it rang. I wanted desperately to talk to Foley, but every time I looked at his number, shining in the darkness under the quilt, I remembered I didn't know what to say to him. He'd say, see, he was right; and I couldn't explain why he was wrong, and why it was so much worse now. In the end I turned the phone off, hugged it against my neck, and curled tighter under the duvet.

I probably saw daylight later than I should have, but I'm sure I was awake. At last, even in the hot darkness, it got through to me that the outside world was lightening, and I peeked out then pushed the duvet off my body, which was wet with sweat and fuzzy from insomnia.

Dawn was insipid and gloomy, but I was glad to see it. I crawled out of my cave, fumbled Jinn's iPod into the dock in the kitchen and turned the volume up to full blast. The bassline of *Good Vibrations* jumped in my breastbone. Sod the G.O.B., I needed noise, full and enveloping and defensive.

I switched on the kettle, but the hissing growl of it unnerved me and I flicked it off halfway to the boil. As soon as I did that, sod's law dictated that *Good Vibrations* hit its quiet bridge, and someone rapped hard on the door. I jumped about a foot.

The Beach Boys chimed in once more with the chorus, and I answered the familiar knock, practically falling into Foley's astonished arms.

'Ur,' he said. His arms tightened round me and I felt his ribcage swell. 'What's up?'

For long moments I couldn't answer him; then I gulped air like a baby gearing up.

'I HATE *being on my own*!' I howled.

'Oh,' he said. 'Yeah. Course.' And his arms squeezed my ribs.

Suddenly I remembered why I liked him. It was the psychic thing. He knew what I needed before I did.

'Let's get out of here,' he said.

I wasn't feeling too fit after my sleepless night and a half-drunk mug of tepid coffee, so as we climbed the cliff path beyond the headland he simply had to hold my hand and pull me up after him. I focused on the roughness of the track, the stones that jutted and the spiky stealthy branches that grew at ankle height. I had to try hard not to trip and fall off the cliff. It was something to think about, and a reason to grip Foley's hand hard, indulging my inner needy-girlie.

It had been so very cold the night Nathan died, and that was only a few days ago. Now spring sun glittered off the water and there were already clusters of daffodils and primroses clinging to the slope and white fulmars like thin kites on the breeze. I wished I was more in the mood. As we climbed higher we could see further into the sea where it lay in rocky lagoons, we could make out every stone and every strand of green weed. The water was that clear, that calm, and out towards the horizon and the far cliffs of the firth it was as silky and smooth as watercolour.

We halted near the top car park to get our breath. At this distance, the single white triangle of sail didn't disturb the painted surface. Fulmars catapulted out from the cliff beneath us and vanished back under again. They must have been nesting in their thousands.

'I warned you, Jinn's DNA didn't prove a thing,' said Foley, out of absolutely nowhere. 'You told them yourself, she got into his car. She did that a few times. He never denied it.'

Cool. He never denied it. Standing there between the earth and the sky, I wished I could launch myself out with the fulmars, because I almost couldn't bear the rage – the brimming, bottom-of-my-guts fury, contorting in a gigantic knot inside me.

I could hardly breathe by the time we got to the top, and that had little to do with the climb. I stumbled up behind Foley into the car park, unfenced, stony and wind-cropped. The sun glinted off the only two cars: a four-by-four people carrier, back window plastered in stickers from Blair Drummond Wildlife Park and Alton Towers, child seats shabby and stained with sick and dried chocolate; and parked parallel to it, pointing towards the cliff, a bright yellow Toyota, soft top down.

Staring at it, I shook Foley off and fumbled in my pockets. House keys. Would that do? I played them through my fingers, jangled them glinting in the sunlight. I dug the sharp ends into my palms. That would murder the paintwork.

But it seemed so petty. Truly petty and not nearly enough. Why on earth didn't I carry something more useful, like a jerrycan of petrol?

Foley was eyeing me.

'Ruby?' He sounded only slightly alarmed. 'Ruby, what are you thinking?'

The advantage of silence. Nobody knows what you're thinking.

'Ruby . . .'

I was getting tired of the sound of my name on his lips. 'Come on,' I said.

Foley wasn't entirely happy about it, but he followed me. When I leaned on the door of the little convertible, I looked up and saw him on the other side of the car, leaning on the other door.

The car park was on a slight slope. It was almost asking for trouble, really. You could tell that from the big sign that said PLEASE CHECK YOUR HANDBRAKE! The cropped grass petered out at the edge, into slightly longer grass and a few stunted daffodils. A little rough ground wouldn't stop rolling wheels if you gave them enough impetus.

I smiled at Foley, not feeling anything. He didn't look at all certain.

I didn't care.

Gulls screeched and wailed overhead, rooks cawed, and for a minute I was on pause. My hand was on the door, and it was metallic and sharp, sun-warmed. It was like touching something alive, but all the same I didn't have any qualms.

I took in everything. The baseball cap discarded on the back seat. The gym bag beside it, one compartment unzipped and a sports water bottle sticking out. Sweet wrappers crammed into the ashtray (so he wasn't too OCD after all). A zipped pouch of CDs on the passenger seat, but I wasn't even remotely tempted to steal them. His music could go with his car. Maybe Jinn had listened to it.

There was the other thing in that car: Jinn's DNA, tangible. The whole vehicle reeked of her. No blood, of course, but Essence of Jinn. I wondered if she'd run from the car, or if she'd trusted him for longer than that and so never got the chance. Maybe he'd pulled it to a halt, and creaked on the handbrake, and turned to smile into her laughing, flirting eyes and her sparkling face. And lunged.

Before I could change my mind, I climbed into the driver's seat and tugged the handbrake. It jerked up smoothly and I eased it flat. There was no give, no slight roll. I frowned and turned to Foley.

'It's in reverse.' He pointed at one of the pedals. 'That one. Push that one.' When I pressed it with my foot, he leaned across me and shoogled the gearstick into neutral.

I smiled. Everything was so polished and smooth and oiled.

Tom loved this car.

Glancing up at Foley, I smiled again. He wasn't trying to stop me. He was just watching, careful, uncommitted. For now.

I opened the car door and got out the traditional way. Facing the cliff, I leaned my weight forward against the still-open door. It was absurdly easy. The front wheels gave, the little car rolled forward a metre, then stopped.

Foley still wasn't arguing. And he'd already contributed. I took that as a signal not from him but from the Almighty. I was the Arm of God, actually. Quite a responsibility.

If the car rolled over the edge, I decided, it was meant to be. If it stopped – well, there you go, Tom was off scot-free. But I didn't think it would stop. I was in the hands of the avenging gods now, and so was Tom Jerrold's car. It wasn't me at all.

I caught a glimpse of a face in the wing mirror, twice as old as mine, grim and intent, crowned with dark salon-red hair that spiked into her eyes. The wickedest elf. I liked her. She had no voice but she didn't need one. There was script across her throat: *Objects in the mirror are closer than they appear.* I grinned at her, and she grinned right back.

I gave Foley the same grin. It was like I could read his mind. He didn't want to do this but he didn't want to disappoint me, didn't want to act like he wasn't on my side.

'We shouldn't,' was all he said. A final plea. 'Ruby.'

It was out of my hands. 'It's only a car,' I said.

We heaved hard on our respective doors, not looking at one another but at the rim of the cliff and the glittering panel of sea. We didn't have to look at each other. We pushed as one, and it was shockingly easy. The car really wanted to go with us, it wanted a magnificent suicidal leap all of its own. Easily and more easily, it rolled with us down the gentle slope of the field. I began to jog, and my twin cat pendants swung free of my shirt, banging my breastbone.

As if from a parallel world, I heard an engine. I didn't care. I heard it cut out, heard a door slam, then another. A shrill yell, a shout of protest. Still I shoved, harder, determined.

It was Foley who hesitated. So much for commitment. I was relying on his effort and our perfect teamwork, so when he slackened I was taken by surprise, and the car resisted its fate for the first time. Under the momentum we'd built, it rolled a little further, bumped, rolled.

Then it stopped, dead.

I gave my own shriek of frustration and spun round to face the interlopers, but I didn't have to. Wide Bertha was in my face, standing there in her flip-flops, all seven or eight square metres of her. She must have been out for a romantic drive with Inflatable George, because he was there too, shouting angrily at Foley, words I couldn't make out. Bertha didn't yell, she just glared at me. I met her glower just as long as I could, then jerked my head aside, breathing furiously, like all I wanted to do was give the Evil Eye to some fulmars.

Bertha's silence was worse than any yelling, and now Inflatable George had fallen quiet too. Foley's shamefaced expression was a picture. I wanted to laugh, and I would have, if he'd met my eyes.

But he didn't. I found I was twisting his silver cat pendant between my fingers.

'It's only a car,' I said at last. I shoved the silver cat inside my shirt, and the Cyclops cat too.

Watching me, unsmiling, Inflatable George walked past me to the cliff edge. He peered down for a few seconds, shaking his head, then glanced over his shoulder at Bertha. So they were psychic too? Unexpected, and unwelcome. I fidgeted, hating the silence. I was the master of silence; in others it scared me.

Bertha shook her head too, and sighed. I couldn't help but turn in George's direction, and as I did so I saw heads bob up above the line of the cliff. A toddler was the tallest of them, sitting astride its father's shoulders. Two older girls came up next, single-file in front of their pregnant mother.

The parents smiled at the four of us and nodded; the girls, the toddler and the in-utero foetus ignored us. They didn't seem to find it odd, this frozen tableau beside Tom Jerrold's car, but then they'd no idea how close they'd come to spectacular Death by Toyota. The father lifted the toddler down, adjusted his specs, smiled and mumbled something about the weather. Didn't those black clouds look like rain any minute? As he creaked open the door of the people carrier he must have felt the need to make more conversation with the open-mouthed idiots.

'Guess we timed it well,' he said, smiling.

You have no idea, I didn't say through my rictus grin. The family had packed themselves into their Honda and bumped off down the rutted track before Bertha said a word, but luckily for me, she'd calmed down by that time.

She gave me a squeeze that nearly killed me, and said, 'Oh, Ruby.'

'Yeah,' I said. 'Bit stupid, really.'

'I wouldn't have minded his car so much,' she added comfortingly. 'But multiple murder's going a bit far.'

'Even the car,' said Inflatable George. 'That wasn't a good idea.'

Foley said nothing. He was impossibly pale, and he didn't look at me. Regret and remorse were painted all over his face. I decided I'd blown it with him.

'Let's go,' said Bertha. 'I don't want you in trouble, Ruby.'

'He killed Jinn,' I said.

It felt like a lamer excuse than it had a minute ago. I almost felt like it was Jinn I'd let down more than anybody.

'I know. Course he did,' said Bertha. 'But you can't do that. You can't do stuff like that.'

George was nudging the yellow Toyota's back tyre with a foot. 'It might have slipped.' He gave me a comforting wink. 'It might have just slipped by itself. Look, he left it in neutral. And he left the brake off, silly beggar.'

I wanted to smile at him but I felt too much like crying.

'Come on,' he said. 'I'll get you all home.'

'I'll drive,' said Bertha. 'I've to get back to work.'

'I'm sorry I spoilt your day out,' I managed.

'Don't be daft. I'm glad we were here.' She opened the door of her little red Clio. 'Come on, Ruby, I haven't got all day.'

I stepped back, shaking my head. 'No.'

'Don't be silly.'

'No, I'm fine.'

'You're not fine at all.'

'You've got to come,' added George. 'Come on. Foley'll see you home. Won't you, Foley?'

I didn't even look at him, because I didn't want to see him not-looking at me.

'I . . . can't. I've got to pick up Mallory.' Foley was shaking his watch, as if there was something wrong with it.

'Where from?' Bertha was suspicious.

'Brownies.'

'*Brownies?*' Inflatable George gave a burst of disbelieving laughter, then coughed and straightened his face.

'Yeah,' said Foley. 'I know.'

'Still,' said George. 'We'll see you home, Ruby. It's not right, you being on your own.'

'No, it isn't.' Bertha glared at Foley.

'No,' I snapped, shutting them up. 'No. I *want* to be on my own. I'm *fine*.'

I wasn't sure that was true, but other things were. Like the fact that the clogged channels in my head were about to burst their banks catastrophically. Like my absolute certainty that I was not going to be around another human being, any human being, in about five minutes' time. Like the fact that I was not going to sit on the back seat of Bertha's car pressed against a boy who couldn't even look at me. I wasn't doing that for a hundred metres, let alone two miles round the airbase to Breakness. I didn't want to feel him shrink away from my flesh as if my vileness was contagious. Not when he couldn't get enough of me the other night.

I didn't want to be near him. Any of them. I wanted them to go. NOW.

'Go on,' I said.

'But, Ruby –'

'*Go away.*'

If I had to speak again the dam would burst. Bertha must have realised that, because she avoided squeezing me again or patting my arm. She folded her bulk into the driving seat, rolled down the window and leaned out as Inflatable George got in beside her. Foley was in the back already. My, he was in a hurry.

'It's going to rain,' she warned. 'Be careful on the cliffs.'

'Uh. Huh.'

I turned on my heel before the car was even out of sight,

and ran back towards the cliff path. At the top, where it divided, I stopped. The black cloud had shifted north towards me and the first cold spring raindrops spotted my face.

The thought of running into Tom Jerrold was unbearable. He'd be down the path to the right, and there might be other people there too, walking up the shore and along the cliffs from Breakness. Apart from his car the car park was empty now; the left-hand path led to rock pools and vertical wilderness, where the only company would be crabs and the crying fulmars. I slithered down on to it and started to walk fast.

It took me a while to reach the big sandstone overhang about three hundred metres along; the grass that encroached on the path was wet and I had to be careful. I didn't usually like the overhang – I'd scurry underneath and out to the other side as if it might fall at any second – but today I stopped in its shelter. I wouldn't mind if it squashed me like a bug. The black cloud was overhead now, filling the sky, and the rain was coming in cold stinging drops. I rubbed them off my face, and slumped down with my back against the cliff face. I wanted to cry now, but the tears were all dammed up, stuck in my neck and the back of my head, and I was too angry. With myself, with Foley, with Jinn. Tom Jerrold could take a back seat for a while. It wasn't his turn.

I shut my eyes, and saw a yellow Toyota careering off

the cliff edge and plunging through a family of five and a half. My, that would have put Alex Jerrold in the shade. He'd never have crossed my mind again. What's more, it would have made me five-and-a-half times worse than Tom.

I snapped my eyes open again to watch the wheeling fulmars instead, and the rain exploding over the sea and turning the translucent watercolour into a grey roiling blanket.

And with no warning at all the stuff in my head burst out and I opened my mouth, but as-bloody-usual, no sound came out. Nothing but tears and more tears and snot, and when I thought my head must surely be empty it started all over again.

Fine. This was a good place to get it over with. I cried the tank dry several times over before the tears stopped quite abruptly, as if I'd exhausted the reservoir.

'Ruby?'

Shit.

Stupid, but I thought for an instant it was Foley. Stupid, because it wasn't his voice and nothing like it.

It was Inflatable George.

Just as well I was running on empty. I felt like I'd been sitting there for hours, but I know it wasn't more than ten or fifteen minutes. I know because I checked my watch, and because the rain hadn't been long gone. Flurries still spattered into my little shelter, but the worst of the deluge was over, and that kind of hard rain never lasted long here, but blew out over the sea. Now even the black cloud, the one that had seemed to fill the world, had torn apart and dissolved, and patches of blue shone through. In fact the sky beyond my shelter was mostly blue, till George blocked it.

He leaned in. 'Aw, Ruby. I knew you weren't OK.'

Dammit. My lip trembled again, like a bad cartoon, but luckily there weren't any more tears left in my head. I gave him a weak smile. I realised I was glad to see him. Maybe I needed company after all.

I was embarrassed about the state of my face though. I was not a beautiful weeper. I went blotchy and puffy and my eyes receded into my head. I'd seen this in a mirror. It wasn't good.

'Sorry,' I said.

'Don't say that. Are you OK?'

'Yeah.'

He gave a slight apologetic shrug. Ducking under the rock, he sat beside me with his back to the cliff.

'We just got to the main road and I said to Bertha, "I've got to go back. We can't leave Ruby on her own." But she had to be at work, so I walked back myself.'

I decided not to ask what Foley's input had been, or rather his non-input. Instead I gave George a scornful look. 'I just wanted to be on my own. I wasn't about to do anything stupid.'

'Yeah, of course. Of course, I know that. But – well. I'd have felt bad. Us just leaving you here on your own. After – you know. Everything.'

'Thanks,' I said. 'That's nice.'

'I can get you back. We can walk along the shore. It's shorter than the road.'

'I'm OK. Honest.'

'Well.' He tilted his head to give me an ironic wink. 'It's not like you were acting all normal.'

I sniffed and grinned, wiped my nose with my sleeve. 'No.'

The air was surprisingly warm now and we sat in companionable silence, watching the fulmars swoop out. The gorse that crawled across the cliffs was clotted with yellow, the colour tropically intense, the coconut scent strong on the air. After the storm the air was a little clammy. I liked looking out from this dark shaded place into the bright day; it was like being invisible.

'You shouldn't dwell on it,' said George. 'On Tom and that. You can't.'

I shrugged. I felt terribly lethargic, almost as if I didn't care any more, but it was nice of him to try and make me feel better. I let my head flop round and did my best to smile at him. 'Honestly, you can go back. I'm fine. I'm not going to chuck myself in the sea.'

'Course I won't go. You need looking after. A bit.'

Yeah. Jinn gone, and now Foley gone too. I wasn't good at hanging on to people. A bit of a jinx myself. The thought made me massively, miserably tired, and if I could have leaned against his big bulky shoulder and fallen asleep I would have done, right there.

But I was still Ruby. Ruby-On-Her-Own, Ruby-I-Can-

Manage, Ruby-I'll-Be-Fine. I rested my arms on my knees, hunched my shoulders, felt my two little cat pendants swing clear of my shirt once again. I rolled Foley's one between my fingertips. Maybe I had to take it off now. Maybe I had to give it back.

George gave it a distracted look. 'Anyway. Don't dwell on it,' he said again. 'It'd drive you mad. Wondering all the time. Getting angry. And it maybe *was* Nathan.'

'No. It wasn't.'

'Honestly, Ruby, who's more likely? You'd have to be pretty sick. That's more Nathan than Tom, Ruby. You've got to admit.'

'You can't tell. You can't tell if someone's sick, just by looking.'

And Nathan never said *I didn't kill her*! The dog never barked in the night. But there was no point trying to explain that to Inflatable George. It was something I knew only in my gut.

'Still . . .'

I shook my head. 'Nathan loved her.'

'Well, but if he loved Jinx that much, maybe he was jealous. Crazy jealous.'

It took a moment. It took a moment of thinking –

Yes, jealous.

If he thought about it.

If he thought about Jinx . . .

Only a second or two, though, and then the world ground to a halt.

The planet stopped turning and the fulmars stopped crying and the sea stopped heaving below me.

Nausea lurched up my gullet. I leaned forward, elbows on my knees, and closed my eyes.

Not looking at Inflatable George. Couldn't look for a moment. Was that dangerous?

But I had to think. I wanted him gone before I opened my eyes again. If I just kept my eyes shut. Stayed here, curled beneath the sandstone outcrop, nothing in my eyes but the blood-bright glow of the sun. Nothing else here but the smell of the ocean and the sound of gulls and fulmars. He might go.

Please.

George took a small breath. I think, on the intake of it, he swore.

He must have been thinking too.

I raked up a handful of dry sandy grit, sharp under my fingernails. My fingertips found shell fragments, tiny stones.

'Why did you do that?' I asked. My voice felt terribly small beneath the cliff; it didn't even reach the stone overhang to echo.

'Do what?'

'Why did you call her Jinx?'

We sat on in silence.

Stupid me. Stupid Ruby. I hadn't had to ask that. I could have stood up and smiled and said goodbye and walked away.

Except I couldn't. It wasn't just that I needed to know his answer.

It was that he knew fine what he'd said too. He knew as soon as he said it.

The silence stretched for half a minute maybe, or maybe two and a half. I wouldn't know. Time had gone rubbery and elastic. I folded my arms tighter round my knees. The sparkling sea pitted my tight-shut eyes with light. Fireworks on the inside of my lids. Shades of red and glitter. Stardust. I blinked my eyes sharply open.

George was very still beside me.

'Well,' he said at last, 'it was in the papers, wasn't it? When they weren't calling her Jacintha.'

Oh, God, yes. The relief was huge, battering through me so that I felt dizzy. I gave a huffing laugh.

He didn't laugh. Not at all, so I stopped too. I thought about how long it had taken him to think about it.

'Oh,' I said. 'Oh, that's fine.' I stretched my mouth into a smile. 'Fine. I think I want to go home now.'

He didn't stand up to help me. He didn't move. He nodded at my neck and said, 'I like your pendant, by the way. Where did you get it?'

Surprised, I looked down at it. 'Foley gave it to me,' I said, holding the silver cat between finger and thumb.

'No. The other one.'

'Oh!' I held out Cyclops cat, peering at its winking eye. 'It's a long story. I really need to go.'

'I've seen it before,' he said.

'Well,' I said. 'Jinn had it.'

'No, no,' he said. 'Before Jinn.'

No, I wanted to say. *Jinn had it first.* But I knew now. Panic lurched through me. I could get away with the Jinx thing, but I couldn't get away with Cyclops cat.

And besides, it was why he was here. He'd seen it on the clifftop. An invisible fist punched me lightly in the diaphragm.

'It was that girl had it,' he said. 'That girl Roberta.'

I said, 'Her name was Marley.'

'Was it?' His eyebrows rose.

I wanted to be sick and I wanted to cry. I wanted Foley. I wanted Jinn. I wanted something to hit a man with. I wanted somewhere to run, other than *up*.

I couldn't have any of those things. No one was climbing the cliff path towards us. Nobody was around but the fulmars, wheeling and mourning. Clutched tight in my palm, a shell fragment pierced my skin.

'Oh, Ruby,' he said. 'I'm sorry about all this.'

I tried to stand up but he grabbed my arm.

'Don't be sorry,' I gabbled. 'Why are you sorry? I'm fine. I want to go.'

'I didn't mean to do it, Ruby. Not Jinn. I didn't want to.'

He leaned closer. Fear scuttled across my skin with his whisper.

'I had to do it. She made me do it. It was her fault, Ruby. You *have* to understand that.'

Couldn't speak. My throat was the gullet of the narrow cliff path, all rock and sand.

'She was a good girl, Jinn. Despite – you know? She was only trying to help him, that useless creature Nathan. She was trying to get him clean. I'd never have done it to her, never. It was her own fault.'

He hadn't let me go. He wasn't going to.

He tensed, his fingers tightening. 'She wouldn't listen to me! I told her I just found the cat, I told her that; I found it in the road. And you know, she wanted to believe me. She did! It was Baird, bloody Baird. He thought it was easy money. He thought they could blackmail me!'

I wondered where Jinn had found it, Marley's little cat. In his lorry?

And then I thought, *No.* I remembered her rummaging in his jacket, looking for something to steal. Finding more than she bargained for. I remembered her pale face: horror and disbelief. She wouldn't have *wanted* to believe it.

But she couldn't ask me, certainly couldn't talk to Bertha. So she'd have asked Nathan what to do, and he'd have known. He'd have known exactly what to do.

Oh, Jinn.

I remembered George standing outside Dunedin. Him and Nathan, glaring at each other like I didn't exist. He'd gone there to negotiate. Of course. I thought about the fight I'd witnessed: Nathan thinking he'd found a way to stop her working the streets; Jinn horrified at what they were doing instead.

You're the one that says we need the money! You are!

'Jinn liked you,' I mumbled.

'I liked her! Ah, Rubes, she was beautiful, your sister. She *glittered*. So lovely, she was so lovely, and inside too. She didn't want me to have done it. She didn't want Bertha getting hurt. Bertha all over the papers. She didn't want Bertha's heart getting broken, and see what happened? It got broken anyway.'

He was trembling.

'Just some money, she said. Just enough to pay their debts, that's all, and she'd never tell anyone. As if I could *ever* have left it at that. And the stupid thing is she really wanted an innocent explanation. For the cat, you know? She'd have believed me. Nathan wouldn't, but the trouble is, she went and confided in him, didn't she? If it hadn't been for him . . .' He took a breath. 'I didn't *mean* to do it'.

'What? That girl. Roberta. Marley.'

'You did,' I said.

'No. She was a mistake, a terrible mistake. She was wandering around at night, she didn't want to go home, she was running away. She was so mixed up. I thought she was one of *them*. It was such an easy mistake. She was a lost soul. I did her a favour, Ruby, I really did. But it was a mistake. I didn't mean to kill her. And I didn't *want* to kill Jinn.'

Terror ripped down my spine, sending my whole body

into a spasm of fight. I kicked him, tried to twist away, but he was strong. The hand on my arm tightened fast. I tugged and yanked, weakening, but his grip was hard. I whimpered.

'Shh. I'm not going to hurt you, Rubes. I wouldn't do that to you.'

Wouldn't *mean* to, wouldn't *want* to. Liar. I kicked and struggled, tore at my arm.

'It was Nathan's fault. Wanting Jinn to blackmail me. She wouldn't have done it. She was so soft. She loved him so much but still, she wanted me not to have done it. It was her own fault.' He kept right on talking, ignoring my squirming, like he was talking to himself. Making his excuses in advance. 'And I shouldn't have said that stupid name *Jinx* there! Putting you on edge, getting you all tense. Oh, Ruby, you are so right. We all need to watch what we say, don't we? You've got the right idea, Ruby. You've always had the right idea.'

Not always, George.

But now.

And here's another.

I stopped fighting, went limp. He wasn't expecting that, wasn't expecting the struggle to stop. And as he keeled off balance, he wasn't expecting me to lunge at him with another fistful of grit and sand.

I slammed the dirt into his eyes. I think I screamed as I ground it in, hard, hard as I could, while his head thrashed and snapped to try and avoid me. He squealed and squirmed and his hand slipped off my arm. And I leaped up and started to run.

Behind me he was swearing and yelping, like Nathan had, but he was running too, stumbling. He was between me and the car park; I couldn't run anywhere but north, up the shoreline, higher and higher as the path climbed. I darted glances at my feet, sliding and slithering, my breath sobbing in and out. I couldn't seem to catch it properly. I tripped and stumbled on a root, and by the time I lunged forward again I could hear his breath almost at my ear. Furious breath.

'RUBY!'

Trying to catch me with my own name.

'Ruby, you GET BACK HERE!'

I was afraid it might work, his voice loop round my throat and yank me back. I gave a cry of fear and jumped; the path was giving out. It was landslips and wet grass now. I screamed. Useless. I ran.

Fingers clutched the back of my shirt, toppling me off-balance. My right foot skidded on sodden daffodils and I fell forward on to my hands. He seized my belt.

'I tried to EXPLAIN. DAMMIT.'

I slapped ineffectually at him with one hand, trying to clutch handfuls of grass with the other. To my right stones and sand tumbled off the edge. So far down. I was only breathing with my throat. Couldn't get air into my lungs.

'Listen. LISTEN. I haven't got a choice. I've GOT to do

it. You're not happy anyway, you STUPID GIRL. DON'T FIGHT ME.'

I kicked, rolled on to my back and kicked again, like a pathetic beetle. He grabbed an ankle, dodged and flailed for the other one, dragging me closer to the edge.

'It's FINE. You're just going to jump. It's FINE and QUICK. Don't FIGHT.'

His shouts battered my ears. I couldn't understand. His eyes were red and raw and I think one eyeball was bleeding. I couldn't hear him. I could only hear girls' voices, a chorus in my head. My own voice maybe, just amplified. *Let go let go let go let go.*

I let go. The coarse grass tuft slipped through my fist, cutting into my palm, and I had to grab for the path itself. What was left of it. A fistful of path.

'No you DON'T.' He jerked away, ducked his head, shut his raw eyes still sharp with grit. I had to throw the dirt at him, wildly. He flung his hands up to his eyes, skipped back.

There wasn't a path behind him, just a metre of landslip. He fell on to his side with a grunt, and grabbed for the long grass just like I had. His feet were over the edge but he was hauling himself back up. Still half blind.

I wanted to get up and run but I couldn't, couldn't, my legs wouldn't carry me. I scrambled on to my hands and knees. He tried to grab me with one hand, but he wasn't secure enough, and he clutched the grass again. I picked up handfuls of grit, fast as I could, flung them at his face, hard as I could, not daring to go closer. But it was in his eyes and he squealed like a girl. He let go of the grass, slapped his hands protectively over his face.

His feet still flailing at the ground, his fingers belatedly grabbing for a handhold again, he slid, bumpily, over the edge.

I heard stones roll and bounce and fall, but I didn't hear him, and I didn't dare look. I backed hard against the cliff wall, not daring to look over. If I looked I'd fall too. Even now I felt as if I was floating in air.

Except I wouldn't float. I'd land like Alex Jerrold, a bag of meat on the rocks below. No truck to break my fall.

I stared at the edge, waiting and waiting, because I knew. I was waiting for the jolt in my chest that was a human being hitting the ground. It hadn't happened.

The edge shifted slightly; long grass was tugged flat by the weight of a climbing body. I heard breathing.

His knuckles appeared. White, bent almost backwards, gripping a jutting slab of stone. They crept higher, painfully, millimetre by millimetre. The other hand came up too, fingers curling over the edge of the stone slab. The stone wasn't more than half a metre wide and a dark widening outline showed where it was working loose from dry roots and grass and sand.

He breathed rage through his teeth, gasping with pain.

I didn't know if I could live with myself. I just knew I wanted to live anyway. I couldn't kick his fingers, I couldn't do that, but I stuck my heel into the widening gap between stone and cliff, and I prised it out and further out, till the stone came away and his fingers with it, and I heard his surprised intake of breath. And then time stopped. Something that wasn't stone or sand bounced down the precipice.

Silence. I shut my eyes, and the jolt in my chest was like an extra heart stopping.

Epilogue

He'd bought a chocolate flake to go in my ice cream. When he handed me the cone I stared at it, wrinkling my nose.

'You did say vanilla.'

'Uh-huh.' I took the flake delicately between thumb and forefinger and handed it to him. 'Here. You can have that.'

He took it, stuck it next to the flake in his own ice cream. We were sitting on the sea wall, looking out towards the dunes, the town at our backs. The world, or the Breakness bit of it, looked vibrantly bright. The rain-storms had kept on coming for weeks now. The water fell in a torrent from a black sky, then when it was over and the sky was blue again, the world was summer-green and power-washed, glinting bright. It would be slippery up on the cliffs. I bit my ice cream.

'He's out of hospital today. Straight into jail.'

I hesitated, nodded. 'Good.'

'So stop shivering. Aren't you glad?'

'Aren't you?' I turned to examine Tom Jerrold's face.

Inflatable George didn't fall. He went right to the bottom of the cliff, but he didn't fall so much as slither. He might have died if he'd fallen properly through space, but he didn't. He had his life. And that was my payment, I think – that George did not fall. He had his life.

But I had mine back too. Fair's fair.

I could have had a bit longer in the house, the house Lara and Jinn and I had shared, but I didn't want it. It was too haunted, and I didn't mind ghosts but I minded the sadness. When the council gave me a new place, a one-bedroom flat that was half of a duplex, I left behind the windmills and the plastic sun-faces and the wind chimes, and whatever would survive from last summer's B&Q bedding plants. (I did take the ugly gargoyle though. I couldn't leave him behind. He wouldn't find anyone else who'd love him the way we had.)

Occasionally I'd pass our house – I had to make a detour, it wasn't a corner I'd ever pass accidentally – and our garden fripperies were still there. A bit faded, their sparkle dimmed, but the new people hadn't bothered to get rid of them. That made me wish I'd got rid of them myself.

The tyres and the old blanket were gone, of course. I didn't ask what had happened to them.

My new place was on the edge of Breakness. Not the sea side, of course – the houses there were in too much demand – but overlooking the flat fields and the pig farm and the airbase, with the hills and Glassford in the hazy distance. I was lucky to have a view like that.

I had goats, that was the funny thing. Not my own, obviously. A patch of field abutted the duplex garden, between a pig village and a cottage that was more of a shack. Some hippy types lived there, with barefoot kids and a small pottery business and a few ragged chickens. The first time I heard them call out to the goats, I was thrown off balance by the plumminess of their voices. Father hippy used to be a stockbroker and the barefoot urchins, it turned out, went to a private school by day.

The goats and I enjoyed the joke. I'd go down the end of the garden and feed them leftovers – it was true about goats, they'd eat anything: toast crusts, tomato skins, the end of a cheeseburger, the cardboard core of a loo roll (that last one was an accident). They had evil eyes and wicked natures, and the nanny goat scared the hell out of mother hippy, forever ambushing her between the cottage and their vegetable plot. Jinn would have loved those goats. She'd have got the joke, totally.

I was happy in my new home, and only occasionally missed the old one. That's why I kept making a detour to see it: just to cure my nostalgia. The place didn't seem to have anything to do with me now, or anything to do with Jinn.

'I'm glad,' said Tom at last.

He'd taken a long time to think about that one, taken it very seriously. I had to think hard to remember what the question had been.

'I mean, I'm not glad he's alive. I couldn't care less,' he

said. 'But it's true what they say. It would have been an easy way out for him if he'd died.'

'He'll be inside for life,' I pointed out. 'For ever, they told me.'

'Aye. Till somebody wants to marry him and starts a Facebook campaign.'

'Cynic,' I said. 'Never happen.'

'You hope he's in for good? You must do.'

'Uh-huh.'

'Oh, Ruby. I wonder if you'd have said the same about me?'

Who invented ice-cream cones? They aren't even nice. Dry as sticks once the ice cream's gone. I chucked the remains of mine at the river. This time it drifted downstream for a second or two before it was shanghaied by a gull.

'Sorry about that,' I said.

'Yeah. Well, I don't know what made you think you could push a Toyota over a cliff.'

I wasn't sure he was right, but, 'Sorry,' I said again. 'I thought – I really thought it was you. Who killed her.'

'Why? Why would it be me?'

'I dunno. Because I wouldn't feel so guilty if it was? I dunno.'

'You do feel guilty, yeah?'

God, my face must have clashed with my hair at that moment. 'Alex told you what I said that day?'

'Uh huh.'

Well, I'd guessed that, hadn't I? I just hadn't known it for sure before.

'I'm sorry,' I said. 'I'm really sorry.'

'Yeah.'

'I didn't.' I licked my lips, cleared my throat. I didn't want to sound like I was making excuses. 'I didn't mean what I said to Alex. I didn't mean . . . I'm not saying I'm not responsible. Just. You know. I wanted you to know I didn't mean it.'

'I know.' He almost looked at me, almost smiled. 'Thanks for going to see him.'

Well, he didn't need to thank me. It hadn't been so awful. No question of Alex reclining palely on a Victorian sickbed; he'd been in a high-tech sort of wheelchair, propped up. And the atmosphere hadn't been brilliant, but we'd exchanged some awkward conversation, and we'd both said 'Sorry' at exactly the same moment, which nearly made Alex huff a laugh.

'He's liking the book. When do you need it back?'

'No hurry. I borrowed it off an old girl in Oak Tree Court. Said I'd take it back next month.' Which I would. This time.

Now that we'd got Alex off our respective chests, the atmosphere was nicer. Tom snapped the end off his cone, scooped out a baby ice cream, ate it whole. That gave me a tug inside my ribcage.

I was right the first time: there's nothing you can do. Things stay done and said. You can't undo or unsay.

Nobody could atone for Alex's lost future, and nobody could atone for Jinn either. But why should I have the satisfaction anyway? There was nothing I could do now to stop Alex jumping. I couldn't take back what I said then, but I couldn't wallow in it either. It was like Foley said: Got to live with it. Got to live with it.

Tom leaned back on his elbows and gazed at the sky. 'I wasn't there for him. I don't feel great about that, but the little fecker jumped all by himself. I didn't push, you didn't push. I don't want to be angry with him for ever but I don't want to excuse what he did. Not to my mum or dad or anybody. What he did, *him*. We've all just got to live with it. The selfish little bastard.'

'I wish it hadn't happened,' I said.

'Me too.'

He stood up, gave me a smile. 'I'll see you around.'

I got to my feet too. It felt like a formal moment, and not just because he was in his suit and tie. I thought I should shake his hand but I wasn't sure how, so I just said, 'Bye.'

He waved a hand as he walked off.

I watched the river flow fast out towards the sea, and the kids running over the rickety bridge to the beach. *Trip-trap trip-trap*. When I checked my watch again, it was time for my afternoon shift.

I came to a breathless halt when I saw Wide Bertha. She was sitting on the leather sofa in the salon window, reading a celeb magazine, her bag beside her.

Clarissa said, 'That's Bertha Turnbull in to see you. Hasn't got an appointment.' She gave me a hard stare, like it was my fault. 'She wouldn't take no for an answer.'

'Oh,' I said.

'Don't forget you've got Mrs Bolland at two.'

How could I? She of the brick-melting face.

I felt sick and I didn't want to turn and approach Bertha, but Clarissa was giving me the evil eye. So was Mrs Bolland, head full of glittering foils, waiting to get them rinsed out.

I stood in front of Bertha, but I couldn't say anything. At last she sighed and folded the magazine neatly back at a middle page.

'You don't come to my house any more, so I thought I'd come here.'

'Well,' I said, 'I . . . Want to sit here?' I pointed at one of the styling chairs.

She stood up fast and marched across. Sitting down, she tweaked her thin fringe, then glanced up and met my eyes in the mirror. Her tight smile didn't show any teeth. She flourished a photo in the magazine.

'Pink highlights. Like her, here. You promised.'

I grinned. Couldn't help it. 'Pink.'

'Yes. Can you manage to talk to me long enough to do it?'

'I can't – I've got somebody else just now. And I'll need to do it at your house. I'm not qualified . . .'

'But you'll come round? Stop being a stranger?'

'Course I will.'

'That's what I like to hear. All right. I'll go, then.'

I swallowed hard. 'I'm sorry about –'

'I'm due at work,' she interrupted sharply. 'Oh, by the way, he's wanting a word and all.' Bertha nodded at the window.

I shut one eye, drawing out a strand of her hair to examine it closely. 'Who is?'

She jerked her thumb. I had to look. Beyond the displays of wax and gum and conditioner, beyond the spotlit plate glass, beyond the impatient traffic, I saw a boy hunched against the far wall of the surf shop. He glanced nervously up and down the street, anywhere but at the salon. A small girl, bored stiff, was kicking his shin rhythmically.

'Oh,' I said.

'Poor Foley. He was angry about the car thing. Upset. But he got over it, you know. Now he kind of thinks he let you down.'

Well. He bloody did.

On the other hand, he did put the car in neutral and help shove it. And I kind of let him down too, just by expecting him to do it.

'Well,' I sighed. 'Everybody thinks that sometimes.'

At that exact moment I caught his eye, so I lifted my comb and waved it diffidently. He tried not to smile too hard as he raised a hand in return. Mallory thrust up her middle finger and flourished it at me.

'I'll see him after work,' I told Bertha.

'I'll tell him.' She stood up.

'Can you do Mrs Bolland now?' Clarissa waited till Bertha had left, but she sounded cross.

Remembering I did still need a job, I swallowed hard and forgot Foley. Funny how nervous I felt. She wasn't so bad when you got started, Mrs Bolland. You just had to chat to her. Warm her up. Act like she was a human being.

I didn't have Jinn to do that sort of thing for me any more, so it was time to start living with it. Even at the dark deep end that was Mrs Bolland.

I tweaked her foils and smiled at the old bat in the mirror. She could melt bricks but I'd seen worse.

'So, Mrs B,' I said. 'Are you going somewhere nice for your holidays?'

By the same author

Shortlisted for the 2010
Royal Mail Awards

OUT NOW

Acknowledgements

A criminally clueless author would like to thank former police inspector Avery Mathers, former police detective Sharon Birch, and Michael McKenzie at Grampian Police Media Office, Carol Findlay at Moray College, and Kerrie Morrison. All the mistakes are, as always, mine.

I'm grateful also to my fabulous agent, Sarah Molloy; and to Emma Matthewson, Isabel Ford and Sarah Taylor-Fergusson at Bloomsbury, for enthusiasm and patience above and beyond the call of duty.